I0545403

# LAKE
## Covington

# LAKE Covington

A SMOLDR ANTHOLOGY

RED ROGUE PRESS

Lake Covington
SMOLDR
Red Rogue Press
Copyright 2020 by SMOLDR
Cover copyright 2020 by Nick Roetto
Interior Illustrations copyright 2020
by Nick Roetto

All rights reserved. Printed in the United States
of America. No part of this book may be used or
reproduced in any manner whatsoever without
written permission except in the case of brief
quotations embodied in critical articles and
reviews. For information, address inquiries to
Heather Cuthbertson, SMOLDR Editor-in-Chief:
HCuthbertson@smoldr.org.

ISBN: 0-9969239-6-9
ISBN13: 978-0-9969239-6-5

# Contents

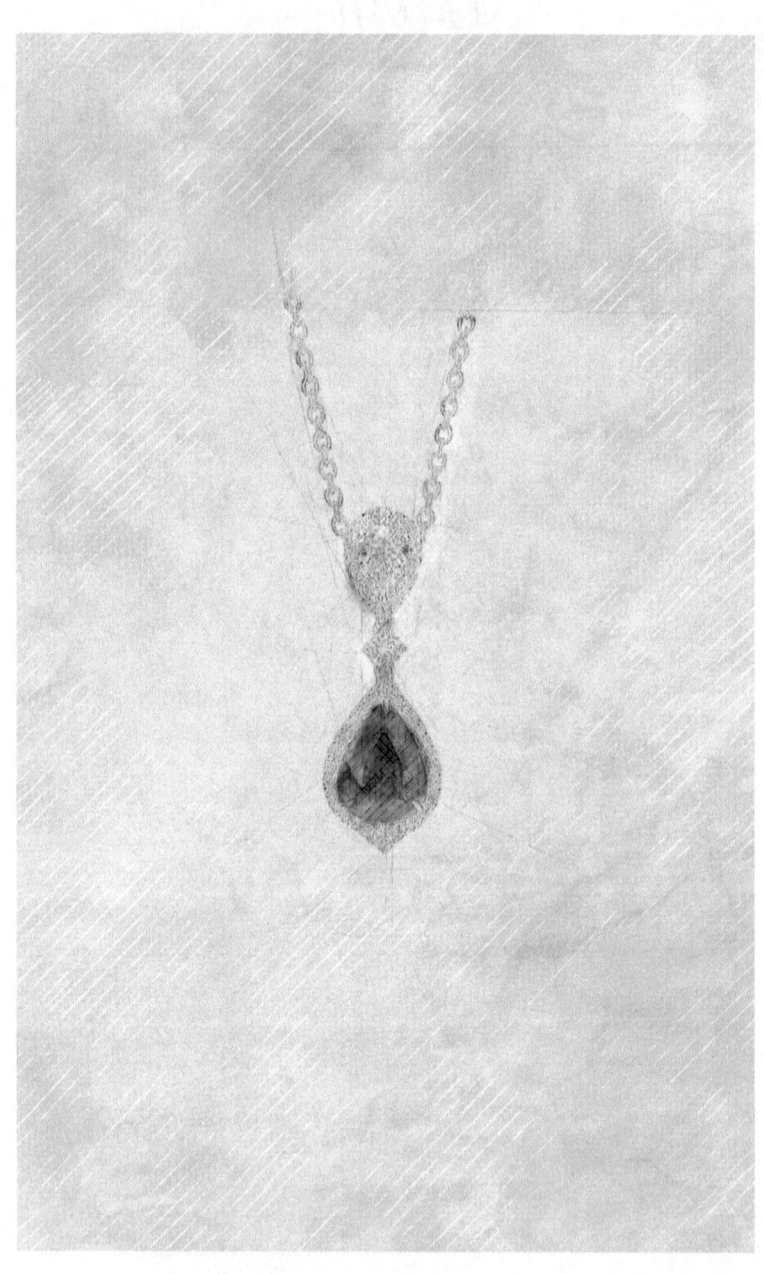

**LAKE COVINGTON**

# Forever Masterpiece

## VOLANNA DAL'ZIEL

### Lake Covington, 1880

*K*ate Sheffield was a woman on a mission, and currently, that mission entailed wrangling two small children out of the ballroom. No easy feat, that. Their governess was ill with a headache, again. The woman, in Kate's opinion, was useless.

When Kate took the position as head housekeeper to the newly appointed Mayor, she hadn't expected the additional duties of nursemaid. Yet, here she was, holding her hands out to two suspiciously dirty twin boys, their faces wreathed in mischievous grins.

"Thomas, Adam," Kate said, moving her hands to her hips. "I've had quite enough. Your tutor is waiting for your lessons and you've kept him too long."

Thomas, with his strawberry hair and freckled nose, frowned. "But wc want to play cowboys and Indians."

Adam nodded in earnest. "I'm the cowboy," he said, hopping up and down.

"I just bet you are," Kate said under her breath.

"What did you say Miss Sheffield?" Thomas asked.

"Never you mind." Kate looked around the ballroom, relieved to see the area remained relatively clean. The hoodlums hadn't much time to disrupt the decorations for the upcoming ball and, for that, Kate was thankful. "Move along you two. I've plenty enough to do today without fixing your messes."

"Awwww," Adam said, shuffling his feet.

"Cowboys do not whine, Adam," Kate said. She softened her reprimand with a wink and he smiled in return.

It wasn't long before she had them up in the schoolroom and she was back to her duties, directing staff and logging items received by local vendors. They were setting up for a grand ball, the unveiling of the mayor's new mansion. The event, as Mayor Golligher put it, had to *razzle-dazzle.*

Whatever that meant. Americans still had the ability to boggle her mind.

The mayor had spent the last three years and lord knew how much money building his palace, and now he was ready to show it to the public. Kate had been tasked to make the event run as smoothly and efficiently as possible, and she had every intention of doing so. Even if the smells from the kitchen, the sounds of the string quartet tuning their instruments, and rich-linen draped tables had homesickness clouding her heart.

The day Kate stepped foot on American soil was the day she pushed her past far behind her. Drudging up those memories would put her in a foul mood and she hadn't time for that.

"Miss Sheffield," the butler said from behind her.

Kate sucked in a breath and twirled around. She was standing in her small office off the kitchen in the servants' quarters, tallying up the remaining napkins and cutlery. "Goodness, Hidley, you surprised me."

"I do beg your pardon, Miss," he said, his face showing no ounce of expression. "The painter is at the front door. You asked to be informed the moment he arrived."

Kate nodded. "Of course. Thank you."

The butler left and Kate straightened her apron. Mayor Golligher had commissioned a renown American painter for a self-portrait. It would be the finishing piece to complete the *Extravagant Extravagance,* as the Mayor so called his home.

She left her office and made her way towards the front hall. As she reached the stairs, she caught sight of the striking figure below, and her foot caught along the carpet, pitching her forward. Her body tensed for the painful landing.

\*\*\*

Christian Jones wasn't used to waiting. Hell, he was typically the one making others wait, so standing inside the Mayor's palatial brick mansion, in the receiving hall no less, he couldn't help but feel his impatience rising.

He was an artist, dammit. Couldn't they have taken him to the parlor? Offered him a drink?

Yet, being commissioned for the mayor of Lake Covington's portrait was a job, and career boost, he couldn't deny. If he was going to make it big one day in New York, this was just the ticket. The fact that this opportunity blossomed from his hometown was an added bonus.

His attention shifted from the interwoven marble floor to the sweeping staircase before him. It rose until his gaze landed on what had to be the most stunning woman he'd ever seen.

His breath caught as he watched her glide down the stairs. Her dark curls were pinned atop her head, some of the strands escaping their pins, framing her heart-shaped face, pert nose and full lips. Her hips swayed and he swallowed, watching her hand glide along the cherry wood banister.

Her eyes caught his before she reached the bottom of the stairs and his breath whooshed from his body. She made an unintelligible sound and tripped, pitching forward. He reacted without thinking, rushing forward, and caught her before she hit the ground.

Her body tensed underneath his hands and he pulled her into his chest, the softness of her curves sinking into him. He liked the sensation it aroused; he couldn't deny that.

"Oh Lord," she said, her face scrunched up in worry. Her cultured, English accent made her all the more desirable and something unfamiliar stirred inside him, causing him to set her on her feet.

"Careful there," he said.

She pushed her disheveled hair out of her face and assessed her clothing.

"Are you all right?" he asked.

She nodded, brushing her hands down her apron. "Thank you," she said, more to the ground than to him.

He placed his hands behind his back and waited. He had clear instructions to meet the housekeeper prior to the portrait and something told him that the flustered woman in front of him was her. The silence and her obvious discomfort gave him a moment to inspect her from head to toe, and by the time his eyes found hers a jolt ran through him.

They were the purest green he'd ever seen.

He had to paint her.

"You must be Mr. Jones," she said.

His fingers itched to trace the graceful line of her cheekbone, brush across her full bottom lip, trace along the vein jumping at her neck and down the soft swell of her breast, modestly hidden behind her navy and cream uniform.

Never in his life had he had such an urge to put his brush to canvas and it was a feeling he was afraid he would never be able to fulfill. He wasn't one to dally with the help, even if a portion of his anatomy disagreed.

"Yes, I am," he said. "And you are?"

She bowed her head. "I'm Miss Sheffield, head housekeeper. If you'll follow me?"

He followed behind, his eyes glued to the gentle sway of her hips. She was speaking softly, pointing out this and that, and yet he heard nothing but the throaty purr of her voice. What the hell was wrong with him?

Before long, she deposited him in the drawing room, with its massive floor-to-ceiling windows overlooking an impressive English garden and cobbled walkways that beckoned him to explore. The sudden urge to ask Miss Sheffield for a stroll was quick to dissipate when he turned and found he was alone in the room.

***

Kate's body was on fire. Never had a man pressed so intimately against her, especially a man such as Christian Jones. All she'd felt was hardness and warmth.

One rarely saw such a display of manliness in England, least of all here.

She knew it to be rude to just leave him in the drawing room, but she feared if she spent one more second with him she'd undoubtedly embarrass herself further. If there was one thing she prized above all, it was her pride. And her manners.

It wouldn't do for the mayor's housekeeper to throw herself at his guest. Even if her body screamed to do so.

Shaking her head, she told the nearest footman to fetch the mayor and she went back to her duties. It was work, not their houseguest, that would calm her uneasy nerves. Of that, Kate was sure.

Later that night, as was her usual custom, Kate walked the gardens, pushing back the homesickness that threatened to overwhelm her. She missed her old home, her grandmother, God rest her soul, and her friends. Yet this new life far outweighed the prospect of a forced marriage, and she told herself, as she was wont to do several times a day, that fleeing England was the best thing she could have ever done.

Even if she found it hard sometimes, she loved her independence and the feeling of satisfaction that followed a hard day's work.

She took a right, heading towards the gazebo and her feet faltered as she saw Christian sitting on a stone bench beneath a lamppost.

He said, "We meet again."

The soft timbre of his voice shot through her and she stopped in her tracks. It was a voice she'd tried, and failed, to forget all day.

"Mr. Jones," Kate said, turning to the right.

He stood beneath a lamp's glow, his hair on fire like a halo, his eyes dark and promising.

"I wasn't sure if I'd see you again," he said.

Too soon, he was close and her feet refused to move away. "Oh?" she said, her voice breathless. Had he pined to see her, as she'd pined to see him? But she couldn't; it wasn't done. She was a servant now and he, he was a renown painter, famous in his own right.

Who was she to wish for another touch? Or even more daring, a kiss, perhaps?

Oh Lord, she thought. She wanted him to kiss her.

"When I saw these gardens earlier," he said, taking her limp hand and pressing his lips to the inner side of her palm. "I thought about asking you to join me for a walk."

Her knees almost buckled at the touch and she was amazed she could still stand. "Oh?" she said again.

He laughed, and heat flushed down her cheeks into her neck. She sounded the fool, she knew.

"God, I want to paint you," he whispered.

Kate gasped. Had she heard him right? He wanted to paint her? "I beg your pardon?"

He cleared his throat and dropped her hand.

"Oh, forgive me." He chuckled. "Let me try again."

"It isn't at all proper, Mr. Jones, for us to be alone out here," Kate said, interrupting him.

"Oh?" he said, mimicking her earlier responses.

She wasn't impressed, even if she felt a smile tugging at her lips. "I should go in," she said, instead.

"Wait."

\*\*\*

He didn't want her to leave, not yet. He wasn't done investigating the feelings Kate was awakening within him. Never had a woman caused him such duress. His mind was on fire and his hands craved to paint, to worship, to touch.

She was beautiful tonight, her curly auburn hair escaping its pins in wild disarray. His fingers twitched to reach out and thread through the silky strands, to draw her close, and closer still. To taste her lips, just once.

And yet, he feared once would not be enough.

"What I said was true." The sound of his voice, even to him, was gruff. "I need to paint you."

Her lips parted and her tongue darted out, wetting them. Everything in him tightened painfully.

"I'm sure that's quite improper, Mr. Jones," she said.

"Proper be damned," he said. He stepped closer and felt her breath exhale out between them. He should, in this moment, walk away. Because she was right. It wasn't at all proper for him to be speaking to her this way. She was unmarried, there were no chaperones around, and blast it, she was a servant. Yet still, the feelings she was arousing within him were growing too strong to deny. "You're magnificent, Kate. Let me capture it."

She shook her head wordlessly.

He gave in to temptation and reached out, snatching a curl between his fingers. It was softer than it looked. And he was pleased she didn't move away.

Night fell over them as he threw caution to the wind and pulled her to him. Her curves and warmth melted into him. He leaned down and stole her lips, swallowing her gasp and delving inside. She tasted sweet, like chocolate and peppermint, and he deepened the kiss.

She moaned and collapsed further into him as his hands traveled down, pressing her more intimately against his raging need. She stiffened and pulled away. Before he could grab her hand to pull her back, she was gone, leaving him panting, aching with unsated desire.

"Damn," he said into the night. He may have just ruined his one chance. Because Kate, well, she was like no woman he'd ever met. And if he had his way, he'd be the only man to ever taste those lips again.

For two days Kate made herself scarce avoiding the areas she knew Christian would be present. The feelings he elicited within her were foreign, intense, and all too addictive. She feared she'd throw the one chance she'd been given at a new life at his beautiful artist's hands.

The servants were abuzz. It seemed this was Christian's hometown, and at the tender age of sixteen he'd set out on his own to make his name. And make his name he had, painting famous singers, actors, royalty. He was a legend. Kate couldn't deny that small voice inside her head, or heart. Perhaps they had more in common than she thought. Crafting a future of their own making.

"Miss Sheffield, that looks lovely on you," Joséphine LaCoste, the housemaid, said. Like Kate, she too hailed from Europe though on the other side of the channel. She was known amongst the town as the local gossip. "Christian Jones won't be able to keep his eyes off you." Her French accent made this sound all the more sordid.

Kate brushed her hands against the deep green silk, loving the texture, as soft as a baby's cheek. The corset dress cinched tight at her waist and flared at her hips, accentuating more of her bosom than she was used to. However, the color was magnificent.

"I have no desire to have Mr. Jones' eyes on me, anywhere," Kate said.

Joséphine snorted. "*Oui*, what woman wouldn't want that man's eyes, or hands for that matter, on them anywhere?"

Kate gasped. " Joséphine!"

"Oh *ma chérie*. I've seen the way you've been avoiding him. And every time he sees you, *oh la-la*, his eyes they are eating you alive."

"That's nonsense."

"No, *ma belle*. What is nonsense is the fact that you haven't taken that man by his lapels and—"

"That's quite enough, Joséphine." The images the woman was painting were enough to have Kate fanning her cheeks. "Thank you for your assistance. I should go down and check preparations are in order before I join the masses."

"Kate," Joséphine said, grabbing her wrist. "You have a chance here, *chérie*, at the possibility of love. I've known Christian since he was *un petit* and let me tell you, there's no man finer. Don't deny yourself the chance at happiness."

Kate swallowed and gave an imperceptible nod before escaping her modest bedroom, brushing past the cracked porcelain basin by the door. The mayor had been kind enough to purchase this dress for her, requesting her presence at the ball, where she would play the in between of hostess and party planner while he showed his new mansion to the who's who of Lake Covington. She normally didn't mind these types of situations, and yet, the thought of seeing Christian dressed in tails had her entire body heating to a most uncomfortable degree.

Was there a possibility for more, with him? Her heart fluttered at the thought. Could Joséphine be speaking the truth? She had some reputation as a matchmaker, and her skills were in high renown. Kate shook the thought away and focused on her duties.

Upon entering the ballroom, excitement swelled in her belly. Soft candlelight illuminated the parquet floors, setting them aglow. Pushed against the wainscoted walls were tables upon tables of delicacies, champagne, and handmade decorations, little bags of small paintbrushes and ripped canvas. The string quartet was due to begin, then everything would be complete.

Memories of her childhood flittered across her mind's eye and so when a warm hand pressed against her lower back she squeaked out in surprise. Twirling in silk and wonder, she caught sight of Christian's dazzling smile before his hands grasped her at the waist.

"God, you're captivating," he said.

His eyes were like fire, branding her immobile. She wanted to lean in, melt against him, and never let go.

"You've been hiding, Miss Sheffield," he said.

Her cheeks heated further but she didn't take her gaze away.

"Come with me," he said, taking her hand and leading her towards the French doors and out into the moonlight gardens.

"Mr. Jones," she said. "I'm needed in the hall for receiving."

Even to her, the excuse sounded pitiful. And her feet, Lord help her, refused any and all commands except to follow Christian.

***

For two days, and two sleepless nights, thoughts of Kate invaded his mind. And now, finally, he had her alone. His fingers itched to touch her, to run along her cheek, down her neck, across her collarbone and beyond. He wanted to trace every nuance of her pliable body until she begged for him to take her.

Every time he'd heard a story of love at first sight, he'd scoffed at the idea. And yet, now, after knowing Kate, he felt the fool. From the moment he saw her something inside of him kindled to life. He'd heard of being struck dumb by love. Never having been one to experience said emotion, he hadn't realized that was what was happening until now. Yet here he was, trying his damnedest to capture the moment, his world exploding in color and texture so vibrant it almost hurt to see. How could he have never believed love existed in this way?

His hand found its way to his pocket again, where a family heirloom sat hot against his leg. The precious necklace, which once belonged to his great aunt, Mary McClellan, was the last piece of family history he had. And when his aunt passed it on to him, he knew one day it would go to the woman he would call wife.

And that woman stood before him, trembling with what he hoped was need.

"Kate," he whispered.

She swayed closer to him.

"Tell me you don't feel this," he said. His voice was more forceful than he meant it to be, and her body jerked.

"I have to go," she said. Her throaty voice raked across him. Without thinking, he reached into his pocket and took out the necklace. The gold, interwoven chain glittered in the moonlight, and the red ruby pendant glowed.

She gasped as his fingers brushed against the back of her scalp, the tender flesh at the tip of her spine. His fingers tingled as he hooked the clasp. When he looked down his breath caught.

The gold warmed her skin, and the gem flashed between the shadows of her breasts. Her lips matched the color of the jewel and her breath was coming out in short little gasps that drove him wild. He leaned down and captured those lips in his and sunk deep, pulling her hard against him. Groaning, he deepened the kiss, and excitement raced down his body as she eagerly responded.

He pushed her up against a stone statue of a cherub and ground his hips into hers. The sound she made at the back of her throat had him reaching for the laces of his trousers but before he could untangle them he heard the faint sounds of footsteps.

"Damn," he said against her lips.

"Christian?" she asked.

When he looked down into her face, her bewildered eyes stared up at him, clouded in hazy desire.

"We should stop," he said. Even to him his disappointment rang clear, but the last thing he wanted was for someone to find her in this state. Her, here and now, this vision was for him and his eyes only.

"Oh God," she said. "Oh my God." She pushed away from him and walked a few steps away. "I can't believe...."

"What's wrong?" he asked.

"This, this is all wrong," she said.

He couldn't deny he liked it much better when she was writhing beneath his hands, instead of gesturing with them.

"There is nothing wrong with this," Christian said, irritation rising.

Her hands fluttered at the necklace around her neck.

"It was my great aunt's," he said.

"Christian," she whispered.

He took that as a sign it was all right to move closer but the sound of voices drawing near signaled his time was running out.

"Meet me back here, tonight, at midnight," he said.

Kate shook her head.

"No, don't say no, not yet."

"I..."

"At midnight, Kate," he said. "At least give us that." And before she could deny him he left her on the stone pathway, surrounded by glowing lights and the scent of roses, starlight glinting in her hair.

*** 

Kate forced herself, through a daze, to carry on with her duties as head housekeeper. She directed guest and staff to proper locations, observed dancing and gently nudged bachelors towards wallflowers and away from gossiping mamas. She managed the catering, keeping plates and glasses full, and all the while, she could feel Christian's gaze searing her very soul.

The very fact that he was in the same room as her, mere feet away, caused her breath to quicken and her heart to race. She felt lightheaded, yet still she pressed on. Colored lace and satin, intermixing with perfume and the press of bodies, was making her dizzy. Her ears rang with each thump of her heart, in tune with the stringed waltz cascading through the ballroom.

The moon rose high in the sky, and before she knew it, the last guests were spirited away in their carriages. The mayor was rhapsodizing about the success of the evening, his excited banter following him down the hall towards his own chambers. Eventually, she was alone in the hall, and she pressed her hand to her heart, willing it to settle.

The time was fast approaching, and Christian was expecting her in the gardens. Half of her wanted to run to him, to throw caution to the wind and take Joséphine's advice. Perhaps this was her one chance at happiness. Yet, that tiny voice in her head, the constant companion of her years of tutelage on an unmarried woman's proper behavior, cautioned her to stay. To finish her duties and go to bed.

Alone.

The jeweled necklace Christian gave her hung heavy between her breasts, and she brushed her fingers against the gem, remembering the feel of his hands on her body, his fingers tickling her flesh.

Goosebumps rose along her skin and her body quickened. She wouldn't, nay couldn't, deny her feelings for Christian any longer. He was magnetic. She was the moth, and he the flame. The thought of not knowing his touch again almost brought her to tears. Christian made her feel wanted and safe, treasured as no man had ever treasured her before.

She raced from the entryway and down the corridor to the ballroom. Her steps echoed in the silence. Most of the sconces had been extinguished. Yet she didn't mind the dark. The moon lit her path, and she followed it eagerly.

Pushing the French doors open, she welcomed the cool night air along her skin. She raced along the cobbled walk, past stone statues and benches, moving towards the small garden maze, where in the middle, a large fountain of a woman resided, half clothed in the fashion of the Greeks, her delicate hands holding a harp.

Christian was there, leaning against the side of the stone pool, the sound of water trickling and night things singing in the shadows. A sense of calm enveloped her as she took him in, the tight black breeches, form fitted coat, and his disheveled hair. It was obvious his fingers had run through the silken strands more than once, and she longed for those fingers on her now.

"Christian," she whispered.

His head snapped up and his dark gaze pierced her, making her immobile. She trembled with need and desire and something else she couldn't describe.

"I wasn't sure you would come," he said. He remained leaning against the fountain, yet his body was coiled tight like a tiger, ready to spring.

"I almost didn't."

He pushed off the fountain and took her in his arms. She melted into him, each part of her body singing with pleasure at the touch of his hardness against her. Something settled in her heart and bloomed.

Right. He felt so right.

*** 

The feel of her soft, pliant body folding into him made all of him harden further. His hips strained into hers at their own accord and the breathy sounds she was making at the back of her throat drove him to distraction.

He captured her lips, his hands finding their way to her derriere and squeezing, lifting her high and hard against him.

"Tell me to stop," he said. His words rang out harsh between them. "If you don't, I won't be able to."

Her only response was to open for him further, and his tongue delved deep, swallowing both their moans. His fingers moved swiftly then, unlacing the deep green dress, only to flatten against the warm skin of her back. She arched into his touch, her own hands frantic, searching for purchase.

Switching positions, he perched her bottom upon the lip of the well, one hand splaying in her hair, pins scattering all around them, the other pushing up her dress, running along the inside of her silken knee, a tender thigh, only to delve deep into moist heat.

She cried out, her hips lifting off the stone seat.

"Mine," he whispered into her mouth. "Say it," he said.

His fingers continued their relentless assault until she sobbed out his name. "Yours," she cried.

The last bit of sanity that held him back snapped. He quickly unlaced his trousers, his raging need springing free, and he positioned himself at her entrance.

"Look at me," he said.

Her cheeks were flushed, a tendril of hair fell over one of her eyes and the sleeves of her dress were down at her elbows, her delicious breasts rising and falling with each breath. The ruby necklace gleamed against her flesh, branding her as his. She was a vision, a goddess bathed in moonlight, desire filled eyes staring up at him with need, and want, and all the things he felt himself.

"You're mine," he said. "Forever."

She cupped his cheek. "Forever."

When he entered her, they both cried out.

*** 

"Stop moving," Christian said.

Kate sighed, attempting to ignore the itch on her shoulder. Every time she attempted to forget about it, another place on her body began to bother it. It was relentless, and positively frustrating since Christian wouldn't let her move.

She should have never agreed to sit for this painting.

"Are you almost done?" she asked. She'd been still for too many hours to count. How long did it take to do a portrait?

It'd been three weeks since she'd given herself to Christian that night at the fountain, and not for one moment had she regretted it. Wearing the forest green dress now, with her hair curled and piled around her shoulders, brought back the delicious memory of their first time.

"I know that look," Christian said.

His deep voice had the uncanny ability to make her knees weak still.

"What are you thinking, Mrs. Jones?"

Kate laughed. Happiness swelled in her chest as she looked over at her husband, his head tilted to the side and his eyes warming. It was the same expression he'd worn as she'd walked down the isle of the old stone church, the sound of the dual brass wedding bells pealing into the morning air, announcing their union. Sans the paint he currently had smeared across one cheek and his half undone shirt.

She loved this man before her, with his artist's hands and loving touch. That day she tripped on the stairs and fell into his arms was the beginning of the rest of her life.

Joséphine LaCoste was right. Christian was her chance at happiness.

He was hers. Forever.

"I knew it," Christian said, bringing her out of her thoughts.

"Hmm?"

"I believe I've done it."

"We're done?" Kate asked.

"A masterpiece," Christian said, grinning as he turned the canvas to face her.

Is that what he saw when he looked at her? She didn't look like herself, not the woman she saw every day in the looking glass. Her eyes seemed larger, more vibrant, and her cheeks were as rosy as her lips. The ruby necklace he'd given her blazed against the deep green of her dress. He captured every detail, every shadow and texture of her. And everywhere she looked, she saw his testament of love.

"My goodness," Kate said, eyes wide. "Is that even me?"

Christian stood and moved toward her. Reaching out he tucked an errant curl behind her ear. "That's exactly how I see you."

She felt her heart melt. "I love you," she said.

He leaned down and brushed his lips against hers once, twice.

"And I love you," he said. "Now, I have another painting in mind, but this time, you aren't to wear anything, except..." he grinned, "the necklace."

Christian kissed her mid laugh, and she sunk into him, into the kiss, and into her future.

**LAKE COVINGTON**

# All I Want is You

## STACEY BRYANT

On a beautiful July day, Aryn stood on the shore watching the sunrise over Lake Covington and decided to let go of everything negative and focus on the positive. She breathed the morning air and fingered the dangling silver charm bracelet on her wrist until she found the engagement ring charm and removed it.

Charles Thomas Winston III had given her the trinket on her twenty-second birthday as a promise of his commitment. When deemed "on the road" to the White House, he broke things off and attached himself to Taylor Brenton, who, with her Fifth Avenue style, was bred to be on the arm of the future president. The two-carat diamond he placed on Taylor's finger should have been Aryn's, not the cheap-ass costume-jewelry promise she held in her hand. She should have known her ex would turn out to be a jerk. His bright red aura became less passionate and more clouded toward the end. She packed up and moved to Lake Covington shortly after.

Aryn let the silver charm slide like rainwater off her fingertips, as payment to the Lady of the Lake. Aryn hoped the matchmaking mermaid would accept her offering and find her a suitable partner. Working at Cuppa Café she often heard stories of how couples had met after dropping a token into those waters. Aryn was ready to find love, and she had her eye on one man in particular.

***

Evan Jacobs was close to a breakthrough, but he knew if he didn't answer his sister's call, he'd be on speed dial. Devin, his nosey twin sister, texted or called every day. He promised her he'd take a break from his work, get out of the single-car garage turned man cave, and enjoy the summer. Evan quickly finished the line of code he'd been struggling with, then closed his laptop. "What's up?" he asked, putting his sister on speaker.

"I'm reminding you to not get lost in your work and stand us up tonight," Devin said.

"I wouldn't dream of it." Evan glanced at his watch. "I've got to go. Jack should be here any second."

"Where are you going?"

"Our daily coffee run."

"*Daily?*" When Devin drew out the word, he realized he screwed up. She'd behave like a dog with a bone.

"Since when do you frequent coffee shops?"

Since the coffee shop had the most beautiful barista working there. Aryn. The first time he went, she had set a latte down before him with an algebraic equation drawn in the foam. He hadn't ordered a latte—hadn't even known what it was and didn't much care for it. Last week he ordered another just to see what else she'd draw. He'd been surprised to see a Superman logo. Puzzled, he thanked her and joined Jack at their usual booth.

His sister's voice snapped him out of his rumination.

"There must be a girl involved. Who's is it?"

Evan hesitated, but when he didn't answer right away, she added, "You might as well tell me or I'll tell Mom you're holding out. You don't want her getting on you, do you?"

He wiped his hand down his face and groaned. Both his sister and his mom were relentless. While his sister galivanted, as his mom put it, he'd always been perfectly content in front of a computer. "I don't have time to date. Besides, I love what I do and I'm committed to work. Jack has allowed me to rent his garage for the summer only. Work is more important right now." He'd given someone a chance, a two-year chance, and she'd left him at the altar. He didn't need to go through that again.

Jack and he had been friends since grade school. When Jack moved to Lake Covington, he offered his garage to Evan so he could concentrate on work. Only work. Except Devin had interfered and Jack had promised her to get Evan out of the garage at least once a week. Meeting Aryn had changed that.

Jack walked into the garage and pressed the button to raise the door.

"I've got to go, Dev. See you tonight."

\*\*\*

By the time Aryn got back to her cottage on the edge of town, she was running late. She needed to grab the dozen mermaid mugs she'd removed from the kiln yesterday and dress for work.

Aryn jogged upstairs to her bedroom and changed into a white tank, a pair of boyfriend jeans, and pulled on her blue Converse. She removed the band from her wrist and tied her blonde locks into a ponytail as she ran out the door.

After securing the box of coffee mugs to the back rack of Big Red, her vintage balloon-tire cruiser bicycle, Aryn set off toward downtown. She did her best sales during the summer months. Her coffee mugs were in high demand, and the tourists didn't mind paying fifty dollars for a custom hand-thrown mug. Between working at Cuppa Café and selling her pottery, she would have enough money by the end of summer to buy a larger kiln.

Sweet and savory smells wafted from the food trucks lining the side streets around the marina. The Fourth of July festival was tomorrow. It was a popular event that started with a parade of sailboats, followed with a picnic in the park, and then ended with the largest fireworks display in the area. A sea of red, white, and blue banners dotted the streets, baskets of patriotic flowers hung on every old-fashion light post, and American flags lined the sidewalks.

Aryn chained Big Red to the bike rack outside the café, unstrapped the box, and carried it inside. Cuppa Café, located on the busiest corner of historic Main Street across from the courthouse, was the spot for locals to get their caffeine fix. Even with the big-box coffee stores that had come to town, tourists stopped by for the quaint charm on their walk to the lake.

Hints of chocolate, warm cinnamon rolls, and the ever-present aroma of fresh-brewed coffee filled the air. Patrons lounged in the cozy leather armchairs, at the tables, and booths. A George Winston song played on the overhead speaker system. Aryn nodded to a few regulars as she made her way to the front counter.

Megan glanced up from wiping down the espresso machine as Aryn approached. "Hey birthday girl," she said. "Thanks for working today."

Megan owned Cuppa Café. She'd hired Aryn on the spot and they quickly became best friends, laughing and crying over many a late-night latte. Megan's light green aura had shined brightly and Aryn knew they'd get along great. Megan was a healer and Aryn needed healing.

"Happy to help." Aryn walked around the counter and placed the box on the table in the small kitchen area. "I have a feeling it's going to be a good day."

Megan already had the first mug unwrapped and was oohing and ahhing by the time Aryn tucked her knapsack under the counter. Always her biggest supporter, Megan gushed over everything she made.

"They're gorgeous...the colors. Amazing." Megan held one of Aryn's favorites with the background painted in a celestial blue. The mermaid sat on a rock and gazed out to sea, her long brown hair flowed down her back, and her green and silver scaled tail with a yellow and orange fin wrapped around the mug. Megan peered inside and placed a hand over her heart and sighed, "There's even a jewel painted on the bottom. It's perfect."

Megan was one of the biggest believers in the Lady of the Lake and loved telling the story to anyone who'd listen, including Aryn.

"You know tourists. They love the myth," Aryn winked.

Megan snapped pictures of the mugs and uploaded them to the café's Facebook page.

They watched the growing likes until the bell above the door chimed and a couple holding hands walked toward the counter. Their auras glowed bright pink, and Aryn knew she'd be drawing hearts in the foam of their lattes. That was all she'd been drawing lately; it seemed everyone was in love except for her. She toyed with the bracelet around her wrist. Hopefully, her luck would change soon.

The couple set two of the mermaid mugs on the counter and ordered large cappuccinos. While Megan wrapped the mugs in bubble wrap and placed them in a bag with the Cuppa Café logo stamped on it, Aryn made their drinks. She could draw a double heart design with her eyes closed. She set their coffees on the counter. "Enjoy."

Megan came up behind her. "Are you making any more of these mermaid mugs? I have a feeling we'll sell out this weekend."

"Good. That means I'll be that much closer to buying a new kiln." Aryn wiped down the counter. "I have another batch ready to paint. I'll have them for you on Monday."

Aryn looked up when the door chimed. An elderly woman walked in the café. Aryn sighed. She wanted it to be someone else.

Megan nudged her. "You know he rarely misses a day."

"I don't know what you're talking about." Aryn felt her cheeks flush.

"Don't give me that. Evan Jacobs. The one you can't keep your eyes off, the one who—"

"Okay, stop." Aryn had her eye on Evan ever since he first walked through the door of Cuppa Café. His orange-yellow aura, indicating his scientific mind, fascinated her, but the way he looked through her like he could penetrate her very soul— swoon-worthy.

When Evan came into the café, Aryn had a hard time focusing on work. Sometimes she'd catch him glancing her way and hoped he was attracted to her too and not studying the menu behind her. She hoped to get more of a reaction from Evan with her new design. She'd been practicing a week to get an Albert Einstein face drawn in under two minutes. If this didn't get him to talk to her, she didn't know what would.

"No more worrying. He'll be here." Megan said. "Instead, let's talk about your birthday. We're still on for tonight, right?" Megan asked.

"I can't believe you got us reservations at Chez Charbon. How'd you manage that?"

Megan smiled. "I may have reminded Chef Henri when he was in last week that he owed me a favor."

The bell over the door chimed again, and this time Evan and Jack walked in.

"Well, speak of the devil," Megan whispered.

"Good afternoon ladies," Jack said as he stepped up to the counter.

"Hi guys, your usual?" Megan asked.

Jack said, "Yep, I can't wait to see what Aryn has in store for us today."

Megan leaned over the register. "Did you know it's Aryn's birthday?"

Both men grinned at her. Aryn felt herself blushing and cursed her fair skin. She took a breath and started brewing the espresso and heating the milk. When the coffees were ready, she armed herself with a toothpick and spoon and went to work. It didn't take long for her to set the finished drinks on the counter in front of the men.

Jack looked at his design first. She'd drawn a set of handcuffs. This morning one of the café's regulars came in talking about the arrest Jack made last night. She'd thought it fitting, and Jack's laugh confirmed that she was right.

Evan looked down at the design, smiled, and said, "Did you know that Einstein rejected the distinction between past, present, and future?"

Aryn's heart fluttered. It worked. He talked. "I've heard that, but I believe our past, no matter how painful, defines us, the present is our gift to enjoy, and our future is full of exciting possibilities."

Evan placed a twenty-dollar bill in the tip jar. "Happy Birthday."

He walked off, leaving his coffee behind.

Jack rolled his eyes and grabbed the two lattes. "Guess I got it."

Evan went to his usual booth in the back corner without so much as a glance backward as he scribbled something in the notebook that he kept in his front pocket.

Aryn groaned. "Well, so much for dropping my charm in the lake this morning."

Megan squealed. "It's about time you offered something to the Lady of the Lake."

"Mine must have been a dud."

"Don't worry," Megan said, hugging her. "The Lady always comes through."

\*\*\*

Aryn arrived at Chez Charbon early. She wore her little black dress with a flared skirt and her black suede heels. She thought she better look her best if the Lady of the Lake chose to work her magic tonight. She held the heavy wood door open for an elderly woman who frequented Cuppa Café. "You look beautiful, Mrs. Johnson," Aryn told her.

Mrs. Johnson touched her styled hair. "Thank you dear. I'm having dinner with my sister and her husband."

She waved goodbye as the hostess greeted Mrs. Johnson and whisked her away.

Aryn spotted a seat at the bar. The Flower Duet coming from the speakers reminded her of when she had taken part in the set design for the production of Lakmé in college. She hummed along and slid onto the high stool; it was like a soft and comforting dark chocolate truffle. She placed her matching sequined clutch in front of her.

The bartender finished serving a beer to the person on her left and then turned to her. "What are you having?"

"Pinot Grigio, please."

As the bartender turned away, Aryn glanced at the man next to her and jumped in surprise. "Evan?" She couldn't believe her luck. Then again, she had a feeling her birthday this year would be one to remember.

"Oh, umm... Hi Aryn."

"Are you waiting for someone? Your girlfriend?"

"No. My parents and sister."

Aryn had been using coffee designs to get Evan to talk to her for a month, but the way he kept glancing down at her chest made her think that maybe she'd been going about it all wrong. She had his undivided attention.

Evan's phone vibrated with an incoming text. Aryn glanced over to see who was texting him.

Devin.

"My sister," he said and picked up his phone. Frowning, he sent a short reply.

"Bad news?" Aryn asked.

"More like a warning. She said my mother is up to something. With her, it's liable to be anything."

This time Aryn's phone buzzed with an incoming call from Megan. Aryn covered her left ear to drown out the rising chatter around her. "Are you on your way?"

"I'm running late. The security alarm at the café is going off and I need to head back to disarm it. Wait for me, okay?"

"Of course. Do you want me to meet you there?"

"No, it's probably a false alarm. I'll try to hurry."

Aryn ended the call.

"Is everything okay?" Evan asked.

"Megan is treating me to dinner tonight. She ran into an issue at the café, but she'll be here."

Evan took a drink of his beer and fidgeted with the coaster. Aryn sipped her wine, trying to think of something to say and keep him talking. It was the longest conversation they'd ever had, and she wanted it to continue. His aura glowed a bright pink, a sign he was interested in love, and she knew she needed to keep him talking to have any chance.

"You mentioned a sister. Is it only the two of you?"

Evan downed the rest of his beer. "Just us. We're twins."

"Wow. Does she look like you? I mean, you know as much as she can, being a girl and all—" Aryn bit her bottom lip to stop herself from sounding like more of an idiot.

Evan chuckled. "We have the same color eyes and hair, but I'm a couple inches taller."

Another long pause threatened to stall their conversation. "So, you know when my birthday is, when's yours?"

"November tenth."

"Scorpio." Aryn couldn't believe her luck. No wonder she'd been attracted to him. Scorpio was one of the best signs for Cancer.

"Favorite food?" Aryn asked.

"Italian."

"Chicken Parm – yumm."

A tall brunette with the same golden eyes as Evan tapped him on the shoulder. The woman leaned forward and whispered, "Incoming," to Evan and then nodded toward a redhead, who was standing next to an older woman.

Evan stood and reached for Aryn's hand, squeezing it. "Hi everyone. Mom, Dad, Devin, this is my girlfriend, Aryn."

Aryn stumbled to her feet, hoping her shock didn't show. "So...so nice to meet you all. I've heard a lot about you."

"Honey…" his mom stared at Evan. "Why didn't you tell us you had a girlfriend?"

"Umm." He placed his hands in his pockets.

"It's fairly new," Aryn said, jumping in. "Evan wanted to surprise you." She turned to the woman Evan's mother brought along. She felt bad for her. "I'm sorry, this is awkward."

"I'll say." The redhead's eyes shot daggers at Evan. "I should go. Excuse me."

***

Evan tried to tamp down his frustration. Devin had warned him his mom intended to set him up tonight and he was tired of the constant matchmaking. He hadn't meant to put Aryn in an awkward situation, but now he feared his impetuosity would ruin his chance with her. "Mom, who was *that*?"

His mom waved the question away. "A lovely girl that I met at the salon in town. I was telling her how you were single and how much I was looking forward to grandchildren."

"Mom!"

"What?" she asked, acting as if she were shocked. "You can't blame me for trying to make sure you're nice and settled."

Before Evan could reply, his dad held up a blinking black box and gave it a little shake. "Our table is ready."

Evan grabbed Aryn's hand and turned to Devin. "Give us a minute."

Devin nodded and followed her parents.

As soon as his sister was out of sight, Evan said to Aryn. "I'm sorry. I panicked. I appreciate you playing along, but I can go in there and explain everything."

"No." Aryn said. "I mean…it's okay. I get it. Really. Obviously, you don't want to be set up on a blind date. We can pull this off, but if we want to do a decent job, first things first."

She bent forward and kissed him on the mouth.

He longed for more than a single kiss. Somehow nothing seemed more exciting than fake dating. Life was about to get much better. When she pulled back, he said, "Thanks," and immediately felt like the biggest idiot.

The hottest girl in the place kissed him and he said thanks. He took a breath. But despite her unforgettable soft lips he needed to focus more on work and less on a relationship. He couldn't go through the same disaster as last time.

He waited as Aryn sent a quick text to Megan telling her where to find them. Then she grabbed his hand and led him into the dining room. "Come on, Einstein."

Quiet conversation filled the room and his stomach growled from the smell of freshly baked baguettes. They found his parents' table, which overlooked the lake.

"Excuse me," Evan said, catching the hostess's attention as she walked by. "There will be six of us. Will that be a problem?"

"No. Not at all. We'll set another place. One moment, please."

"Who else is coming?" his mom asked as the hostess brought the extra seat.

"It's Aryn's birthday today," Evan said, sitting across from his sister. "I invited her friend Megan to join us."

Megan arrived a few minutes later. After they ordered, the questions began.

"Where did you meet?" his mom asked.

Aryn jumped in before Evan could respond. "At Cuppa Café, where I work," she said. "I was smitten the moment I saw him."

"How long have you been together?"

"Oh," Aryn looked at Evan and smiled. "Not too long."

The questions continued throughout dinner. Evan had to hand it to Megan and Aryn, they really played the part and he was glad he didn't have to talk much.

Devin asked Aryn, "Will we see you at the Fourth of July celebration tomorrow?

Aryn nodded. "Absolutely. We'll be there."

"With bells on," Evan said, glaring at his sister.

Megan stood. "I need to head home. It was great meeting everyone."

His family said their goodbyes to Megan. Once she was gone, Aryn leaned against Evan. "Can you give me a ride home?"

***

Evan lifted Aryn's bike from the back of his truck and followed her to the door. He said, "It amazes me how you can ride a bike in that dress."

"Since it's my only mode of transportation, I make do."

Once inside, Aryn set her clutch and keys on the table in the foyer. "We need a plan for tomorrow," she said.

Evan hoped she didn't want to cut and run, but he felt bad for forcing her into a fake relationship. Aryn was fun to be around. He enjoyed her easy laugh and her ability to talk to anyone. All things he struggled with. "You don't need to feel obligated to go along with this charade."

Aryn grabbed his hands. "I don't mind."

Her hair was down, a stripe of pink framing her face. She smelled sweet and musky. Aryn licked her lips, and the action sent a jolt of electricity straight through him. It was as if the air pulsed between them.

"How about a glass of wine?" she asked.

Evan didn't much like wine; he wanted something else.

He looked into her eyes and closed the small distance and kissed her gently, his mouth moving over hers. He stepped back a little. "I've been wanting to do that all night," he said.

"I hoped you would."

When Aryn left for the kitchen, he walked around her small living room admiring the eclectic mix of art hung on the walls. Stacks of books on sculpture covered most available surfaces, and an old trunk served as a coffee table. Next to the television sat a pile of DVDs that he remembered from his teenage years—titles his sister made him watch.

"Here you go," Aryn said, handing him a glass of wine. She kicked off her heels, went to the couch, and tucked her legs under her.

He sat down beside her, trying hard to take his eyes off her perfectly shaped legs.

"I feel bad for having roped you into our family drama."

She took a drink. "I'm enjoying myself. I like you, Evan. Besides, if we break it off now your mom will have more women lined up to take my place. Unless that's what you want?"

"Not at all."

"Then it's decided." She set her glass on the table.

Evan wasn't sure what was supposed to happen now. Conversation wasn't his strong suit, especially with attractive women. He looked around the room and spied the movies. "What's your favorite movie?"

"Are you kidding me?"

"What? That's not a good question?"

"It's not, *not* good, but I can't come up with a favorite. Ask me my favorite ending."

"Okay. What's your favorite movie ending?"

"*Sixteen Candles.*"

Evan shook his head. "*Sixteen Candles?*"

Aryn's eyes widened. "Don't tell me you've never seen it. It's a classic."

He went along with it and waited for her to summarize the movie before he fessed up and recited the only line he could remember: "Hey, sexy girlfriend."

"OMG." She slapped him on the arm. "You did see it and you just let me sit there like a fool telling you all about it!"

"You know I have a twin sister, right? Of course I've seen it." He laughed. "So why do you like it so much?"

She shrugged. "I don't know." She grabbed one of the couch pillows and hugged it. "I guess I related to Molly Ringwald's character and the way she seemed to be a side note to her parents' busy lives. My mom and stepdad would forget about my birthday a lot. They were always working or traveling. It's not a big deal. I had au pairs who remembered."

Evan gave Aryn's hand a gentle squeeze.

The day was warm and the breeze light. Aryn met Evan and his family at the park for the Fourth of July celebration. She and Evan took part in the three-legged race, ate too much caramel corn and cotton candy, and went for a long walk along the lake holding hands. At nightfall, Evan held her as they watched the spectacular fireworks display over the lake.

Evan's parents and sister were due to head back home the next day. Evan promised to call her after they left, but three days passed without a word and he didn't show up at the café with Jack. When Aryn pressed him about Evan, the officer's confident orange aura changed to dark pink. Aryn knew he was making excuses for Evan.

Aryn had made her move on Evan, made it clear that she was interested, but she refused to pursue someone who wasn't into her. Once before she'd fallen for a man who left her. She wasn't going to make the same mistake again.

One night after closing, Megan stopped by with burgers and fries from Mojo's. She placed the takeout on the kitchen table and unpacked the food. "How are you feeling?"

"Depressed. Sad. Dejected." Aryn plopped a salty fry into her mouth.

"Have you tried calling him?"

"No."

"Going over there?"

"What's the point?" She ate another fry.

"Maybe there's an explanation."

"Doubtful. The charade is over. He needed me. Now he doesn't. Period."

Megan tried to comfort her, but nothing she said helped. Aryn felt foolish for believing in the Lady of the Lake.

***

Evan couldn't concentrate. He stared at his computer screen, not accomplishing anything. For the first time in his life, he felt lonely. He had friends, well, Jack, but he missed *her*.

Aryn had ignited a light inside him. He no longer wanted to spend his days shackled to his computer. He'd been trying to ignore her, thinking he needed to work, but he was an idiot—she showed him he could do both. He hoped it wasn't too late to get her back. It was time to take another chance on love.

Evan needed a plan, and if he wanted to win her back it had to be good.

***

Aryn placed a mound of clay on the center of her potter's wheel. She closed her eyes and breathed deeply to center her mind and body and let her hands do the work, but all she could think of was Evan.

With a gentle downward pressure, Aryn pressed, centered, and created an opening from the top of the clay. As she widened the opening and pulled up, the mound wobbled off center like a tilt-a-whirl gone mad. Her focus gone and the piece ruined, she cleaned up the mess. Her phone dinged with an incoming text from Megan. Aryn wiped her hands on her stained apron and checked her message.

> Just got a call from the alarm company. Alarm going off. Can U go check? I'm an hour away.

Aryn texted back:

> Absolutely.

At least she could help a friend and be productive tonight.

Aryn parked her bike in front of Cuppa Café and got off. Jack waited for her at the front door.

"Hey Jack."

"Thanks for coming, Aryn," he said.

"No problem. What do you think? Another false alarm?"

"Yep. I've already gone in—all clear, but you'll need to enter the password."

"Okay, sure." A bright orange glow emanated from him. He was awfully excited about a false alarm. She wondered if it had been a slow night for Lake Covington's police department.

Jack held the front door open for her. "I'll be right behind you."

Aryn entered the code, and the alarm silenced.

From the corner of her eyes, she saw a flicker of light from the kitchen area. She stepped around the front counter. Evan sat cross-legged on the table with a cake in front of him, candles burning, their flames dancing like glimmering stars in the distant sky. *If You Were Here* by the Thompson Twins played softly in the background. He had recreated the final scene from *Sixteen Candles*. Her stomach fluttered and her pulse quickened.

"What?" She wiped a tear away. "What are you doing here?"

Evan said, "I'm sorry. I've been a jerk. I've been hurt before."

"So have I."

"Can you forgive me?"

Aryn nodded.

Evan held out his hand. "Come...sit."

She climbed up onto the table across from Evan. "You remembered."

"Make a wish."

Aryn looked down at the cake then back to meet Evan's eyes. "It already came true."

*Thank you, Lady of the Lake.*

# Lake Covington Herald

February 11, 2019

## This Day in Lake Covington
**CONNOR LANE**

The Great Storm hit Lake Covington in 1919, dropping two inches every hour for nearly a week. February 11th, the sixth day of the storm, the weight of the water proved too much for Moyer Dam. As I stand at the door of what the locals call the New Church, I can look out at the lake and see the bells of the original church sticking out of the water. It's a jarring sight, and a constant reminder of the tragedy that happened that fateful day.

"I was a baby when the dam broke," Edna McCray, Lake Covington's oldest citizen tells me, as she looks at the bricks and corroded brass. She has a golden chain in her hand, and a locket dangles in her grip. "We lost my oldest sister, Olivia, that day. Shattered my poor mother's heart."

Many of Lake Covington's older generation have a similar story. The water that flooded the valley took over four hundred lives, over a hundred of which were never recovered. In an ironic note, seven months before Moyer Dam gave way, it had passed an inspection, despite cracks and leaks in the dam and its abutments.

Under the pressure of the rain and the runoff brought by the storm, the massive concrete wall crumbled and collapsed. The citizens of Lake Covington had only minutes to evacuate. The water rose high enough to inundate Main Street and the entire town square. The nearby town of Diggs Junction fared better, having a few more minutes before the water arrived and sitting higher above the water table.

Perhaps the constant reminder of those old church bells is what makes the citizens of Lake Covington so aware of how the catastrophe shaped the town not only physically, but in the way its people interact with each other. The town's relief efforts that 11th of February bonded them in a way that has lasted, and according to Edna McCray, will continue long after she's gone.

"We meet here at the church every year on the anniversary of the flood," she tells me. "This way, we never forget."

I couldn't have said it better myself, Edna.

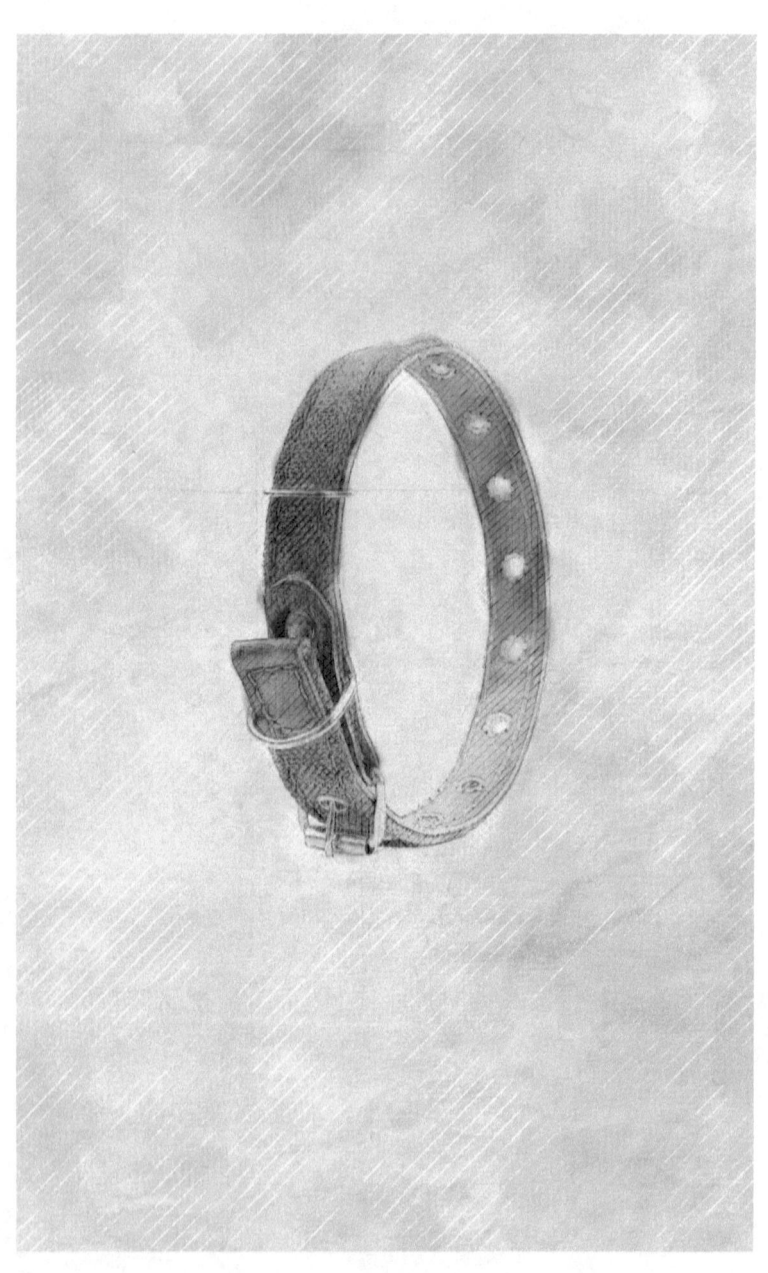

# Wagging the Dog

## NANCY CANU

*T*aylor turned the clippers on, drowning out the schnauzer's growl. "I agree," he said, adjusting the dog on the grooming table with his free hand. "I'd growl too if somebody was going to shave my butt. You'd growl more if it was hot wax, trust me."

He'd groomed the cavalier, the two labs, and the doodle earlier. For now, he had this trim to finish, and then maybe he could restock the front of the store. A full day. A profitable day. Which was good, because Pet Project might be his dream come true, but he hadn't quite factored in how much work this dream would require. Converting a derelict former pharmacy into a grooming salon was a lot harder than it looked on those renovation shows. Not to mention taking a lot longer. And costing a lot more. A helluva lot more. The only saving grace was living upstairs essentially rent-free. Not that he had any regrets, oh god, no. Being around dogs all day was the best thing he could imagine.

Taylor stepped back from the table and checked the schnauzer over. "You, little man, are done. No more scary clippers." As he put the dog into a crate, the front door chimed and he glanced at the security monitor. He didn't recognize the dog, a big poodle mix, although the owner was vaguely familiar. Somebody he'd seen on the boardwalk? Maybe. Between fishing, strolling, or grabbing a bite to eat, everyone in town went there. That didn't seem right, though. Working around the docks? He spent a lot more time over there, checking out the sailboats. That had to be it.

When Taylor came out front, Kimmy the cashier had her eyes glued to her cellphone. Taylor hissed at her, and she scowled and hunched her shoulders. "What? He just came in."

Rather than lecture her—again—on customer protocol, Taylor pasted on a welcoming smile. "Welcome to Pet Project," he said, coming around the counter. "How can we—" Damn.

Muddy water dripped onto the floor under the dog. The large, hairy, wet dog. The large, hairy, extraordinarily filthy, wet dog. Taylor took a deep breath—bad idea—and coughed into his fist. Would pulling his shirt over his nose be rude?

"Lake water. And roadkill. Not in that order."

Oh. That voice. Deep and smooth as melted dark chocolate. Taylor checked the guy out, thinking of all the things he'd like to hear that voice say, and...no. Definitely no. Too scruffy, most likely straight, and...no. Taylor didn't do blue collar. He did guys with suits and stock portfolios and manicures, guys whose cars had heated leather seats and whose condos had killer views. Not that men like that were thick on the ground around here, but Lake Covington wasn't exactly the back of beyond. He had hope. Not a lot, but some.

Taylor tried on his professional smile. "So, you're here for a bath?"

The guy with the filthy dog looked at Taylor, brown eyes crinkling at the corners, and his mouth quirked up on one side. "I was thinking just the dog."

Taylor snorted, and the smile he got in return started an odd buzz in his chest. Had he thought those eyes were brown? They were hazel, with gold and green flecks. Not even close to handsome, not with that crooked nose and long jaw, but nice eyes. And a sense of humor. And a dog.

The guy glanced down at the dog, who made a happy face and wagged his tail, sending an arc of brown water across both front doors. "Oh fuck," the guy said, clapping one hand over his forehead. "I am really sorry about that."

Taylor had to feel bad for him. "No worries. Let's get—" he eyed the dog "—him into the back, and Kimmy will give you some forms to fill out."

The guy made an indefinable noise, sort of a resigned groan. "Forms?"

Taylor didn't find that noise sexy. Nope. Not one bit. "Name, address, phone number, dog's info, basic liability release. No big deal, just standard stuff. And payment information, of course."

"Jesus," the guy muttered, and sighed. "Okay. About how long is this gonna take?"

"Well, if all he needs is a bath, about three hours. If he's got a lot of mats, then I'll have to shave him—more like four hours, then. We'll call you when he's ready."

Another sigh. "Yeah, that'll work. Thanks." The guy shook his head at the dog. "I'll see you later, I guess." He didn't sound all that happy. True, not everybody loved dogs the way Taylor did, and he tried not to judge. Much. The guy handed him the end of—a piece of rope? Really?—and Taylor's good intentions flew right the hell out the window.

He must have made a face, because the guy winced. Not totally clueless, then. "Sorry about that. He's not usually on a leash, and—"

"Not a problem. Don't forget to fill out the forms." Taylor headed for the back, dog in tow, before he said something unforgivable.

***

Taylor had never driven this far up along the lake and wasn't exactly sure where he was. Good thing he had Google Maps, because he was pissed off enough that following simple directions was about his limit right now. The mailbox at the end of the gravel driveway said Kaye, so this must be the right place, except there was no house. Only a weird looking—what the hell was that supposed to be, anyway? A houseboat?

Taylor parked the minivan next to a big-ass pickup truck and got out, scowling at the thing tied to the pier. It looked like a pontoon boat and a summer cottage had a fling. Whatever. Kimmy had called earlier to confirm that Taylor could drop the dog off because the grooming was taking longer than anticipated. That was the polite version. Taylor's version was obscene and wouldn't win him any customer appreciation awards.

He went around, opened the back hatch, and let the dog— Caesar, according to the forms—out of the crate, getting a good grip on the flimsy polyester leash and choke collar combo he had to use because Francis X. Kaye couldn't be bothered to buy his goddamned dog a leash and collar.

Deep breath. He could do this. Hand over the dog and get the hell out of here.

He made it almost all the way to the pier, Caesar clinging to his side, before Kaye appeared, stepping out of a door on the side of the floating whatever the hell it was. Kaye looked at the dog, looked at Taylor, frowned, and asked, "What happened?"

"What happened?" Taylor's right eye started twitching, and his mouth took over. "Aside from the mats? There were burrs— burrs—like, everywhere, *and* he had fleas. I gave him a flea treatment, because I had to, and there had to be fifty of the little bastards in the tub, plus more dead ones when I *shaved* him." He was on a roll now, and it took him another couple sentences—he'd had hours to work up a good head of steam— to notice two things.

One, Kaye was standing there, calmly watching Taylor and not seeming particularly offended about Taylor's rant. And two, Caesar was looking around like he'd never been here before.

Shit. Taylor cut himself off mid-sentence. "He's not your dog, is he?"

Kaye shook his head, mouth curling in a lopsided smile. "Nope. Somebody dumped him, end of last summer, and he's been hanging around the docks since last fall."

"Okay. So." Taylor breathed in. Let it out. Oh man. "Can we forget all the shit I just said?"

This time, Kaye's smile showed a chipped front tooth. Not attractive. Except it kind of was. "Yeah. Um, look, I just put burgers on the grill. I gotta go check on them. Come on board for a minute?" He shrugged. "It's okay if you—"

"Sure." If being social would aid a potential client's memory loss regarding his behavior, Taylor was all for it. That had to be somewhere in his business plan.

"Come on board, then."

Taylor stepped forward and the dog swarmed toward Kaye, wagging his now-whippy tail and bounding onto the deck, hip-checking Taylor in the process. Taylor stumbled, and let go of the leash rather than fall into the lake. Kaye grabbed his flailing hand. It was nothing, simple politeness, but Taylor's body noticed. Kaye's hand was warm and dry and firm, and his fingers gripped with the right amount of pressure, a fleeting impression of easy strength, of someone used to physical work.

"Thanks," Taylor said, and maybe he imagined that Kaye didn't let go right away. "Mr. Kaye—"

"Frankie." His smile lit his hazel eyes and Taylor found himself smiling back.

"Taylor. Taylor Beckett."

"Pleased to meet you, Taylor." Frankie slipped the leash off Caesar and led the way through a small living room and past an even smaller kitchen, none of which Taylor actually saw because he was watching how Frankie's shoulders narrowed down to a truly nice ass and muscled thighs. Which had to be the height of stupid. Not his type. Not even with the pretty eyes and warm smile. Or the dog.

Taylor walked through the open sliding glass door and stopped in his tracks when Frankie stepped aside. Lake Covington stretched out in front of him, blue and serene, all the way to the trees crowding the opposite shore. "Oh my god. This is amazing."

"It is, right?" Frankie slid four burgers off the grill and onto a plate, turning off the gas at the same time. "I didn't even care that the houseboat was a wreck when I bought it. The view was worth every penny." He cleared his throat. "Look, I'm really sorry about the dog. Caesar. I honestly had no idea. We didn't have dogs growing up. Well, my uncle did, but that was a Lab— not like they really need haircuts and stuff."

Taylor fumbled his way into a comfy deck chair, mesmerized by the view, and Caesar flopped down by his feet with a heavy sigh. "And I'm sorry I went off on you like that, I just thought you..." He wasn't sure where to go with the rest of that sentence.

"Were a complete asshole?" Frankie offered Taylor a crooked grin.

Taylor should not be feeling any tug of—anything. Scruffy guys were not his thing. Not even ones whose houseboat had a killer lake view.

Frankie shook his head. "It's okay. I get it. Look, could you recommend some dog food and stuff? The guys at the dockyard put food out for him, but I'm pretty sure it's crap from the supermarket, whatever's cheapest."

"Why do they call it a dockyard when it's not?" Taylor muttered, tugging one of Caesar's ears, and was surprised when Frankie laughed.

"Yeah, I asked the same thing. Turns out it was one, back in the day, and nobody ever changed the name even when they stopped building boats there." His smile was kind of addictive. "You know about boats?"

"A little," Taylor admitted. "My grandparents had a place in Vancouver, and I'd go sailing with them whenever I could. You?"

"My mother's family owns a marina down near Redondo Beach. In California. I worked there summers during high school. Then I went to work with my father's family on the piers." He shrugged.

"So pretty much the same thing you do now," Taylor said. According to Kimmy, his source for all things Lake Covington, Frankie was in charge of maintenance for the docks.

"Um, no." Frankie opened a mini-fridge, and offered him a bottle of the local microbrew. Taylor wasn't going to refuse a cold beer, not today.

Frankie opened one for himself and sat down in another deck chair. "I was a dock worker. A longshoreman. I loaded and unloaded cargo from ships for fifteen years in Portland." He tilted his head, studied Taylor for a second or two. "I needed a change. I saw an ad for the job at the dockyard and jumped on it." He shrugged again. "I like it here. And the scenery's nice." His smile was definitely flirty, and the pit of Taylor's stomach went hot.

There'd been no one since he moved here. Between the renovation and getting Pet Project going, he had zero free time. And even though statistically there had to be some other gay men in town *and* everyone in Lake Covington had to know he was gay by now, not one guy had so much as given him a look. He knew he was handsome, knew his sandy hair, blue eyes, dimples, and lean swimmer's body made an attractive combination. So, yeah, he didn't understand it.

Frankie's sideways glance made Taylor want to say yes to, well, whatever. "Do you want a burger?" Frankie asked, and Caesar scrambled into an alert sit, ears pricked. Frankie laughed at him, shaking his head, and Taylor's heart tumbled. Only because he was a sucker for anybody who liked dogs. Not, you know, because of anything else, like the easy way Frankie laughed.

"I meant Taylor," Frankie said to the dog, voice dry, "but I guess you can have one too."

"A burger would be great," Taylor said, trying not to laugh, and meant it.

"So what kind of dog do you think he is?" Frankie asked, after Caesar inhaled his two burgers, and both humans sat down with burgers, chips and another beer.

"Poodle and something," Taylor said. "Maybe golden, maybe some hound. You never saw him around before he showed up at the docks?"

"Nah. I mean, one of the guys said he saw him early in the summer, but lots of people come through with dogs, you know?" Frankie tossed Caesar a chip and laughed when the dog caught it. "Good boy."

Did Taylor's heart do a funny thump at that indulgent laugh? Nope. Nope, nope, nope. "So how'd you end up with him?"

Frankie shook his head, longish dark hair sliding forward over his forehead, and the early evening sun highlighted reddish strands. "He started hanging out with me in the office whenever I was there. Probably for food, maybe the A/C, but he was good company." He glanced at Taylor and raised an eyebrow. "Better than some of the guys I've dated, that's for sure."

Taylor took a swig of beer, emptying the bottle. He debated for all of a second about another drink, trying hard to ignore the way his heart had sped up. One beer was polite, two was being friendly, three bordered on, what? A date? No. There would be no dating. Taylor always went out with guys better looking than him, and he wasn't ashamed to admit it. Frankie was not Taylor's idea of handsome, he was—okay, he seemed like a nice guy. He had a dry sense of humor. He liked dogs. That wasn't enough.

Frankie leaned over, ruffling Caesar's ears, and opened the mini-fridge. He set one beer on the table next to his plate, and held another one out to Taylor, no expression on his face. That wasn't true. There was appreciation in that hazel gaze, and a bit of resignation. Taylor guessed that Frankie figured Taylor was going to say no thanks, he had to go, the burger was great, see you around. Because they both understood Taylor was out of his league. Right?

Except Taylor wasn't the guy with the sweet car and the trendy clothes and expensive haircut anymore, was he? His Land Rover was gone, traded in for the minivan and much-needed cash. He hadn't bought new clothes for two years, and the unisex salon in town gave him a trim every couple months. He'd ditched the idea of being a veterinarian to become a dog groomer, for god's sake. Got his certification and some solid experience, and then took the money set aside for vet school and bought the pharmacy, stretched what was left over to do the renovations.

Taylor reached out for the icy cold bottle and shivered when his fingers brushed Frankie's. "Thanks." He liked the hint of a flush on Frankie's cheekbones, liked the slow way Frankie smiled, liked the spark of heat that flashed between them. "So," he said, settling back in his chair, "are you a powerboat or a sailboat man?"

Frankie's grin was wicked. "You do know that 'how's your boat running' is code for 'I'm waiting for engine repairs, how about you', right?"

Taylor laughed, and picked up his burger. "Point. But if you had to choose—"

"Sailboat. Hands down."

Two-plus hours of talking and two more beers later, Taylor figured he was still okay to drive. Which was a good thing, because calling an Uber was probably not an option, not up this far around the lake. "I really need to—"

They both stood up at the same time, and Taylor hesitated, caught by the look in Frankie's eyes. Not heat, not exactly, but definitely want. Definitely.

"Um." Taylor swallowed, realized he was frowning and tried to stop. He'd had a great time, but staying would send the wrong message and he needed to go. He tilted his head to one side, eyes drawn to Frankie's mobile mouth. No. That would be a bad idea. It would.

One of them moved, and Taylor wouldn't take bets on it not being him. Frankie's lips were like his hand—warm, dry, firm, and full of possibilities. Their tongues met, slow at first, a little tentative and a lot of heat. Frankie tasted of beer, and up this close his skin smelled like sun-dried sheets. Taylor needed, wanted, more, and slid his hands around Frankie's waist as he deepened the kiss. The body underneath the loose T-shirt had no softness to it at all, and Taylor hummed when Frankie shivered under his touch.

The kiss went on, building momentum, better than a first kiss had any right to be. Frankie grabbed a handful of Taylor's T-shirt and tugged, once. Taking that for a hint, Taylor broke away and pulled the shirt off over his head.

Frankie groaned, almost a growl, sending a ripple of goosebumps across Taylor's skin. Frankie traced both hands down Taylor's pecs and over his abs, hooking eight fingers into the top of Taylor's jeans to drag their lower bodies flush. Taylor hit pause long enough to get Frankie's T-shirt off. Oh, sweet. Work muscles, not gym muscles, and not manscaped, either. Taylor shuddered a little at the pleasant rasp of hair against his belly and went back to kissing Frankie, determined to find his buttons and push every single one.

It was a good plan, and it carried them up the narrow staircase to the surprisingly spacious bedroom and onto the big bed. Frankie was panting hard and so was Taylor, and by the time they were both naked Taylor didn't care what they did as long as Frankie kept touching him with those capable and rather knowledgeable hands, calluses and all.

"Don't stop," Taylor murmured, and bit down on Frankie's shoulder, grinning when Frankie gasped.

"Wasn't planning on it," Frankie told him, rolling until Taylor straddled him. In the dim light, his teeth flashed white. "Take your time." His smile got a little wider, doing strange things to Taylor's gut. "I sure will."

Taylor woke up the way he always did—sound asleep to wide awake from one breath to the next. He was naked, pleasantly sore in several places, wrapped around a lightly snoring Frankie, and he needed to get out of here right the hell now.

He managed to slide out of bed without waking Frankie up, and then tripped over Caesar in the dark while searching for his clothes. He patted the dog, who flopped back down with a heavy sigh.

Dressed, he turned around for one last look and found Frankie watching him in the moonlight. "I have to go," Taylor croaked, not sure why his throat was so tight.

"Yeah." Frankie shrugged using his shoulder and head at the same time, eyes closing briefly. "I figured that out. Be careful driving home."

Taylor retrieved his shirt, his shoes, and his keys from downstairs, and didn't fall into the water getting off the houseboat. All good, right? But after starting the minivan, he sat there for way too long, forehead resting on the cool steering wheel.

He needed to go home. This had been—maybe not a bad idea, but not a good one, either. Frankie Kaye was not Taylor's type of guy, and in the long run? Better to stop now, after one night, and chalk the whole thing up to beer and not having gotten laid in a while. That was all it was.

Taylor set his jaw, put the minivan in drive, and headed for home.

***

"Taylor Beckett? Oh my god—I can't believe it."

The familiar voice stopped Taylor dead, right in the middle of counting out the register. Of all the people he'd never imagined showing up in Lake Covington, Piers Wolters was top of the list. It was on the tip of his tongue to ask how Piers could stand to be this far from Portland—and therefore civilization—but there he was, white-blond and blue-eyed, walking through Pet Project, graceful enough to make models weep with envy.

He was never less than perfect, ever, not even the morning after a night of heavy drinking and wild sex. Taylor knew this from experience, an entire eighteen months of it, a year and a half of going everywhere with the gorgeous, gregarious heir to the Wolters fortune.

Piers came around the counter and caught him in a hug, surrounding Taylor with the smell of money. Or Clive Christian No. 1, which was almost the same thing. His white linen trousers were tastefully wrinkled, and his dark blue polo shirt cost more than Taylor's entire outfit. His deck shoes would pay Pet Project's utilities for a month. Maybe two.

"So this is where you've been hiding yourself," Piers murmured, brushing his nose along Taylor's ear. The intimate touch left him flat—no thrill, no rush, no nothing, unless vaguely annoyed counted. "We should go somewhere and catch up. It's a little early for dinner, but I found the most amazing little shack that serves local seafood." He looped his arm around Taylor's shoulders and grinned at him, perfect white teeth on full wattage. "You know you can't say no to me."

That wasn't quite true. After that last party, waking up still drunk, sandwiched between Piers and a naked man Taylor had never seen before, Taylor got dressed and left Piers's townhouse. He'd gone home, and once he was sober, he called the realtor in Lake Covington and told them yes, he wanted to buy the pharmacy. From party boy to entrepreneur in one frightening leap.

"Sure," Taylor said, almost on reflex, and wanted to slap himself. "Just give me a minute to finish this up."

Piers raised his eyebrows. "I heard you ran off into the wilds somewhere, after you left me." The twinkle in his blue eyes and his tone of voice implied Taylor should deeply regret both things. "When did you open this charming little shop?"

Charming little shop? Really? Once upon a time, Taylor thought Piers was clever and funny. Right now? Not so much.

Frankie would never—yeah, not going there. That ship had left the dock and set sail for parts unknown. Taylor had managed to avoid running into Frankie for a couple of weeks now, a good trick considering Frankie was now a regular customer at Pet Project. One-night stands happened, and you moved on. Right? Right. It didn't mean anything that Taylor found himself wanting a second night. Or afternoon. Or day. Or to talk some more. Sit on the deck with a beer and—

Taylor closed the cash drawer. Hard. He'd finish this later. "So what brings you to Lake Covington?"

Piers didn't roll his eyes, but it was close. "Trent—you remember him? Of course you do—he said we had to come for the Regatta. I don't know what he was thinking. My god, you must be going out of your mind here. I mean, look around. What do you do for entertainment?"

"I work." Taylor had no idea what to call the dull burn south of his heart. Seething? "There hasn't been time for much else." He knew his smile looked fake and didn't care. "I like it here. The people are nice, there's plenty of dogs to keep me busy, and I'm my own boss." God, that sounded hopelessly lame.

"Poor baby," Piers said, laughing, and draped an arm around Taylor's shoulders.

Torn between shoving Piers and being polite, Taylor looked away, toward the front doors. Outside, on the sidewalk, he caught sight of someone who might have been Frankie and his stomach clenched around a ball of nothing.

It was definitely Frankie. He'd gotten a haircut and shaved, and he was dressed up—a light blue oxford button-down and jeans that showed off his long legs. Frankie paused, hand on Pet Project's door handle, and met Taylor's eyes through the glass. Glanced at Piers, still with his arm around Taylor.

Then Frankie nodded, once, and walked away.

No. No, that wasn't right, he needed to—

Piers laughed, and Taylor nearly jumped. "Local talent?" Piers tipped his head in the direction of Frankie's disappearing back, and his mouth curled up on one side. "If that's all you have to work with, you must be spending a fortune on porn."

For one long, long second, Taylor remembered the electric feel of Frankie's stubble on his skin and the way they'd moved together, his easy laugh and how Frankie had watched him the whole while, crooked smile and all, and the warm, confident glide of his hands as he—

Without quite knowing how it happened, Taylor was half-way to the door. He paused, turning around fast enough to see a surprised Piers. Only for a moment, though, and then Piers was back to blasé and bored. "I'm sorry," Taylor said—he wasn't, at all, but he had manners—and dredged up a bright smile. "I have to go see a dog about a man."

\*\*\*

Frankie wasn't on the street, and his truck was nowhere around. Taylor stood on the sidewalk, late afternoon sun in his eyes, heart pounding, and decided he needed a plan.

First, he went back to his apartment. Since he didn't have sackcloth or ashes handy, jeans and an almost-new white T-shirt would have to do as groveling attire. That out of the way, he took a very fast, very thorough shower—he was being optimistic here—and shaved with more care than usual. No cologne, no hair product. If he was going to do this, he was going to be who he was now, not the spoiled brat he'd been with Piers. Somebody who might—might—deserve Frankie Kaye.

He drove out of town, palms sweaty on the steering wheel, and couldn't breathe when he pulled up at the houseboat and Frankie's truck wasn't there. Shit. Caesar bounded off the houseboat and greeted him when he got out of the minivan, and for once a dog was less interesting than a person. "I'm an idiot," Taylor told him. "One phone call. That's all I had to do. I don't deserve to have thumbs."

Caesar barked, and Taylor spun around at the sound of tires on gravel. He followed the dog over to the truck, thinking one of them was guaranteed a civil greeting at least.

The passenger door swung open and Caesar jumped into the cab, tail thumping on the dashboard as he licked Frankie's chin. "In the back," Frankie told him, laughing as he fended the dog off, and Taylor's stomach took a dive at the warmth in his voice.

Caesar did as he was told, leaping between the front seats into the rear of the crew cab. Taylor stared, not sure what to say to this clean-shaven, dressed-up version of Frankie, who chewed the inside of his lip and looked away, drumming his fingers on the steering wheel.

Taylor hesitated, mind a complete blank. Then he saw the faint flush along Frankie's cheekbones. Still tongue-tied, Taylor climbed into the passenger seat and shut the door. The cab was outright luxurious, with comfy dark brown leather seats, woodgrain trim on the dashboard, sat-nav and a fancy radio. He glanced out the windshield at the houseboat, remembering the outrageous view from the back deck, and how perfect sitting there and talking with Frankie had been. Okay, so not a condo. And Frankie was never going to be the kind of guy who got manicures or wore designer clothes.

Taylor snorted, smothering a laugh. He was an idiot.

"What?" Frankie asked, and the wariness in his eyes just about killed Taylor.

"Are you going on a date?" Taylor asked, which had to be the stupidest thing he'd ever said, although now he understood the whole heart-in-your-throat thing.

Frankie's cheeks went red, and he glanced away. "I was— you know, that new barber shop opened, and I wanted to— what's wrong with that?" he snapped, when Taylor laughed.

"Nothing," Taylor said, the absolute truth, and to prove it, he stretched across the console and kissed Frankie. For one horrible second, nothing happened, and Taylor knew he'd messed things up beyond fixing. Then Frankie's lips parted, and somewhere in the middle of the best kiss Taylor had ever given or gotten, the center console ended up jammed into his hip, and Caesar licked his wrist. He broke away and leaned his forehead against Frankie's, grinning. "Nothing's wrong. Everything's perfect."

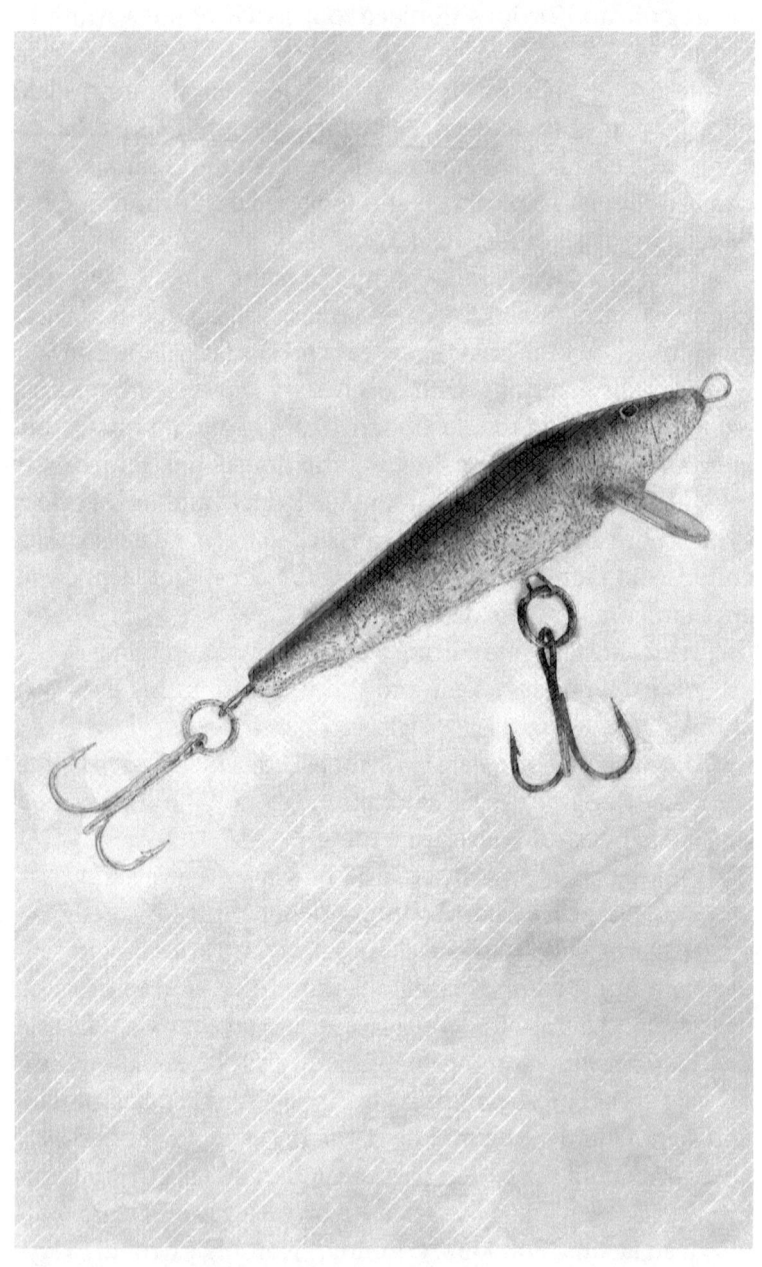

**LAKE COVINGTON**

# Hooked

## HANNAH MORSE

"**W**atch out!"

Coffee in each hand, Amber dodged the tech pushing the portable x-ray machine down the ER hallway. Her meeting didn't start for another twenty minutes, but she'd carried over the nursing school adage that if you weren't at least fifteen minutes early for something, you were late.

Budget meetings were never fun, but she'd worn a brand new pair of pink scrubs, had the eyeshadow to match, and she'd pulled her long, blonde hair up in a high ponytail. Hopefully, if her ex showed up, he'd see how over him she was. He'd been a mistake. A big one. She'd fallen into the relationship with Brad, a pharmaceutical rep, while she'd still been mourning her father, which was why she hadn't seen the warning signs that he wasn't worth her time. She still had to put up with seeing him at work, but her head was in a better place than when she'd met the jerk.

Amber had grabbed a coffee for a coworker on the way in. Today was supposed to be her day off, but a text had arrived bright and early that morning giving her a time and place for a last minute meeting to finalize purchases ahead of a hospital accreditation inspection. So much for her plans to spend the day lazing by the lake. Maybe she could make it tomorrow.

Radios crackled and voices overlapped as she threaded her way through the busy emergency room. She found Julia and pressed the coffee into her friend's hands.

"You're a life saver," Julia said.

"I try. How's today been?"

"The usual, one thing after another." Julia nodded towards the room she'd just exited. "This guy got bitten by a fish."

Amber sipped her coffee. "A big one?"

"Not so much, but he's sure it's going to end up infected. He's kind of cute."

Amber rolled her eyes at her friend. Julia had been trying to set her up on a date for weeks, ever since Amber had decided she was ready to start dating again. Brad hadn't broken her heart, not really, but she'd still taken a while to want to get back on the proverbial horse anyway.

She took a drink of the bitter coffee as she peeked into the room. The guy was examining his bandaged hand with a frown, and he wasn't her type at all. He was too tall and looked like he got his fashion advice from an issue of *Game & Fish*. Amber had always gone for guys in suits with expensive haircuts. Her dad used to snort and say love didn't have a price tag, and that someday she'd learn better.

Amber inhaled deeply and turned back to Julia. "He looks like a lumberjack, and that's so not me."

"Whatever, you like hiking, and camping. I thought that was one of the problems with Brad."

"There were a lot of problems with Brad. Is he going to be at the meeting today?"

"I saw him earlier. Sorry."

"Ugh. As if a meeting on my day off isn't bad enough." She patted her hair to make sure it was still in place. "At least nothing else should go wrong."

*** 

The meeting had been a disaster. Amber's proposal for new thermometers had been shot down because she needed to provide more justification for the model she'd wanted, and Brad had smirked at her the whole time.

Her little hatchback whined as she pushed the gas pedal down harder, wanting to get home to her little house on the other side of town. Netflix and a glass of wine would do wonders for her mood. The engine coughed as she turned onto Main.

"C'mon," she muttered, patting the steering wheel. The car had been a gift from her father for finishing nursing school, and she loved it because he'd picked it out for her. The glossy red paint hadn't been his favorite color, but he'd known it was hers. The engine sputtered again, and Amber's stomach dropped.

Luckily, the sign for Nash's Fix & Fill was just up ahead. Kelly, the owner, had kept the original 1950s sign, and while the place looked like it was from the last century, Amber knew from experience that the service it offered was top-notch. Thanking her lucky stars, Amber turned her blinker on. The engine died as she made the turn and she rolled to a shuddering halt near the front doors. She got out and winced at the angry hiss and acrid smoke coming from the front of the car.

Kelly Nash stood outside her shop, arguing with a man Amber recognized. It was the flannel-shirt wearing patient that Julia had been caring for. Ignoring him, Amber waved to Kelly before heading inside and taking a seat on one of the red leather benches. The place was decked out in a 1950s style with white tile, chrome galore, and red highlights. It was one of her favorite places in town, and she had fond memories of sitting on this bench with her father while the family car had an oil change or the radiator flushed.

An Elvis song played on the jukebox under the window, and Amber hummed along as she scrolled through emails on her phone. Then she started flipping through her social media feeds. Nothing exciting seemed to be happening to anyone, and she clicked back to the home screen. Ten minutes had passed already. She glanced outside. Kelly was still with the lumberjack. *Great.* Amber was never going to get home at this rate. She'd have to interrupt and tell Kelly her car needed work, and then get a ride home.

Amber walked toward the front door, scrolling through her contacts for someone who could come get her. She wasn't going to ask Brad, though she still had his number because he was contracted with the hospital. He hated her car and had wanted her to upgrade, and right now she couldn't deal with him saying *I told you so.* Amber's finger hovered over Julia's number, wondering if she'd gotten off work yet. Just as she was about to call, the door to the shop whooshed open. The lumberjack barreled through, nearly colliding with her. He had a tackle box and a fishing pole in his hands.

"Hey," she said, not pleased at nearly being run over.

The man mumbled what might have been an apology as he stepped towards the counter. Something tugged hard at her sleeve. "What the—"

The guy spun around. "Oh, hell," he said. "Stay still." His voice was a deep rumble. "My damn lure hooked you."

Sure enough, on her sleeve was a silver lure. She frowned and wondered if it'd torn her pretty scrubs. There wasn't a big hole, yet. Amber reached to remove the hook before it did any more damage.

"Wait," the man said. "Don't touch it. It's got a couple barbs and isn't going to let go of you easily."

"Well, can you get it out?"

"Yeah, just one second..." His eyes dropped to the badge that was now twisted in fishing line. "Amber."

She lowered her hands to her sides as he leaned in close to inspect the hook. "This braided line can't be cut without the right tools." He was speaking more to her shirt than to her. "Which I don't have at the moment, but if I can get the hook out, I should be able to untangle you."

He smelled woodsy, like pine and sunshine. She couldn't help but look him over, and she had to revise her earlier opinion. His dark hair hung just long enough to start curling, and he had a little more than a five o'clock shadow on his cheeks. The scruff suited him. He wore a plaid shirt, jeans, and boots that looked like they got some use. "Do you have a name or should I call you fish guy?"

"Fish guy is absolutely appropriate." He straightened, and Amber had to tilt her face up to look into his warm brown eyes. "I'm Jude, I study the fish in Lake Covington for the Department of the Interior." His skin was tanned, like he did spend a lot of time outside.

"Explains why you're going around flinging hooks." Amber glanced down at her sleeve. "So what about this one?"

"Yeah, it's in there good, might take a few seconds to get loose."

He bent over her arm again and Amber held still while he carefully gripped her sleeve.

She asked, "Isn't it kind of dangerous to just have a fishhook flying around?"

Jude grunted. "I don't, usually. I was pulling stuff out of the boat. The trailer has a wiring issue. I should have dumped everything in the bed of my truck, but I was hurrying to finish the paperwork."

"I don't think you saved any time."

He chuckled. "Good point."

She admired the smooth metal of the lure. It was shaped like a fingerling fish. Even having spent plenty of time fishing with her father, she'd never seen its match. He would have liked it.

"I don't think I've ever seen a lure like this one. Did you make it?" Amber asked.

Jude shook his head. "I found it alongside the lake when I went to launch my boat one morning, just sitting on a rock with nobody around. I call it my lucky lure. If I'm having trouble catching what I need to, it does the job. Do you fish?"

"I used to. My dad and I would go. We'd pack a lunch and spend the afternoon. We never landed many, which is why he said it's called 'fishing' and not 'catching.'" She studied the line of Jude's jaw as she sorted through her feelings of grief over her father. She didn't get to talk about him much. Her mother had died when she'd been tiny and her other relatives didn't live close. "He passed away several years ago, and I haven't been since." She hadn't realized how much she missed spending time with someone with a fishing rod in her hands.

Jude's fingers faltered. "I'm sorry," he said softly.

Amber sighed. "I should really go more. He'd hate that I haven't been for a while. Work's been keeping me busy."

"You work at the hospital?"

"Healing Waters. You've probably seen it when you're out on the lake."

"Gorgeous, big white building on the west bank? I sure have. I think a bunch of renovations just finished up."

"The research center is amazing. I'm proud to tell people I work in the ER." Her dad had beamed whenever he'd told anyone that's where his little girl worked.

Jude's expression became sheepish. "I was there earlier." He waved his bandaged finger. "Fish bite. Everyone was very nice."

Amber was impressed that he didn't try to come up with a wild story to try and impress her. Jude was all kinds of cute, and she couldn't believe she'd ever thought he wasn't her type. Had she been wrong this entire time? Certainly, she'd been off base when it came to Brad and his fancy car and tailored clothes. Maybe her dad had been right, and she'd been looking for love in the wrong places this entire time.

"I'm glad we could help you," she said. "Was it a poisonous fish?"

"No," he laughed. "But the bite was nasty, and I needed it cleaned out and some antibiotics."

"Hazardous work you do." Amber couldn't quite stifle her laugh.

"Just because it wasn't a twenty-foot great white doesn't mean it didn't hurt." He pouted and her gaze became captivated by the curve of his lower lip. She didn't even notice he'd removed the hook until he straightened up, the lure and hook in his hand. "And there you go, all free."

"Thank you," Amber said. Jude nodded and quickly tied a series of knots in the line to keep it in check. The sure way he moved made heat wash down her body to settle between her hip bones. "Nice knots." Her voice came out oddly high-pitched. Sometimes, late at night, she'd imagined someone tying her up and having their way with her, but before today she'd never met someone that made that fantasy seem like it could be reality.

"I was a boy scout," he said, giving her a crooked smile that looked more delectable than it had any right to. "Y'know, before I had a doctorate in biology."

Amber didn't have a chance to reply since Kelly opened the door and stuck her head in. "Jude, that trailer is a real piece."

"I know, but I believe in you. I'm sure you can get it working."

Kelly heaved a sigh. "Doesn't mean I won't complain. And tomorrow sometime will be the earliest. Hi, Amber, what's up?"

"My car's engine croaked."

Kelly looked sympathetic. She knew how much the hatchback meant to Amber, since Amber told her every time she brought it in for an oil change. "I'll try to fit it in tomorrow. I've been swamped lately."

"That'll be fine." It wasn't, exactly, because there went Amber's plans to soak up some sun yet again. She needed a vacation.

"Cool, then I'll see you both later." Kelly closed the door and Amber watched as Jude carefully wrapped the fishing line, lure, and hook around the rod so it wouldn't catch on anything else.

"How are you getting home?" he asked.

Amber pulled her phone out of her pocket. "I was just about to call a ride when you ran me over." She tapped the screen, but nothing happened. After a few button presses, the battery symbol flashed at her.

*Perfect.*

Groaning, she flopped onto the red leather bench and dropped her head into her hands. "This isn't my day." There'd been no relaxing, just meetings, Brad, and a broken car.

"I could give you a lift," Jude said, sitting beside her and placing a hand on her arm.

She looked up at him.

"Are you working tomorrow?" he asked.

"I'm off."

"I could give you a ride back here too. What if we had lunch together first? Maybe at the lake? I could bring my fishing gear."

"I'd like that," she said. She'd like it a lot. The prospect of spending more time with Jude made her feel giddy, as if the sun had suddenly appeared from behind the clouds when she'd been expecting rain. Her dad would have laughed so hard if she'd told him she might be falling for a fish guy.

The corner of Jude's mouth ticked up. "I think my lucky lure might actually be lucky."

She bit her lip. "And why is that?"

"Caught you, didn't it? I think you might be the catch of the day."

***

Water lapped at the pylons of the short dock, and the air smelled of summer. Jude breathed in a lungful as he rounded the front of his old truck to pull open the door for Amber. She slid out and tilted her face back to soak in the sun. The light cascaded over her face, and he was happy that the weather had cooperated with them to be able to go to the lake. There'd been a lot of sparks the night before and he was hoping for a few more today.

"Spending time fishing was a great idea," she said, eyes still closed. She was in jean shorts and an old T-shirt, which was a good look on her. Any look would be good on her, if he was being honest. Her hair was up in a ponytail, a few strands left curling around her face.

Her weekend casual made his jeans with holes in the knees and his faded band shirt feel extra shabby. He should have gone with one of those flashy ensembles from the big sportsman's store. Not that Amber had looked at him funny when he'd picked her up. She hadn't said anything, either.

He needed to stop worrying.

Shaking his head, Jude pulled the rods and bait box from the back of his pickup. He turned towards Amber just in time to watch a dragonfly dive bomb her. It landed on her arm and her eyes flew open.

"There's a bug," she hissed, staring at it.

"A nice one. He's huge. *Anax junius.*"

Amber's mouth fixed in a tight line. "I'm glad it has a name, but I need it to go away."

The dragonfly was calmly running its front legs over its huge eyes.

Jude said, "You could move. That might make him fly off."

"What if I hurt it?" She bit her lip.

He liked that she was concerned about the safety of an insect that'd made her its impromptu landing spot. Most people would just try to get it off as fast as possible and risk damaging the delicate wings.

Jude put the gear down and walked towards her. "I got it." He ran his fingers lightly up her arm until the dragonfly took off. "There you go," he said. He could see the goosebumps rise on Amber's skin at his touch. Electricity shot straight through his middle. He inhaled sharply and dropped his hand.

"Thank you." Her voice was quiet, and for a moment he got lost in her eyes. They were nearly the same green as the dragonfly's body. He swayed closer to her for a long moment and his gaze fell to her pink lips. He wondered how she tasted.

Amber laughed awkwardly and snapped into action. She ducked around him and grabbed a cooler out of the truck. He sighed as he went to collect the fishing gear and followed her onto the dock. Watching her hips sway, Jude wished he'd spent a little less time in college frantically climbing the academic ladder. He had no idea how to flirt.

Describe the life cycle of the stickleback in excruciating detail, yes. Let a beautiful and intelligent woman know he was into her, not so much. But he was smart; his honor roll listings said so. He could figure this out.

"This is my favorite spot," Jude said as he carried the tackle box to the end of the dock. "The water's deeper than it looks here, there's a tree for shade—" he gestured at the willow that grew beside the dock "—and that all means there's fish. Plus, it's out of the way. Not a lot of boat wake."

Amber set the cooler down and gazed out over the water. It shone bright blue in the summer sun, and the forest around it was a rich green. A breeze blew in off the water, cool and fresh. It ruffled her hair and he could smell whatever fruity shampoo she used. It was sweet, just like her.

Jude kicked his shoes off, removed his socks, and sat on the sun-warmed boards to dangle his feet in the water. The water felt blissful as it swirled around his ankles. He sighed in contentment as he wiggled his feet and snapped open the bait box. After a moment, Amber removed her sneakers and ankle socks, revealing pink polished toenails that disappeared under the surface as she sat beside him.

"I came here a few times with my dad," she said, "and it feels like it's welcoming me home. Now if I can just remember how to cast a line."

"It's like riding a bicycle."

He handed her a pole. After a moment of inspecting it and the lure on the end, she flicked the line out towards the water. The reel hummed as the line spooled out, and there was a plop as it hit the surface.

"See?" he whispered close to her ear.

Amber grinned. "Still got it." She pressed her thigh against his, and he forgot what he was doing for a moment, content to simply feel her close to him. "Are you going to use your lucky lure?" she asked, tone teasing, and he snapped back to reality.

"Not today. It works better when it's trailing behind a boat." He carefully attached a hook complete with silicone bait to his line.

"Or in an auto shop?"

His cheeks warmed. "I think I used several weeks' worth of luck when I made that catch."

She patted his knee then let her hand rest there. It was very distracting, and he had to try several times before he cast the line out correctly, sending the hook past hers. They sat without talking for a few moments, and he listened to the birds twittering in the willow, trying to match the calls to local species.

Amber stretched a leg out and circled her toes in the water. "After being on my feet so much this week, they appreciate this," she said, glancing to where the upper floors of the hospital were just visible over the tops of the trees. Her fingers flexed around the pole. "I think my dad would be happy I'm here."

"Your dad sounds like a good guy." Jude felt like he had a lot to live up to, her father must have been an amazing man to have had such a wonderful daughter. Amber grew quiet, staring out across the water. He wanted to see her smile again and sorted around in his mind for something, but mostly came up blank. He could at least fill the silence. "Yesterday, I read this fascinating study relating to the yolks of fish eggs."

Her nose wrinkled. "Yolks?"

"The part of the egg that feeds the baby fish?" he said.

"I know, it's just, imagine trying to make sunny-side up fish eggs." She giggled and leaned her shoulder against his.

He chuckled as a thrill washed down his spine. "Or over easy. You'd need a very tiny spatula."

"Soft boiled in itty-bitty egg cups."

"Scrambled."

"These would all taste terrible, wouldn't they?" she asked.

He put the rod in one hand and slipped his arm around her to rest a hand on her hip. "Probably, but it's still funny."

"I'm glad you get my sense of humor."

"I'd like to get all of you—" he broke off as he mentally kicked himself. That had been far too much of an innuendo for a first date. "Wait, that wasn't...I'm going to stop talking now."

Amber looked up at him. "Smooth. Better kiss me to make up for it, fishman." Amber's eyes were bright, and the tip of her pink tongue brushed over her lower lip.

There was a faint tug on his line as he held his breath and lowered his mouth to her soft lips. She tasted sweet, like ripe berries. Jude deepened the kiss, his lips gliding over hers. Her teeth gently caught his lower lip, nibbled, then let go. Sparks of bright heat sizzled through him.

He brushed back a stray lock of hair from her cheek and cupped her face. Amber gasped softly, and his tongue found its way into her mouth.

Her fingers gripped his shirt and his hand found the hem of her tee. His fingers snuck underneath until he could spread them out over her back, touching as much of her skin as possible. Amber made a soft noise of enjoyment against his mouth. She twisted further towards him and there was a splash as her foot kicked the water.

It was followed by a louder splash, and Amber jerked back. "Fish," she said, turning to grab her rod.

"What?" he asked, dazed from the kiss and having her in his arms.

"Fish on the line."

Jude took a moment to process what she was saying. "Oh, right, fish. Better reel him in."

Her eyes returned to his face, and her smile, with its slightly smeared pink lipstick, was wide. "I think I already have."

# Lake Covington Herald

March 30, 2019

## This Day in Lake Covington
**CONNOR LANE**

You can't drive through Lake Covington without seeing the Mayor's mansion. It stands almost as tall as the clock tower on the courthouse, and its setting on the hillside on the western shore of the lake gives it a bird's eye view. When it was built in 1879, it was the largest building in Lake Covington. To this day, it remains one of the largest buildings in town.

Lake Covington's first mayor, Herbert Golligher, wasn't what you'd call a humble man, but he was a man of means. He served six consecutive terms as mayor and saw Lake Covington go from a backwater berg to a tourist destination for the wealthy, and a mecca for outdoorsmen.

In Golligher's opinion, a man who oversaw a town of a few thousand should live in a home that could house as many in a location where he can also oversee them. When Golligher set out to build his palace, he brought in bricks by the wagonload and had the stones for his Doric columns quarried in

Renton, seventy miles away. The project took three years and two hundred craftsmen to complete, but when it was finished on March 30, 1879, it was easily the most expensive and laborious operation the county had ever seen.

Golligher claimed at the time that he built the entire mansion with the proceeds from a silver mine he owned, but after his death, records of this mine could not be found, nor could anyone in his employ pinpoint its location. Most of Golligher's fortune had been built as a land baron, so it's conceivable that the mine had been sold years before his death, but the lack of a record cast a dark light on the Lake Covington's longest-tenured mayor.

The mystery of how Herbert Golligher built his home remains unsolved, but it further solidifies his place as the most enigmatic man in the town's history. His legacy cannot be denied.

**LAKE COVINGTON**

# Flood Gates

## NOEL STARK

### Lake Covington, 1919

The bombs were close. He could feel the recoil of the howitzers through the ground as he crawled, his ears throbbing from the blasts. Geysers of dirt and metal shot up beside him as he covered his neck to protect himself from the shrapnel whistling overhead. He tried to move forward but the morass that was No Man's Land only sucked him down, its gaping maw hungry for his soul.

Thick Belgian mud clutched at his body as though the very hands of those dead soldiers who died before him were desperate to drag him down to hell. A farmer whose future once depended on the earth, Isaiah knew the muck he now slithered through would be his grave.

Like a fresh breeze, his memory conjured a lifeline: lips the color of coralroot orchids, soft and pliant, moved to form words only he could hear... *Keep going.*

He kept going.

As the rain fell harder, the mortars grew closer. He despaired he would never again smell brown pine needles lying thick on the forest floor, never feel the cold frost on his hands during the spring calving, never hear the soft throaty laugh that was only for him.

That was when he saw it. A light. A light that burned beyond all sense through a dirty window among sodden trees.

Trees? There were no trees. They had all been shorn down by years of infantry fire. But the light was there, sparking hope in his heart, calling to him.

He surged forward with a roar, yanking his body from oblivion's grasp, desperate to survive. But the next mortar was too close. He heard the tremendous crack and then his head exploded in pain followed only by black.

***

Olivia McCray finally felt heat. She'd been trying to get a fire going for what seemed like hours, patiently wooing the tiny sparks into flames until they began to fill the room with warmth. She threw on an extra log despite knowing she had to conserve. It had been raining as hard as she had ever seen for hours and there was no way to know how long the storm would last. She'd hauled in a wheelbarrow full of wet logs from the cord outside in hopes they would dry. But, considering how much rain they had taken on, it was a faint possibility.

She paced the length of the cabin in a panic. On each circuit, she stole glances at the man passed out on the cot she had dragged as close to the fire as she dared.

Abruptly changing direction, she checked his prone form for the umpteenth time to see if he was alive. She ghosted her hand across his lips, holding her breath, testing for the exhalation of heat and moisture.

Olivia found him just outside the door, collapsed underneath a broken tree branch snapped off by the high winds. Barely conscious when she urged him inside, he had immediately fallen into a stupor after she dropped him to the cot. There was no time to think about the consequences of his presence, her only goal being to get him warm, to bring him in to safety.

She stripped him of his drenched and muddied clothes, terrified he would catch his death. She put her hand to his forehead, testing for fever as her eyes roamed the bare skin along his neck, across his sculpted shoulders, and down his muscled arms.

Her breath caught at the sight of his raw red hands. She saw his knees and elbows were deeply gashed as well. He had been crawling, but why?

Olivia wondered if she should wake him, to make sure she even could, but she was reluctant. When he woke, everything would change. Right now she could still have her fantasies, her hopes, her anger. She could still play out the perfect lines and the perfect ending to the reunion that had almost come to pass.

She cursed her cowardice. Isaiah Washington was here. With her. Alone. This was her chance. She was a woman now, a strong and confidant woman who had put her mousy ways behind her. Hadn't she?

Outside the storm continued to rage. The rain bombarded the roof as a flash of light burst through the windows. Olivia began to count: one...two...thr—

The thunderclap tore at the silence and Isaiah's lids snapped open. In an instant Olivia's whole world upended as he pulled her down to the cot and pinned her flat with a ferocious growl and murderous intent. His half-crazed stare harbored no trace of the boy she knew.

"Isaiah," she gasped. "Isaiah, it's me. It's me!"

His body stilled as awareness slowly crept into his features. "Olivia?"

She nodded as aggressively as she could while he still held her fast. She watched as a squall of emotions swirled through his caramel eyes, as though he battled between past and present, dream and reality.

On instinct she tried to ground him in the moment. "We're in the McPherson cabin and there's a storm outside. You were hurt—unconscious—and I dragged you here. You're safe. We're safe."

The weight of his body relaxed, surrounding her like a heavy blanket. The rain battered the roof and the thunder rumbled through the hills as their heavy breaths deepened and fell into sync.

Isaiah's eyes heated, turning from caramel to chocolate. Olivia could feel his cool skin through her wet slip and suddenly yearned for him to drop the two inches that separated them to take her lips. But instead alarm flowed into his features as realization hit and he scrambled away taking his warmth with him. She instantly felt the chill sweep back.

He towered over her wearing a look of deep concern. "Are you all right? I didn't hurt you?"

"I'm fine. I'm fine." She pushed herself up from the cot to sit.

She watched him assess her body, disregarding her words, when he suddenly snapped his eyes back to hers in horror. "You're indecent!"

A nervous giggle bubbled out of her mouth. "So are you."

He looked down at himself and gasped at the sight of his small clothes. One arm flew to his chest and the other to his nether regions as he vainly tried to cover himself like a pin-up girl whose beachside changing hut had been toppled by a cheeky wind.

Olivia giggled outright at the sight of this huge, masculine specimen trying to recover his modesty until he lunged for the blanket that was inconveniently pinned beneath her and pulled, causing her to roll off the bedding, then the cot, and onto the floor with a thunk.

He flew to her side, dropping the blanket and pulling her to her feet. "I'm sorry. I'm sorry." He tried to right her but only blushed anew at the contact. He stepped back and covered himself again, looking around at everything but her while she awkwardly pretended to brush out her bedraggled slip.

Olivia pushed out a torrent of words. "You wouldn't wake and you were soaked through and you would never have warmed if I hadn't taken your clothes and I'm much more covered than you and there's only one blanket so you should really have it."

She fell silent. The sounds of the storm filled the cabin.

Isaiah kept his eyes on the floor. "I was unconscious?"

"I found you only feet from the door. I heard a crack of wood splitting after a strong gust and when I looked outside there you were under a fallen limb." Olivia risked a step toward him. "What were you doing out there?"

His face shuttered and he stepped away, turning to look out the window. His body filled the frame. He'd always been tall but in the three years since she'd seen him last, he had thickened—his shoulders broader, his chest full, his jaw chiseled. He'd become a man. But it was his eyes that had changed the most—their depths told tales of a thousand lifetimes, all of them steeped in misery. His deep voice countered her question. "What are you doing in here?"

Her courage left her in a whoosh. She couldn't tell him the real reason she had gone out in the rain, had come to the cabin. That this had always been their place and she was sure they would find each other here again. So like the coward she was, she went with the half-truths she had told Mama.

"I wanted to take Sapphire out for a ride in the hills and then realized we'd gone too far when the storm blew up. It was coming down pretty hard when I saw the cabin. I thought it would be better for me to stay put and safer for Sapphire to make her own way back."

Isaiah scoffed. "Right. Sapphire. Blue for blue blood."

"She's not from the most noble of lines."

"I wasn't talking about the horse."

Olivia felt her temperature rise. *Not this again.*

She strode over to the fire and jabbed at it with the poker. Sparks flew into the chasm between them. She was angry for being unable to find the words to defend herself, instead falling into the same old role that dogged her every move: *poor little rich girl.*

"Who else is here?" he asked.

She chipped the glowing embers off the logs, watching as they threatened to fly out of the hearth. "What do you mean?"

"The fire, the wheelbarrow, me on the cot. Who did all that?"

She looked at him, perplexed. "I did."

Isaiah snorted as though the idea was beyond all rationality. "You dragged me from outside, put me on this cot, pulled off my clothes, built a fire, and hauled in wet wood?"

Forgetting to be meek, she spun around to face him.

"Yes. Is that so hard to believe?"

Isaiah's intense stare raked over her, raising her skin in goosebumps. His body wasn't the only thing that had matured—his demeanor was one to be reckoned with. His confidence made him still and strong, giving the impression he was relaxed while being poised to spring at any moment.

His mouth quirked up. "You're nettled."

Olivia could feel all the ire and resentment she'd kept at bay begin to lap at her carefully constructed barriers. "I'm not the fragile flower you always thought I was. When I don't have anyone around treating me as though I can't do anything, I make out just fine. It's all of you who need someone to protect, not me who requires it. Isaiah, I swear, you're worse than Mama."

Isaiah's eyes clouded. "Don't you say that."

Olivia let out a huff of exasperation. "The only thing you had in common was thinking I wasn't able to survive on my own. Where you differed was over which of you had more right to decide what would become of me."

Isaiah's face was as dark as the storm outside. "Your mother won that battle."

"What are you talking about?"

"She came to me when you got into that fancy school in New York. She said you had a chance at having the best life could offer and that wasn't with me. I knew she was right and I did the only thing I could."

Olivia could feel dread flood her body. "Which was what?"

He looked away but not before she saw the regret in his eyes. "I stepped aside."

Olivia could barely breathe. "What?"

She watched betrayal push out the regret when his eyes swung back to hers. "And you went. You went. After all our plans. After you told me you loved me. I'd held onto a stupid hope we were something more, that you could stand up to her and tell her no. But the second she said go, you left me."

Olivia threw the poker to the floor with a clang, feeling the years of grief pour out of her in a rage. "The night she told me she was shipping me off to school I ran to you! I ran to your farm and when I got there you were gone. You left *me*."

*** 

Isaiah stared at her, dumbfounded. Could it be true? Could the past two years he'd spent witnessing untold horror, watching his friends kill and be killed over a few lengths of Belgian field been spawned by a few moments of missed opportunity? He'd purposely gone up north to join a Canadian regiment so he would get shipped overseas, as far away as possible. By the time America got into the war he'd already been fighting for two years.

Olivia visibly shook with anger as she stalked over to him. "Your father smiled at me when he said you had enlisted. He *smiled* as though I was the one holding you back from glory. You went to war to get away from me."

"How could I stay on the same continent and be without you? How could I let you have your chance to be free of your mother, to have a better life when I knew I couldn't stay away?"

"But you could have died."

Isaiah saw the anguish in her eyes and he knew he had to tell her now. She would find out sooner or later what kind of man he had become. "I did."

She grabbed his shoulders with surprising strength and her eyes brimmed with tears. "Don't say that. Don't ever say that."

Ignoring his thrumming heart at her touch, he forced out the words she needed to hear. "I saw terrible things. Horrible things. Did some of them too."

She shook his shoulders. "You saved dozens of men who were trapped behind enemy lines. Brought in over forty German soldiers with your regiment. You're a hero."

He scoffed at the ridiculousness of the sentiment. There were no heroes in that war, only survivors. And he still didn't know if he was one of them.

He could smell her though, now, here. He always marveled over her scent—lilacs after a spring rain. How it wafted toward him at the strangest times, filling his senses and raising his blood. Now it had an added note, something musky and deep. It balanced out the sweet innocence with the heady essence of the woman she had become. He breathed in her scent and soaked in her touch—they felt real. But if he was actually still in battle and this was a hallucination, he didn't want to know.

He brought up his hand in between her arms to capture an errant lock that had escaped from her pins. He rubbed his fingers together gently, relishing in its softness. "Your hair is darker."

Her voice sounded sad. "I spend all my time inside now."

The numbness he used like a comfortable blanket began to chafe. Olivia had always been better outside than in, better with horses than with people. She would steal as much time as she could from her etiquette and deportment lessons to ride in the forest or up the mountain, and then to meet him in this cabin. One of the only things that had gotten him through those long, cold, muddy nights during the war was the memory of her hair against the pillow on that cot, blond waves streaked white with the sun. And now that hair had dulled as though the sun had been put away in her absence.

She stepped back from him. "You don't like it."

Isaiah dropped his hand and let her go. He walked over to the cot and sat down, staring into the fire. "Neither of us are the same people anymore. It's good you went to Vassar. You're just as smart if not smarter than those New York girls. It's where you belong."

She paused for a moment, as though considering her response. "I don't know where I belong. It's not here where my mother thinks I'm a doll to dress up, nor there among those women who have never put their foot in a muddy puddle. I always envied that about you—you always knew who you were."

Isaiah couldn't bear to look at her, unwilling to see the hope she still pinned on him. "And who was that?"

"A man of the sun and the air and the soil. A man who understands animals and can care for them."

Isaiah felt bitterness creep into his voice. "There's not much to envy now. I can't work the farm."

Olivia looked over, concern on her face. "What do you mean?"

His shoulders slumped. "I can't lead the cattle hands or take charge of the steer. My brother Abe's got the knack for it but Pa keeps forcing it on me even though it's obvious to everybody I'm no good anymore."

Isaiah realized what he said was true, even though he hadn't admitted it to himself yet, or his Pa. "I can't be in those open fields. Can't watch their hooves churn up the ground."

Olivia made her way slowly to the cot, as if afraid he might spook. She placed a gentle hand in his hair. "Then farm something else."

He felt himself leaning toward her, putting his head on her stomach and his hands on her hips. He was so desperate to have one last moment with her, even though he knew he wasn't the man she needed. But couldn't he be just a little selfish?

His throat convulsed but he forced himself to speak. "When I was... over there, I would stand in the trench and look at No Man's Land feeling sick about what had been done to that soil. I couldn't see life in it, like I always had. I only saw blood and bones and death."

Her hands sifted through his hair, drawing the memory out of him.

He swallowed and kept going. "One morning while I was standing sentry I looked out and I saw this tiny plant sticking up out of the mud, pushing its way out despite all the gore that lay on top of it. And I left my post. I didn't even think about getting killed. I only thought about getting that tiny bit of plant. I walked over to it and scooped it up and brought it back. And I didn't pull any fire, not a single shot."

"What was it?"

"A grapevine." He tilted his head up so his moistening brown eyes could look into her clear blue ones. "You can't grow grapes here."

She pulled back and fixed him with her eyes. He saw a steely determination seep into her gaze, one that was tempered with a fire she had found in his absence. And he knew this was it: this would be the moment of the break. He almost felt relief it was over so he could disappear into this final death.

Her voice deepened into the husky sound he knew so well. "As much as I hated being cooped up inside, I loved being at school. And not for the reason Mama wanted me there—to find a husband and rise to the level of those rich girls. But because I got a chance to think on my own, to use my voice and know it would be heard."

Admiration bloomed in his heart for her. As much as it tore him apart to know this would be the moment where his dream would die, he was joyful she had found her place. Even if it was a place without him.

"I learned so much, Isaiah. And every time I learned something new about the world or myself all I could think about was telling you."

Suspicion filled him. She looked nervous, as though she was on the cusp of saying something big. "Olivia, why are you here?"

Olivia's face became guarded. "I told you I...

"Not in the cabin, in Lake Covington. Why aren't you still in school?"

If he thought he saw steel in her eyes before, it was nothing compared to what he saw now. "I'm here because I won't be apart from you again."

Isaiah burst up from the cot and strode away from her, desperate to find an escape. He shook his head. "No. No. You have to go back. It's what you were meant for. I'm no good for you now. I'm no good for anybody."

She turned to him but she didn't approach. "But you came to the cabin. You were looking for me."

He rounded on her, angry over her willful misunderstanding, ready to drive the point home. He jabbed a finger at the storm. "You know why I was out there? Pa told me I might as well be dead to him now that I can't manage the farm. And I started walking. Blind. With nowhere in mind. And when the storm hit and the thunder crashed I thought I was back in the war. I dropped to the ground and I crawled for miles." He raised his scraped and bruised hands in evidence. "Look at me. I'm broken, Olivia. I'm broken for good."

She moved toward him, talking low but firm. "And you came to the cabin. You came to me."

Isaiah shook his head, flattening his back to the wall as she approached. "I didn't know where I was going."

Olivia stopped inches away, full of confidence and strength. How could this woman be the same person he fell in love with so long ago? That same shy girl that trembled when he touched her? How did they get to this place where he was the one shaking and she seemed so sure?

She rose up on her toes so her lips whispered across his. "I don't believe you."

Then she claimed his mouth. He gasped at the touch, opening his lips. She took full advantage, relaxing into the kiss as she warmed his frozen lips, coaxing life into them as he had coaxed life into that tiny vine. She fed him kisses like rain and sunshine and he could feel his heart begin to beat again as though it wouldn't continue without her.

Something broke inside him and he let out a sob that wracked his body. She wrapped her thin arms around him, absorbing the shocks with her small, strong frame. Passion overtook him like the storm outside and he had to respond, covering her mouth in a deluge of desire and devotion. He bent her back and surrounded her with his body, engulfing her with all the feeling he had locked away from the war, kept so hidden he thought he would never find it again. Until he found it with her. Always with her.

He plunged his tongue inside and tasted the dewy innocence that was tempered with a musky wisdom she hadn't had before. She met him in kind, sampling him, drawing from him, stoking him to a fire he had long since thought burned out.

She pushed her hips into his growing need and he groaned from the contact. She tore away from the kiss only so she could whisper, "Please, Isaiah. Please."

There was nothing else he could do. Isaiah lifted her up and took two long steps to set her down on the table. Her legs wrapped around his hips as they frantically kissed, desperate to draw each other in.

He ran his hands down her body, relishing the feel of her through the silk of her slip, mapping her once again. His thumb found her taut nipple through the fabric, pulling it, teasing it until a moan flowed out of her, deep and wanting. His hand continued down to her thigh, finding its way under the hem until he found her hot, weeping core.

So intent on his luscious task he hadn't noticed her own hand disappearing down the front of his small clothes until he felt her fingers tighten around his shaft. He hissed out a breath at the contact. She'd never been so bold and he retreated to look in her eyes in question. He only saw desire and excitement, a heated curiosity that had been kindled over their years apart.

Their breathing hitched as they tried to give and receive pleasure. Isaiah leaned into her touch, anchoring his forehead to hers, his eyes fluttering closed. As their passion grew the rain continued to pound until it became indistinguishable from the rush of their blood. Isaiah felt her first flutters around his fingers which only hastened his own climax and when he heard her go over, felt her go over, he let himself go to a pleasure so great he thought he had died.

And then an unholy explosion rent through the cabin, and he knew that he had.

***

Olivia couldn't understand what she was seeing. After realizing the terrible crash was not due to their frenzied lovemaking, she and Isaiah pulled themselves together, grabbed their overcoats and stumbled outside. They now stood side by side on the ridge that lay just beyond the cabin overlooking the valley. Or what had once been the valley. Moyer Dam had broken; water tore through its gap destroying everything below with a torrent of water.

The rain kept coming, matting Isaiah's hair against his brow, turning his overcoat heavy and dark. His expression was hopeless as he sank to the ground. "It'll tear Lake Covington apart."

Olivia watched as trees swayed with the force of the flood until they inevitably toppled in and sucked away. The roar of the water filled her ears while the rain bruised her skin, battering from every angle and scraping her down.

An idea took hold.

She dropped down in front of him, feeling the dark, mineral rich earth seep between her fingers. "What if someone were caught in that?"

Isaiah took in the force of the water. "They wouldn't have much of a chance. They'd eventually be washed out to the ocean."

"Never to be recovered."

"Probably not."

Olivia felt a mania bubble under her skin. "What if we disappeared? Everyone would think we had drowned. Taken away by the flood."

Shock crossed his features. "Olivia, you can't mean it. Our families would be sick with worry."

Olivia felt a righteous anger rise with her excitement. "Would they? Or would they have no one to control? No one to throw away? You know that I'll never escape Mama's plans for me—to marry the right man, have the right house, be the proper daughter to reflect her as the perfect mother. She's never cared what I truly want." Olivia curled her hands into fists. She was shaking, not with the cold of the rain, but with fury over what she had become: a simpering child who did as she was told.

"I'll die if I stay." She opened her fists and took his hands in hers. "And so will you. Come with me."

Isaiah blinked. "Leave the farm?"

"Your Pa would give it to Abe. He'd have to. He said you might as well be dead. So be dead."

Isaiah winced at her harsh words but Olivia pressed on.

"You don't want the farm anymore anyway and you said yourself you are a different man."

Shame filled his eyes and he turned away. "If I'm still a man."

She took his head in her hands, forcing him to see her, desperate with the need to make him understand. "You're the only man who has ever shown me respect. The only person who was selfless enough to let me go even though it tore you apart. Respect me enough now to know my own mind. That I know what I'm doing. For both us."

A glimmer of hope sparked in his eyes, soft but insistent. He whispered so low she could barely hear him over the rushing water. "Where would we go?"

The lunacy of the idea burst through her. Where would they go? The notion of freedom was so alien she didn't have any experience of what it meant to actually *choose*.

"Someplace warm. Maybe the coast."

He looked off into the trees, a buoyancy trickling into to his voice. "It's warm there."

She poured surety into her voice. "You could grow grapes."

His mouth softened, his voice wistful. "You could raise horses."

She could feel him tipping. "We could be together."

Isaiah turned toward her, his eyes searching her own. He shyly smiled and repeated, "We could be together."

Olivia answered his smile with her own at a thousand-fold and he barked out a laugh. He looked at her in awe and she knew he loved her. He always had. She knew it to her bones.

The rain washed over them.

Olivia put her hand out in offering and in the time it took to utter a prayer, he grasped it and they rose together out of the mud.

# The Lie That Binds

## KAT VINSON

*J*oy pushed open the door to Mojo's. On the other side was the low hum of a handful of voices. She hadn't been back since quitting bartending after graduating college. Mojo's was too loud, too coarse, and she doubted much had changed.

A couple occupied a small table in the back and two men sat at the bar. A light showing for five o'clock, even for a Tuesday. The music wasn't on yet. The scent of stale beer reminded her of the state of her love life. It had been months since she'd even been on a date.

Uncle Len came out of the back, wiping his hands on a towel.

"Joy! You made it."

She moved across the floor, her feet sticking a tiny bit with every step. She wondered when they were last cleaned. He brought his hands up to pinch her cheeks. She ducked and he laughed. It was an old habit of theirs.

"I'm glad to help," she said. "What do you need me to do? Bartend?"

"Rex has that covered. What I really need is someone to waitress."

She'd rather tend bar than waitress, but she was there to help her uncle out, not complain. She only had to last long enough for Krystal to come back from maternity leave and she'd be off the hook.

"Sure," she said. "I can do that."

Len patted her back and said, "Let's go grab you an apron."

She followed him to the back, the stench of fry oil assaulting her. As they walked past the grill, she eyed the debris from the last burger Len had made. Disgusting.

"How's life at Lake Covington Elementary?" he asked.

One of her students had had a colossal temper tantrum that morning. "Better once summer vacation is finally here," she joked.

Len grabbed a black apron off a hook on the wall and handed it to her. "Can't be much longer. Few more weeks?"

"More or less." After she tied the apron, she stuffed a notebook and pen in the front pocket. She emerged from the back, just as three men came into the bar. Two she didn't recognize but one she did: Russ Kannier.

Her heart stopped and her fists clenched of their own accord.

"Joy Kinsey's back at Mojo's," he said, scorn lacing his voice. "What's the matter? Couldn't handle a bunch of kindergarteners?"

She met his gaze. She'd dated Russ her senior year in high school. She'd mistakenly thought he might be the one, but then he and his douchebag friend Marcus had almost gotten her best friend Autumn killed. After that, nothing about Russ appealed to her, not even the fact he was still unbelievably sexy.

Joy didn't bother answering him and continued walking over to a couple in the back of the room, her mind racing all the way. She picked up the empties on the table and took their order in a daze.

Russ scrutinized her the whole time. It burned through her.

This was going to be a long night. It was going to be an even longer six weeks.

Joy slid the tray of glasses onto her forearm. Rock 'n roll thumped in her chest as she headed over to the one table she'd rather avoid: Russ's.

It had been five years since Marcus and Russ had pigged her best friend, Autumn. If it hadn't been for Joy dating Russ their senior year, Autumn wouldn't have been on Marcus's radar in the first place. But she was, and Autumn completely fell for Marcus's superficial charm. She'd even slept with him; he was her first. For weeks, he strung Autumn along, pretending to like her, so that he could break up with her in the cruelest, most public way possible.

The pigging came to a head at a pre-graduation party.

Joy and Russ had been lounging together on a couch when Russ was called over by another one of his football friends. Joy checked the door for Autumn again, but she wasn't there yet. Russ and his friend disappeared into the kitchen just as Marcus came in carrying a plastic grocery bag full of pig masks and started handing them out to everyone. She wondered what Marcus was up to. With him, it was liable to be about anything.

"What's going on?" she'd asked him. "Where's Autumn?"

"She's coming," he said with an expression on his face that didn't settle right in Joy's stomach. He handed her a mask. "Don't be a downer. Put one on, too." After she donned it, Marcus went on to the next person. Joy looked around for Russ, but the room was crowded and the majority had masks on. Just as she was about to get up, the door opened and Autumn came in. Marcus took one look at her and yelled, "Now!"

Someone came out of the kitchen in a pig costume, oinking really loud and heading straight for Autumn.

Joy looked from Marcus to Autumn, not understanding what was happening or why Marcus was doubled over, howling. Between breaths, Marcus said to Autumn, "We pulled the pig and you're it, you dumb bitch. Oink, oink."

All the guys started laughing and oinking. Autumn stumbled backward out of the room and toward the door.

Joy ripped off her mask in horror and chased after Autumn. By the time she elbowed her way through, her friend had already made it to her car. Joy palmed the driver's side window, trying to stop her, but Autumn drove off with tears glistening on her cheeks.

Hands in fists, Joy marched back inside to confront Marcus and whatever jerk wore the costume but stopped short when she saw the pig suit in a pile by the door and Russ and Marcus chuckling together. Then it hit her. Russ had been called into the kitchen right before Autumn arrived. He'd been in the suit. Joy stared at him in shock and when Russ spotted her, he had the gall to look guilty. She backed out the door and then she was running with Russ right behind her.

"Joy, stop!" He yelled.

"How could you do that to Autumn?" she cried before stopping.

"What?" Russ said, almost crashing into her. "I didn't—"

"You destroyed her! And you got me to wear one of those masks!"

Russ reached for her and she batted his hand away.

"Don't touch me," she said coldly. "I don't want to see you again. We're over."

"Joy, you don't understand. I—"

"You're a liar. Just stay away from me."

In the morning, Joy had found out that Autumn had been in accident after she left the party. A deer had darted out in front of her car and Autumn didn't have her seatbelt on. She swerved to avoid the deer and hit a tree. She had a concussion, a compound fracture in her left leg, and six broken ribs, but she survived.

Autumn refused to talk about that night, any of it, even with Joy. After she'd left town, Joy called her for months. She wouldn't even answer. Only recently had they started to reconnect, but Joy had been too hesitant to bring it back up, worried it would destroy whatever hint of a relationship they'd been able to build.

Joy filled her tray with pints of Budweiser and took them to Russ's table. Russ must have been in the bathroom, so she took the opportunity to actually be friendly to this table. "I haven't seen you guys around before," she said to Russ's friends as she set the drinks down. "What do you all do?"

"Construction," the blond answered. "We're working on the youth center at the Old Grange."

Before she could respond, Russ reappeared. He emitted masculinity in a way she'd always found disturbingly compelling. Even though she hated him, every time she saw him, she felt his strong magnetic pull. After everything he and his friends did to Autumn, it made her hate herself for still finding him attractive even if she wanted nothing to do with him.

"Don't have anything better to do with your evenings than work here?" Russ smirked. "Who feeds your fifteen cats?"

She fixed him with a withering gaze. "At least I don't spend my nights confiscating fake IDs and hauling out drunks like some wannabe cop."

Russ glared at her and she hurried away, knowing what she'd said was a low blow.

Joy tossed her tray down on the bar and poured herself a drink. As she swirled the amber contents in her mouth, she thought about a conversation she had with Russ one night at the park. They'd lain in the grass, looking at the stars—like something out of a cheesy movie scene—and talked about the future.

"I'm applying next week," he'd said.

"To the academy?"

Russ had always wanted to be a police officer. She knew it was his dream ever since he was a little boy. Joy used to joke with him that the only reason why he liked her was because her dad was the Chief of Police.

"I have to get hired on first, but then, yeah."

She squeezed his hand. "Me the kindergarten teacher and you a police officer. It's perfect."

And it would have been, but after Autumn's accident, Joy broke up with him. She told her dad she did it because she found out Russ was doing acid—an unforgiveable drug in the world of law enforcement. It was a lie, but it was payback for Autumn. Her dad blackballed Russ and not just with the LCPD, but everywhere. The moment the hiring office did a background check on Russ, her father was quick to inform them off Russ's drug history. Russ would never be a police officer. The closest he'd ever get was working as a bouncer at The Impulse.

It was what he deserved after what he'd done to Autumn. At least that was what Joy had told herself all these years.

***

The next Monday, Joy came out of the restroom at Mojo's, stopping to check a text that had just come in. It was from Autumn, saying she was coming back to town for the first time since high school. Although Joy was excited, she couldn't help but wonder why now after all this time.

Just then, Marcus—the devil himself, with the much-deserved beer belly and a shiny new bald spot—turned the corner into the dark hall. His eyes were malevolent. Joy's pulse kicked up a notch.

"Look who it is ... Joy Kinsey."

He was staggering drunk.

He lurched toward her. "How've you been? I haven't seen you since what? High school?"

"By the looks of it, better than you. Let me by."

He offered his left cheek. "Not unless you give me a kiss right here."

"No thanks. I'd rather clean the grease trap out with my tongue."

How had Autumn not seen what he was? It was glaringly obvious he was an asshole.

Marcus stepped forward, crowding her. She backed up against the paneled wall. He was getting too close for comfort. Her heart thundered in her chest. The music was too loud. No one would hear if she screamed for help. The only other option was the emergency exit behind her. She could make a run for it, but Marcus might follow her, and she didn't like the idea of being in a dark alley alone with him.

Before Joy could figure out what to do, Marcus grabbed her arm and started pushing her toward the exit. Her feet tangled underneath her. She planted her left hand against the wall to stop herself, but Marcus forced her backward.

"What are you doing, you asshole? Let me go."

She tried to punch his jaw, but she mis-stepped and her knuckles only grazed across his chin. Marcus chuckled. "I like them feisty." He leaned toward her. She could smell the booze on his breath.

Joy cried out for help even though she knew it was futile with the music. Tears started to sting her eyes. How long before Rex or Len would notice she was gone?

Russ appeared behind Marcus, making her gut twist even more. Was he going to join in like he had with Autumn?

"Is there a problem?" Russ asked.

"Mind yours, Kannier," Marcus said, not taking his hands off Joy.

"Yes, there's a problem," she said again, her voice cracking as she stared at Russ, hoping he'd help her.

"Let go, McKenzie," Russ said with more force, dropping a big hand on Marcus's shoulder and pulling him back.

Marcus released her. She could feel the tingle as the blood rushed back into her skin. Joy winced as she rubbed her arm.

"Get out of here, Joy," Russ said to her without breaking eye contact with Marcus.

Joy darted past Marcus. As she did, she heard him say, "Just playing, Joy, like with your friend."

Russ followed her. As soon as they were far enough away from Marcus, Joy turned toward him and said, "Thanks."

His eyes glinted with what appeared to be concern, but that could be the lights from the stage.

"Are you okay?" he asked.

"S...sure," she said, taking a breath. "I'm fine."

"If you're so fine, why is your voice shaking?"

He touched her shoulder, the heat from his fingers penetrating all the way to her heart.

"Drunk jerks are part of the territory, right?" Joy tried to laugh it off, but Marcus had unnerved her. She wasn't sure if it was what he'd done, what he'd said, or both. "I just need to get out of here. I have work tomorrow and still need to stop by the store. You have no idea how much construction paper I go through in a week."

"Aren't you leaving soon? It's almost ten, isn't it?"

He paid attention to her schedule? Joy didn't know how to take that. Flattered, maybe? "You're right," she said. "I'm going to close my tabs out now."

"Let me walk you to your car," he said.

"Oh no, it's okay."

Just as she said it, she saw Marcus swaying as he headed to his table. He winked at her as he slid into his seat. Maybe having Russ walk her out wasn't such a bad idea.

Joy closed out her tabs, said her goodbyes to Len and Rex, and grabbed her purse. Russ waited for her by the door. She felt like a traitor to Autumn for being glad he was there, but Marcus was on a bender tonight and she didn't want to give him another reason to come after her.

Russ and Joy walked in silence through the parking lot. She unlocked her car with her remote and he opened the door for her. The small gesture stopped her. It took her right back to high school when they were together, and things were good and right, and they had their whole lives and dreams ahead of them—lives they'd planned to spend together. Strands of her hair tickled her cheeks as she looked up at him, her heart fluttering. Russ reached forward and pushed the strands behind her ear. His fingers lingered on her earlobe, making a chill run down her spine.

Joy shouldn't be feeling these things. She should politely thank him and go home, but she couldn't tear her gaze away.

Without realizing it, she leaned toward him. Her lips parted. Russ gripped her arms and gently held her in place as their lips met. His tongue slid over hers and he pulled her closer toward him. A needy sound escaped her, and she felt him smile. She moved her hands to his back and brushed her fingertips against the hard muscles. The chemistry between them was intoxicating and she inhaled his subtly spicy scent.

Despite all the years that had passed, Russ hadn't forgotten anything. His mouth moved to her earlobe and he tugged on it with his teeth before massaging it with his tongue. Then he kissed the most sensitive part of her neck. She reciprocated, the stubble scratching her lips and making her need him even more.

Then it was like the spell had broken and all those years flooded back into her memory. All the hurt. All the pain. All the betrayal. She dropped her hands and moved away.

Russ stared at her with a stunned expression.

After a beat, he ran his hands through his hair and laughed. "What the fuck am I doing? You ruined my life."

Joy raised her eyebrows. "Yeah? And Autumn could have been killed. Would that had made the pigging even better?"

"How many times do I have to tell you? That was all Marcus—"

She put up her hand, stopping him. "I told you back then that I didn't want to hear any more of your lies and I don't want to hear them now." She took a deep breath. He wasn't worth the energy. "Thanks for walking me out, Russ. Sometimes I forget that you only pretend to be a nice guy."

***

Joy followed her kids out to the playground for their twenty-minute recess. All day her brain had relentlessly conjured up images of last night's surprise kiss. Russ had smelled like sandalwood and leather and she'd wanted more of him. It disgusted her to be having these thoughts—these desires—about him. How could she want someone she hated?

She stood outside the red brick building waiting for Katie, her fellow kindergarten teacher. Katie's classroom poured out of the door with her friend following behind.

"This morning has been rough," Katie said with a yawn. "Tim's out of town and the baby was up all night."

"At least you found someone," Joy said. "You're lucky. It's horrible trying to date here. Everyone knows everyone."

Joy inwardly groaned. She could only blame it on Russ for sounding so edgy this morning. Why had she even brought dating up?

"Oh, come on Joy," Katie said. "It can't be all bad. Lake Covington isn't that small."

"I've run out of men to date."

"What about Russ Kannier? He's single."

Joy's heart nearly stopped. Katie was a transplant who'd married into the town, so she didn't know their history and Joy didn't have the energy to get into it. "He's friends with that ass Marcus McKenzie and you know that whole saying about birds of a feather."

"Friends? Uh, I think Marcus and Russ hate each other."

Joy shook her head in confusion.

"They had some big blow up and were hauled off to jail. Tim said it had something to do with a girl they went to school with."

Fighting over Autumn, or someone else? Joy didn't know what to think. This did fit with the way Marcus and Russ had behaved last night. Maybe they weren't friends anymore. But even if it were true, it didn't change what they'd done. She'd lost her best friend, thanks to them. Autumn had never looked back when she left Lake Covington. For the first time in five years, she would finally get to see Autumn face-to-face when she came back into town tomorrow.

\*\*\*

Joy glanced over at Russ's table. He was laughing with his construction friends, acting as if last night never happened.

He was drinking more than normal tonight. She must have brought them at least three rounds of Jager.

"Hey, you," Marcus waved his hand in Joy's face as she was staring over at Russ.

Joy growled. "I have a name." Marcus was dangerously close to getting a beer thrown in his face. "What do you want?"

"Drinks."

"You know where the bar is," Joy said.

"Someone's nasty today."

Marcus leered at her as he walked away. As he left, Russ waved her over.

"Another round of shots," he said when she got there.

"Are you sure you need another one?"

"Don't be like that," he said, slurring his words a bit. "It's my birthday. Don't tell me you forgot?"

She had and something about that fact made her feel bad. "Another round." She paused. "It's on me. Happy birthday."

While Joy waited for Rex to pour, she argued with herself. It didn't mean anything. She was just being nice. She'd do it for any other regular. Russ was no different. That was all it was. Just as she was about to second guess herself again, Autumn walked in the door.

"Autumn!" she cried out and ran out to hug her. "You're early. I wasn't expecting you until tomorrow."

"Yeah, I decided to drive on in tonight. I hope it's okay?"

"Of course. I'm happy to see you. It's just that ..." Joy glanced backward. "... both Russ and Marcus are here tonight. Do you want me to meet you somewhere else after we close?"

Autumn shrugged. "No, I'm fine. It's been five years."

Joy squeezed her friend's hand. "Here, come sit at the bar and we can talk for a bit. Are you staying with your parents? I bet they're so excited that you're home again."

They walked to the bar arm-in-arm. Autumn was trying to hide her limp, but Joy knew it was there. It was something she'd had ever since the accident. Joy looked over at Marcus, but he hadn't seen Autumn yet.

Just as Autumn slid onto a bar stool, Russ appeared. "Can I get those shots?"

Joy flinched at his voice. Of all the times for him come to the bar, he chose now. Autumn hadn't been in town five minutes and here he was just to remind her why she left.

"Russ!" Autumn smiled. "Hey."

"Autumn?" Russ leaned toward her. "Is that you?"

Autumn hugged him, all casual and cool, not as if she was embracing the very person that helped humiliate her. Joy stared, confusion bubbling up until her mouth hung open.

Rex put the last of Russ's shots on the tray.

"How've you been?" Russ asked. "Haven't seen you since high school."

"I've been good."

Joy reached for the tray and knocked two shots over in the process. She jerked back to reality when Rex glared at her and started to refill them. What was Autumn doing? Why was she acting as if nothing happened?

"It's good to see you. Take a shot with me. It's my birthday."

"Oh no ... I'm not a Jager girl—"

"Yeah, so. Speaking of." Joy interrupted them. "I've got your drinks, Russ." She left Autumn and followed Russ back to his table. She numbly set the shots on the table before walking away, her thoughts swirling.

As soon as she returned to the bar, she snapped at Autumn. "How could you talk to him like that? After what he did to you?"

"What are you talking about?" She shook her head. "It was Marcus, not Russ. If that douchebag comes up to me, it'll be a different story."

"But Russ was part of the whole thing," Joy said.

"No, he wasn't. He kept trying to warn me off Marcus, but you know me. I just wouldn't listen." Autumn snorted, but it came out almost a sob.

It felt like the room was spinning, but Joy hadn't had a drop to drink. "Russ tried to stop it?"

"Yeah, he did. How do you not know this? You were so close."

"*Were* close."

Russ had been telling the truth all this time. He wasn't the one in the pig costume. Why had she thought that? The magnitude of what Joy had done struck her. She *had* ruined Russ's life for no reason. Russ was a good guy and she was the jerk. No wonder he hated her. He had every right. Only she had no right to hate him.

"Is that why you two broke up?"

"Yes," Joy groaned. "Why wouldn't you have just talked to me about it, Autumn? Told me. You have no idea what I did ... what I did for you."

"You didn't have to live it, Joy. You have no idea how it felt. I couldn't get away from this place fast enough and just forget that my last night here, not spent in a hospital, I was humiliated in front of everyone. EVERYONE. And then the accident ..." Autumn's voice cracked. "I'd never experienced that kind of pain before. Outside and inside. I'm sorry I wouldn't talk about it. I just wanted it to go away."

Joy shook her head. "I can't do this. I just can't."

She raced out the door of the bar, desperate for fresh air. Leaning against the brick wall, she closed her eyes and steeled herself against tears that would come any second. What had she done?

*** 

The next night, Joy's heart pounded as she walked down the sidewalk toward The Impulse, the club Russ worked at.

As soon as she'd left, she'd called her dad. He wasn't happy that it was ten pm, but she couldn't allow the lie she'd told to go on another day. Her dad had been livid that she'd taken advantage of his position and hurt by her betrayal. There'd been some yelling and some tears. She doubted he'd trust her like that again and it was nothing short of what she deserved.

Now she had to tell Russ.

She slowed to a stop when she saw the entrance. The line stretched around the corner and men in fitted leather jackets and women in short, shimmery dresses crowded the sidewalk, the neon sign casting a glow on their faces.

Russ stood by the door in his regular jeans and T-shirt. He was stamping the hand of a woman in a gold dress and towering stilettos. He glanced up and their eyes met. His instantly narrowed at the sight of her.

"I never took you for a clubber," he said when she got close.

Joy steeled herself. "Do you have a minute? I want—need—to talk to you about something. You know I wouldn't have come here if it wasn't important."

"That I do believe," he said and stamped another hand. He turned to the other bouncer, who eyed Joy with curiosity. "You got this for a minute?"

The guy nodded.

Russ waved at her to follow him to the side of the building not filled with waiting partygoers. When they were far enough away, he turned and crossed his arms. "What's so important?"

Joy took a breath. "Autumn told me what really happened. You know...with Marcus. She said you weren't involved. That you actually tried to tell her to stay away from him."

"Yeah? Tell me something I don't know."

"But I didn't know." Joy sighed. "I was just so angry and hurt when I thought you could do something so awful to one of my friends. It felt like you'd done it to me. That I was the one who Marcus pigged that night. I thought you were in the pig suit."

"I told you I wasn't. You should have known me better than that."

Joy nodded. "You're right. I should have trusted you. Believed you, but everything happened so fast and I didn't know. So ... that's why I told my dad what I did."

"I knew it." His jaw clenched. "What did you tell him?"

"That you were doing acid."

"Acid?" he said incredulously, running his hand over his short hair. He looked away from her and then back. "No wonder every department rejected me. I can't believe you would do that to me, when I had done nothing wrong. *Nothing.*"

Joy cried. "I know that now and I'm sorry."

He kicked a loose bit of brick against the wall and grabbed the back of his head.

Tears pooled in her eyes. "I told my dad the truth. I doubt he's ever going to trust me again, but he said ... he said there's going to be an open position soon. He wants you to apply. Demanded it, actually."

Russ blinked a couple times and his arms fell to his sides. The anger drained from his face and his dark brown eyes gleamed with something Joy couldn't identify. She hoped it was happiness. He deserved it after what she'd put him through all these years.

Joy turned to leave.

"Wait," he said. "Don't go."

"No?"

"You know, becoming a police officer wasn't the only dream I lost that night."

She turned toward him and he gently cupped her shoulders with his hands. "I lost you too."

"How can you ever forgive me? After everything I've done?"

"Because even when I hated you, I loved you. You were just a kid. We both were. I should have done more to stop Marcus."

Her heart was flying. Was this really happening? Her bottom lip trembled, and tears slid down her cheeks. They came from sadness and sorrow and happiness.

The sandalwood of Russ's aftershave wafted up her nose as he slipped his arms around her waist and pulled her against his solid body.

She melted into him as his lips found hers. He tasted of the need she felt. All the years of being apart came crashing down upon her and there was nothing she wanted more than him. Her hands wandered down his back and past the waistband of his jeans. He pressed her against the brick wall, and she hooked her leg around his thigh in a desperate attempt to get even closer.

Abruptly, he pulled back and gazed at her. "Joy," he said between breaths.

She looked up at him. "Yeah?"

"I've missed you so much."

Then he kissed her like it was the only thing he'd ever dreamed of doing and she kissed him back the same way, making her own dreams instantly come true.

# Lake Covington Herald

May 22, 2019

## This Day in Lake Covington
**CONNOR LANE**

There are no official records detailing when the town of Lake Covington got its name, or the exact date Percy Covington first stopped here on his trip west. We do, however, know from a letter written by young Mary McClellan that it was on the 22nd of May in 1845 that the Covington and McClellan families joined together at the place that would become our great town—the same fateful day when Mary saw something glittery in the lake. Whatever it was that Mary saw would become something of a local legend and a bit of an icon for the folks of Lake Covington.

The legend tells that Mary strolled the shores of the lake and was enticed into the water by something shiny under its surface. As she waded in, she slipped and disappeared under the water. Fortunately, Percy Covington was there to come to her rescue, and they married that very fall.

Being a transplant myself to Lake Covington, I must admit that I found the story a bit dubious at first. The incident was attributed to a mermaid, who Mary's letter makes no claim at having seen. After the fact, her story changed, and she spoke of brilliant scales that flashed in the sun and hands dragging her below the lake's surface.

Mary's bracelet was mysteriously lost to the waters in the encounter, a fact she claimed was a small price to pay for the love she found with Percy. Since then, hopeful lovers have thrown trinkets into the lake as an offering to the Lady, and now enough coins and jewelry lay along the bottom that the shallow end does indeed sparkle in the sun like glittering scales.

Was there a mermaid, and if so, was she playing matchmaker, or possibly attempting murder? Either way, the town's fascination grew, and the lore of the Lady has permeated every level of Lake Covington life. The lake has become a symbol of love and a destination for lovers, and that may never have happened if Mary McClellan hadn't gone after something shiny on the 22nd of May in 1845.

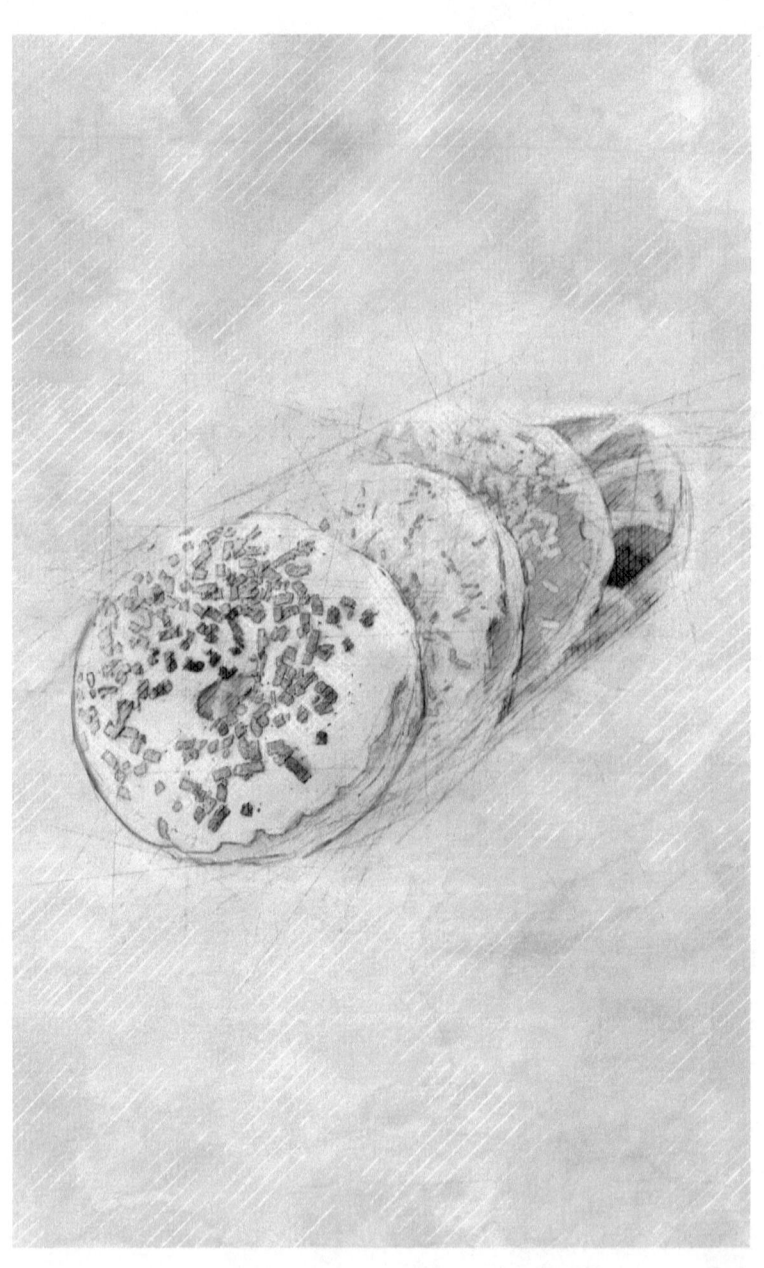

LAKE COVINGTON

# Much More in Store

## CHRIS KANTHER

Casey stood at the doorway to the back room of the Lake Covington General Store and sighed. It was filled with wall-to-wall boxes and dusty relics. For years the back room had been a catch-all for odds and ends and other strange paraphernalia for hobbies and interests of its previous owners.

"What a load of junk," he said.

His grandmother came up behind him and flicked the back of his head. "Treasure, dear, it's a treasure sale, not a junk sale."

Casey arched one eyebrow at the old woman. "In this case, one man's trash is still trash, Grandma."

His grandmother marched forward into the chaos and replied, "Well this one woman hasn't given up hope yet that we'll find something in here worth something."

Casey rolled up his sleeves and started in after her. "When one of us ends up in the hospital, I pray our tetanus shots are up-to-date." They began digging through the junk and Casey was all too aware of the bugs skittering out of the way.

"What exactly are we looking for?" Casey asked as he delicately moved aside a taxidermy owl whose glass eyes seemed to follow him.

His grandmother was cardigan-deep in piles of bedazzled jackets from the eighties. "Anything you can sell at the treasure sale, or barring that, a sack of unclaimed gold nuggets."

After hours of sweaty, fruitless work, Casey went to the kitchen to grab a drink of water. Kitchen might have been a generous description for the run-down commercial space that his grandparents had added on some time in the late seventies. Harvest Gold and Avocado Green counters and appliances told a sad story of disuse for more than a few years. But still, Casey smiled as he looked around, recalling many fond memories of baking with his grandmother for church socials, weddings, bar mitzvahs, and all manner of parties.

The sun streamed in through the windows, and Casey wished it lit up flour instead of dust motes. But neither he nor his grandmother had baked a cake here in years. Casey glared dubiously at the oven, positive that if he looked at it wrong there could be a fatal gas leak.

Throughout the afternoon, the other members of the Lake Covington Historical Society trickled into the store to help sort through the junk: there was Jim and Evelyn, Char, Gordon, and Diane. All were long-time friends of Casey's grandmother, and dedicated to preserving the historic underpinnings of Lake Covington. Including the General Store.

Casey wasn't sure when he had been unofficially inducted as the youngest member of the Historical Society. He liked all the old folks and their wild stories of the "good old days," as if lack of seatbelts and casual smoking could somehow be good. Casey had never been great with friends his own age, and after his grandfather passed away two years ago all Casey's time had been swallowed up by the store.

Once all the members of the Historical Society had arrived, they settled on rusted folding chairs while Casey made them coffee. His grandmother rustled around in her purse and produced a folded document.

"This trash arrived earlier in the week," she announced, as she unfolded the papers with a flourish and settled her cat-eye reading glasses on her nose. "The City of Lake Covington has received notice that the property of address may be unsafe for human habitation and business. An inspector will be by next Monday to evaluate the building for any structural concerns."

Gordon piped up. "There's nothing wrong with this building. Damn fools."

Casey's grandmother looked over the top of her glasses at Gordon. "The cracks in the brickwork outside beg to differ, I'm afraid."

Gordon was about to launch into another tirade when a knock sounded at the back door. Casey went to answer, dreading an early visit by the inspector.

Casey's heart practically stopped as he pulled the door open. "Morgan?"

The smile the police officer returned was radiant. "Officer Cass, at your service."

Casey was thunderstruck. The last time he'd seen Morgan Cass, they had been eating cereal and watching Saturday morning cartoons in their underwear. "What...what are you doing here?"

Casey's grandmother stepped in. "Officer Cass has been assigned to be the liaison between the City and the Historical Society while we finish up our preparations for the upcoming Fourth of July Festival."

The old woman was plotting again. Still, Casey's eyes dragged across Morgan's chiseled jaw with its light dusting of stubble, down his muscular torso, and back to his warm brown eyes. Damn, he had filled out nicely.

Casey tried to pay attention as Morgan went over road closures, police presence, emergency services, and all the other planning necessary to run the festival in downtown Lake Covington. But one question burned in his mind: Where had Morgan been the last ten years?

Casey was dragged from his mental wanderings by Morgan's smooth voice. "And where will you be during all of this, Casey?"

So informal, like no time had passed. That was always Morgan's way. Between the uniform and the easygoing nature, he oozed trust.

Clearing his throat, Casey said, "I'm running a baked goods booth to help support the Historical Society. Lady of the Lake cookies, Dutch desserts, old family recipes we've found in cookbooks and recipe cards."

Morgan smiled. "You were always a good baker. I can't wait to try some."

Casey tamped down on a scream. *You could have tried them for years if you hadn't disappeared.* But before he could say anything, his grandmother interjected.

"Why don't you stop by the house for dinner tonight, Officer Cass?" she asked. "Casey is doing some of the baking tonight and I'm sure he'd love an agreeable taste tester."

Before Casey could protest, Morgan said, "Do you still live in the white bungalow on the corner of Myrtle and Oak?"

Casey's grandmother winked shamelessly. "Lovely you still remember, dear. We'll see you at seven."

With a few parting words to the group and a nod at Casey, Morgan excused himself.

Casey rounded on his grandmother as soon as Morgan was out of earshot. "And when precisely were you going to tell me that Morgan was back in town?"

She patted his arm and gave a sympathetic pout. "When you needed to know."

What he needed to know was what the hell had happened to his one-time best friend?

*** 

Later that evening, Casey tugged on one of his only button-up shirts and looked in the mirror. His arms hadn't filled out like the tree trunks Morgan sported, but he didn't look too shabby. His blonde hair was getting a bit long, but he liked it, even if his grandmother said it made him look like a time-displaced hippie.

His grandmother had pulled a casserole out of the freezer, Morgan's favorite noodle kugel from when they'd been kids, and that's when Casey knew for certain he'd been had.

The kitchen was small, but painted a warm coral color that helped it feel cozy instead of cramped. The cabinet tops displayed vintage tea services saved for special occasions. Casey had many sweet memories here, including coming out to his grandparents and their wholehearted acceptance. As he set the table, Casey asked, "So, how long have you been holding it in that Morgan was back?"

The old woman gave him a winsome smile as she sautéed onions and sausage over the old stove. "I thought it best for you to find out naturally, but then Morgan never called, so I decided to claim my elderly right to be a busybody. He's gotten rather handsome."

Casey coughed the water he'd begun to sip. He knew where she was going with this and was not discussing his lack of love life with his grandmother.

"It's been a while since you and Chad broke up."

Casey decided it was time to invoke his young person right to distract the elderly by changing the subject. "So, the festival preparations are all in order? How much money do we need to make to keep the General Store?"

His grandmother sniffed as she seasoned some green beans. "Don't think I don't know you're hoping I develop topical dementia on the subject of Morgan, but if you must know it's more money than we'll likely make at the festival. I'm almost ready to leave a gift for the Lady of the Lake and offer up a prayer."

"That scaly woman never did me any favors in love," Casey replied bitterly. Just then the doorbell rang. Casey rushed to answer it, and despite his better judgement he felt a little swell go through him at the sight of the figure on the other side of the rippled, colored glass.

Casey opened the door, and Morgan's wide smile revealed teeth that could have been a paint chip sample for "pearly." He was dressed in a blazer and dark jeans, which, Casey was not above noticing, fit him like a glove. Casey felt his stomach doing somersaults.

"Um, here," Morgan said, pushing flowers and a bottle of wine into Casey's hands.

Casey led Morgan into the kitchen. Morgan kissed Casey's grandmother on the cheek and she *oohed* and *aahed* over the flowers.

As Casey took the kugel out of the oven the phone rang and his grandmother answered. "Oh, Char!" she exclaimed in a voice Casey knew was reserved for false declarations of surprise. "I'll be right over. Don't you worry one bit." She hung up the phone and put on her cardigan. "Char's fallen and she can't get up."

Morgan looked alarmed. "Give me a minute and I'll come with you."

Casey just raised an eyebrow and chuckled. The old woman had learned something from television at least.

Casey's grandmother had the decency to look apologetic. "No dear, you stay here with Casey and have supper, I'll let you know if I need anything."

Morgan looked back and forth between Casey and his grandmother. "Are you certain?"

"Quite certain," Casey replied. He was being had for the second time this evening. The chance that Char had actually fallen was infinitesimal, but he couldn't bear to out his grandmother's scheme when she was leaving him such a delicious gift. She took her ancient flip phone, promised to call, and was out the door.

Casey opened the wine and poured two glasses. It was a good year for the local vintage, he noted to himself. Casey handed a glass to Morgan. "I hope you don't have to work tonight, because I don't want to drink this bottle alone."

Morgan took a sip before replying, "Are you sure your grandma's friend is going to be all right? Do we need to call EMS?"

"I'll be sure to let you know if Char's in the hospital tomorrow so you can send flowers," Casey replied dryly. "I'm going to start dessert. What would you like? Pie? Cookies? Me?"

Morgan choked on his wine. His face turned beet red. "I'd actually like to offer you an apology," he stammered.

Casey didn't meet Morgan's eyes as he measured the flour into a mixing bowl. "I confess curiosity has me by the balls. Normally best friends who ghosted you a decade ago don't wander through your front door all grown up with wine and flowers."

Morgan shook his head. "I didn't mean to ghost you. We moved so suddenly."

"Cookies, it is." Casey cracked the egg with too much force, and bits of the shell landed in the batter. He cursed under his breath. "You've never heard of a telephone? FriendFace? Email? You were my best friend. Maybe more. It hurt to lose you." Casey flashed back to his twelve-year-old self crying after Morgan's family moved away. This painful memory stirred another: Morgan's strict, horrified parents walking in on Casey kissing Morgan.

"I was going through a lot back then," Morgan said quietly. "I looked up your FriendFace account so many times."

That was a shock to Casey. He'd figured that Morgan had just forgotten about him. "And why didn't you click *Add*?"

Morgan stared at his wine glass. "Because everything inside me screamed that I wanted to be more than friends, and everything I'd been taught at the ex-gay camp told me that feeling was wrong. Evil. Sinful."

Casey's stomach churned. Now he knew for sure that they'd taken Morgan away because of him. "You moved away from here because they could tell, couldn't they? That a boy who liked baking and sparkly cartoons was probably going to be gay." Tears stung his eyes. "I'm so sorry they put you through that because of me. I doomed you with that kiss."

Morgan set down his wine glass and abruptly hugged Casey. "Their actions can't hurt me anymore. I wanted to apologize in person to you, Case," he said, using his childhood nickname. "You and your grandparents were the best thing in my life. I wish I'd made it back before your grandpa passed."

Casey was trapped between the heat of the oven and Morgan. "Kiss and make up?"

Morgan's lips were gentle as he placed his hands-on Casey's hips and pressed into him. They backed up against the oven, and Casey wrapped a hand around the back of Morgan's head, his fingers digging into the wavy brown hair. Unlike their childhood first kiss, this one was flavored with regret and loss, but also joy and a sprinkling of hope.

Their interlude was interrupted by an ominous thudding sound from the oven.

Casey broke away. "Shit," he said, opening the oven to see the once-red heating element now rapidly cooling.

Morgan looked stricken. "Does this mean no cookies?"

Casey ran a hand through his hair. "This means no baked goods fundraiser, and no chance of raising enough money to save the General Store."

"My apartment's got a toaster oven," Morgan suggested.

Casey's heart swelled. "That's sweet of you, but I'll have to see about using one of the other member's ovens."

Morgan looked thoughtful. "Wasn't there a kitchen in the back of the General Store? It looked old, but maybe it works?"

Casey kissed Morgan again, leaving the other man with a glazed smile. "Grab your coat, you beautiful man, and hope I don't blow us up."

\*\*\*

Casey enjoyed a fine view of Morgan's tight posterior as he leaned over the back of the oven. "The gas lines look secure. I'm going to try turning it on."

"The good news is that if you're wrong at least the insurance should cover the damage from the hellfire that will consume us," Casey replied with a dark chuckle.

Morgan arched an eyebrow. "I don't remember you being nearly this pessimistic when we were kids."

"I was twelve and wore Lucky Charms underwear. I think it's safe to assume I'm a tad more bitter these days."

Morgan laughed. "Are you magically delicious?"

Casey's face warmed as he gave a devious grin. "Look for the end of the rainbow and maybe you'll find out."

"Is that an invitation, or do I need a four-leaf clover for luck?"

Casey turned away, and although he chuckled at Morgan's joke, doubt was his constant companion. "Morgan, you fall back into my life, all sexy and charming, but I'm afraid. Afraid I'm going to wake up from a dream."

Morgan looked crestfallen. "I promise I'm here. For real."

Casey smiled. "Maybe, once this trouble with the store is settled, I can think about being with someone."

Morgan took Casey's hand. "Look, I came back to Lake Covington after the Academy because the only place that still felt like home was where you lived. Plus, you just called me sexy and charming." Morgan gave Casey a god's-honest wink.

Casey groaned, but like the Grinch, his heart felt like it grew three sizes that day.

***

Casey worked feverishly the next day in the General Store's ancient kitchen. He baked batch after batch of scones, breads, pastries, pies, and even did a centerpiece Mermaid cake for the silent auction. Perhaps it had been a blessing in disguise that their home oven had broken, because after he pulled a file box out of the large commercial oven, he could do double batches with ease.

The day Casey planned to set up his booth at the festival, he'd do fried pastries like doughnuts and beignets. Those were always crowd pleasers in the morning. As he tallied the ingredients he'd need for the batter, he heard a knock at the back door.

Looking at his watch, Casey saw it was after nine pm. "We're closed," he said as he opened the door to find Morgan waiting with take-out.

"Word has it you haven't eaten anything today, which I could write up as a felony offense," Morgan said through a smirk.

Casey snatched the fragrant, greasy bag from Morgan and replied, "Only if you promise to handcuff me." Morgan turned red all the way to his ears.

Casey opened the bag. "Super Burgers! I haven't had one of these in forever. And you even remembered I like extra pickle."

"An obscene amount of pickle was how I described it to the cashier," Morgan said, as he leaned over the flour-dusted counter and unwrapped his own burger. After a few bites, he looked around the chaotic kitchen, filled with racks of cooling pastries. "You're selling all this at the festival?"

Casey shrugged. "More than this, hopefully. Word on Grandma's retiree gossip circuit is that Char had a miraculous recovery last night and turned out something like twenty-five berry pies today." Casey pulled a warm sugar cookie off a cooling rack and broke it in half before feeding it to Morgan. "What do you think?"

The look on Morgan's face was practically orgasmic. "I think it's a wonder you haven't opened a bakery and given everyone in this town diabetes yet."

"I'd like to one day. Open a bakery, not give everyone diabetes," Casey replied with a laugh.

Morgan popped a greasy fry in his mouth. "What's stopping you?"

Casey gestured at the dilapidated kitchen. "This doesn't seem like a money pit to you?"

"Touché. But Case, if there's something you want to do, you owe it to yourself to pursue that."

Casey pulled another batch of cookies from the oven. The cozy warmth of cinnamon snickerdoodle spilled over the kitchen. "When did you know it was the police academy for you?"

"When I realized it was the closest I'd get to being Superman," Morgan replied.

Casey fed Morgan another half cookie. "So, all those cartoons really did rub off on you. Too bad you don't also fight crime in spandex."

Morgan laughed. "I'm serious, Case. I'm sure you're great at running the store, but I hate to see you give up your own dream to keep this place up."

Casey shook his head. "It's not like that, Morgan. This store, it was everything to my grandparents, especially my grandpa. Letting go of it would be like letting him down."

"Wouldn't he rather you be happy than do what was important to him?"

Casey let out a bitter laugh. "My happiness detector is busted. My last boyfriend only dated me to see if he could buy this building to tear it down and develop a high-end shopping plaza."

Morgan let out a low whistle. "What a bastard."

Casey shrugged and went back to work. As he rolled out dough, he felt Morgan's arms circle him from behind. "You're a treasure, worth protecting, worth love, and worth your dreams," Morgan whispered before kissing Casey's cheek.

Casey pressed into the other man, intertwined their hands, and soaked in the sensation of being held again. It was nice. He wouldn't deny that. He wanted to be held like this. By Morgan, he realized, but now wasn't the time. "I've got so much work to do, Morgan. Thank you for dinner, really, but I'm going to be baking all night, and since tomorrow is the festival, I know you're going to have plenty of work yourself."

Morgan's grip tightened. "Nothing I would rather do than this."

Casey heart fluttered as he gently disentangled from Morgan's embrace. "Find my booth in front of the store tomorrow and I'll save you something special."

*** 

The day of the Fourth of July Festival was bright and clear, and people turned out in droves. Several streets were blocked off, creating a spacious pedestrian area lined with a long series of booths, games, food tents, and a beer garden. Local musicians played at two different stages, all done in support of the Lake Covington Historical Society. As their primary fundraiser for the year, all hands were on deck to help.

Casey had loaded all the pastries into beautiful displays, and hoped to entice customers with a free cup of coffee to everyone who bought a baker's dozen or more.

He worked the fryer for most of the morning, turning out crullers and other doughnuts, which proved to be a hit with the morning crowd. His grandmother helped, but as head of the society, she was needed pretty much everywhere. The rest of the members stopped by in shifts until noon, but afterward Casey was left on his own.

The line backed up, and Casey could hear a smattering of grumbles ripple through the crowd. He worked as fast as possible but noticed folks checking watches as the line deepened. Casey's panic rose high as a kite until he felt a hand on his shoulder. "Got an extra apron?"

Casey almost cried with relief at seeing Morgan. "Aren't you on duty?"

"My shift is over for the day, so I thought I would see if you needed help," Morgan replied.

"Okay, run the cash box while I fry up a new batch of crullers," Casey directed.

Casey noted wryly that with Morgan working the counter, the ratio of female customers doubled, and he couldn't blame them. Who wouldn't want pastries served by a hot police officer? Even out of his uniform, his tight police academy T-shirt and winning smile brought the crowds.

Still, the booth was cramped, and it seemed like they both kept finding ways to brush up against each other suggestively. Casey wasn't sure if it was that or the hot oil, but he felt positively flushed.

All good feelings died though when he saw Chad in the line. "Nice to see you're still baking, Casey," he said with a false charm.

Casey felt like flicking hot oil at him. "What do *you* want?"

Chad flashed a devious smile. "I was hoping to taste your wares one last time. Before the General Store goes bye-bye." He gave a sickeningly cheery wave that made Casey's hackles rise.

Perhaps Morgan could see the anger on Casey's face, because he stepped in and said, "We're trying to save the store; if you're not interested in buying something to support that cause, kindly remove yourself from line."

"Ooh, Casey, where have you been hiding your new boyfriend?" Chad asked, as he lowered his sunglasses to get a better look at Morgan.

Before Casey had a chance to reply, Morgan said, "If I was lucky enough to be his boyfriend, I would support him instead of trying to destroy his dreams."

Chad chuckled. "Feisty, I like you. Two dozen pastries for me. Did Casey tell you I offered him his own store in the new development? He could have had his own bakery already if they'd sold the General Store to me. Instead, a little bird tells me it'll likely be condemned and torn down, and I'll still get the land." Chad took his purchase, threw down his money with a laugh and walked off.

Casey was shaking with fury, but Morgan squeezed his hand, rubbing his thumb on Casey's hand in calming circles. Casey took a deep breath and the tension drained away. With a shiver, Casey shook off the bad feelings, and got back to frying.

*** 

The members of the Historical Society sat around the money box as Diane and Jim tallied the day's totals. Casey's booth had done better than expected, selling out of the baked goods by the end of the festival. The treasure sale had also done surprisingly well for what Casey had once derided as junk. Maybe people wanted a little history to hold on to after all and the thought gave Casey a flicker of hope.

Diane wrote the final tallies in the accounting book, but when she looked up, it wasn't with glee. "We did admirably," she said, her voice scratchy with emotion.

They crowded around the book, and indeed, the numbers were the best they'd ever done with the festival. But they were thousands of dollars short of the money needed to refurbish the General Store per the inspector's impossible demands.

"All this hard work, all for nothing." Casey sighed. His throat tightened as he thought of the memory of his grandfather being torn down, brick by brick. Casey tried hard to not let the dejection wash over and drown him.

His grandmother rounded on him. "Not nothing. Does it break my heart that we'll probably lose the store? Absolutely. But we're the Historical Society, and I'm sure there are other buildings in Lake Covington in need of our care." Her voice broke on the last word.

Casey balled his hands into fists. "I don't care about other old buildings! This is the only one that matters to me." He was practically hyperventilating. "I worked so hard to save the one thing that mattered to me, and I failed." In his anger, he kicked at the box that had once been inside the oven, spilling its contents all over the floor.

A few dusty trinket boxes and old letters skittered out. One of the letters caught his eye. Casey knelt to pick it up. Though the paper was cracked and yellowed with age, the penmanship was in a beautiful looping cursive.

*My Darling Percy*, it began.

"Oh my stars ..." Casey's grandmother breathed over his shoulder.

Casey was confused. "What are these things?" he gestured to the loose array of items surrounding them.

Evelyn was reading another scrap of the papers. Her bottom lip trembled. "They're love letters between Percy Covington and Mary McClellan."

Morgan looked confused. "Who are they?"

A collective gasp went through the old folks. "Only the founders of Lake Covington!"

Their troubles forgotten for a shining moment, the members of the Historical Society thrilled in the monumental excitement of their discovery. They laughed and cried with Percy and Mary, and when the letters were all read, they began looking through the rest of the box. Inside were an old enamel snuff box, a beautiful fountain pen engraved with the initials MC, two bracelets made of colored glass beads, and the original deed to the Lake Covington General Store.

Gordon asked Casey's Grandma. "Did you know the Covingtons owned the store?"

She shook her head. "Not in the slightest. I knew the building was old, but not that it dated back to the town's founding."

Morgan looked thoughtful. "That sounds significant."

Casey smiled as an idea blossomed. "Significant enough to convince our inspector friend, I think."

***

*One Year Later*

As onlookers applauded, Casey and his grandmother used the ridiculous oversize prop scissors to cut the ribbon in front the newly renovated General Store.

After the discovery of the store's historical significance, Morgan bent the Mayor's ear over the trove of historic items discovered. She had eagerly approved a city ordinance naming the Lake Covington General Store a historic landmark. That bought the members of the Society time to raise money for the restoration. Eventually the members decided to convert the once horrendous back room of the General Store into a small but lovely museum that told the story of the town and the Covington and McClellan families.

It had been a long road to get it there: endless fundraising, bake sales and car washes, more treasure sales. Then came the demo, renovation, and painting. They had worked from daguerreotypes, tintypes, and any other old photographs they could find–anything that gave them an idea of the historic look of the General Store in order to restore it properly.

The best part of the new arrangement, however, was that Casey and Morgan had found an old photograph that showed there had once been a store display labeled Jansen's Dutch Bakery. Casey hadn't known one of his ancestors was a baker. Armed with that bit of information, he was able to persuade the Historical Society that reintroducing Jansen's Bakery to Lake Covington was in the best interest of the new historic theming. Plus, it didn't hurt that it would help provide some much-needed income to keep the building up going forward.

Casey knew they would never have gotten to this day without Morgan. He had been their champion with the City, and always helped when he could with the construction and labor. When Morgan and Casey had officially started dating, Grandma's only stipulation to the match was that Morgan would have to officially join the Historical Society, a move he made without hesitation.

The only thing that could have made the occasion better would be if Casey's grandfather had still been alive to share it with them. The night before the General Store grand reopening, Casey had been feeling nostalgic, and baked Grandpa's favorite rum cake in his honor for today.

For the occasion, in honor of Lake Covington bringing them together, Casey had given in to Morgan. They had gotten their own matching set of beaded bracelets that sparkled in the evening light. The Lady of the Lake would have approved.

A year ago, Casey couldn't have imagined love would find him again. Now the bitterness was drained away. As they looked at the preserved letters and photographs together, Casey reflected that in a strange way, the Covington's love story had allowed him to finally accept his own.

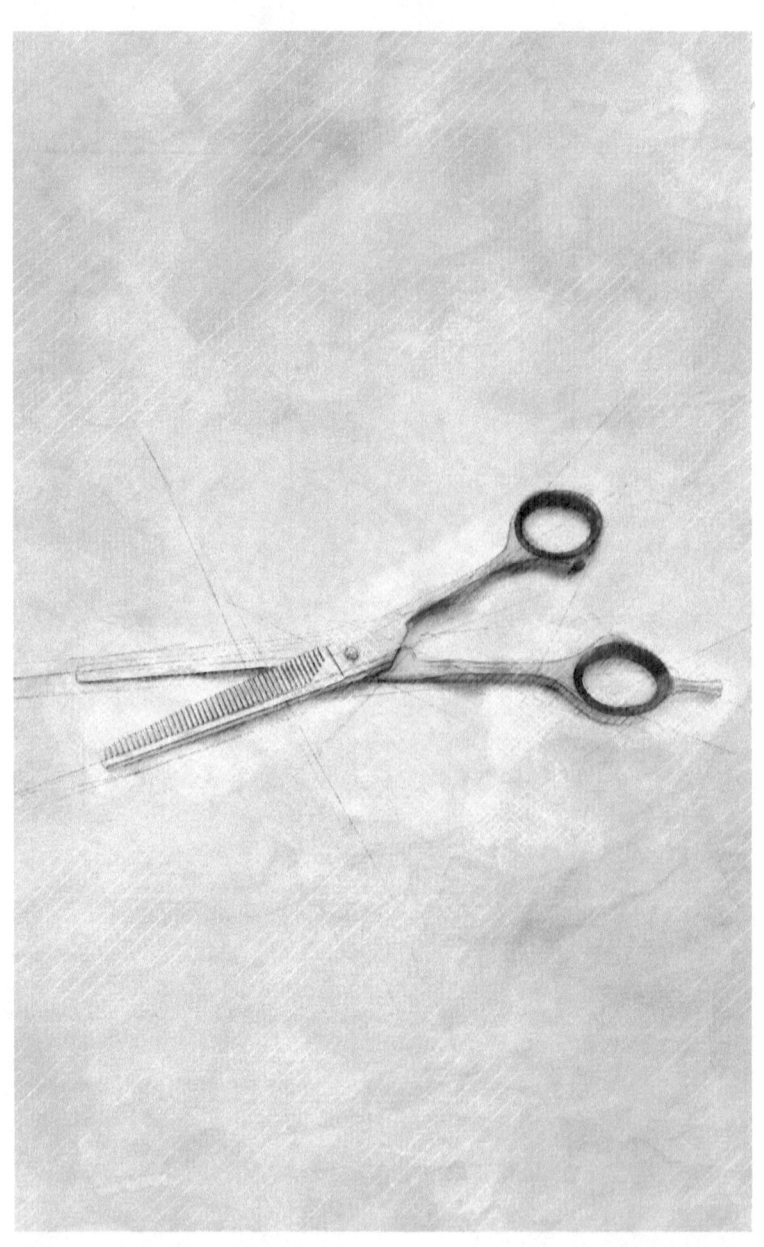

**LAKE COVINGTON**

# A Lana Montgomery Special

## HJ REINHART

*L*ana and Collette watched the man flipping through a magazine in the lobby of the Curly Q Hair Salon. He had an air about him that made women stop and notice. Only he'd been in the salon before and Lana hadn't. All the hairspray she'd inhaled over the years must have finally caused brain damage.

He adjusted the sequined pillow behind his back. He didn't fit the ambiance of the Paris Hilton-inspired lobby with the shag carpet, over-the-top chandelier, and lamps with fishnet covered legs as a base. Lana's boss, the infamous Collette La-Coste, was never one to do anything subtle.

Lana said, "This is the third time he's been here in a month. I don't know what else to cut."

Collette's red mouth curved into a mischievous smile. "I doubt he's coming for the trim, *non?*"

"Ha ha, very funny." Lana's clients tended to be loyal, but more in the six to eight weeks sort of way. She didn't even know his name. The first time he'd come in, there was a bachelorette party getting their nails done, and the second time she was in a text fight with her mom over what happened during the season finale of *Homicide from Hell*. Lana did remember that he was a good tipper, though. "What do you know about him?"

Collette grabbed her phone and scrolled through her calendar. Her nails clicked against the screen. "Here he is ... he came last Tuesday. I remember now ... you were wearing that great black jumpsuit, *oui?*" She chuckled. "No wonder he came back, darling."

"Can you stay on track please?"

"*Zut*, you're no fun. Let us see ..." she squinted at the phone screen. "His name is Gabriel Hoffman." Collette tucked her phone in her bra.

"Is that it?"

"*Oui*, that is it."

"You know everything about everyone in this town and that's all you can tell me?"

Collette handed Lana a black cutting cape. "Tragic, is it not? My great, great grandmother, Joséphine, would be turning over in her grave."

"What's tragic," Lana said as she took the cape from Collette's manicured hand, "is when they find me tied up in this guy's basement."

Collette winked. "Sounds like a good time to me."

"You're impossible." Lana shook her head as she went into the lobby. Gabriel immediately closed the magazine and smoothed down his slacks. He was good looking, she'd give him that, but more in an understated way. Like maybe he was trying not to be. Lana had seen her fair share of muscled meatheads come through, wanting their locks like Ryan Gosling, and trying to act like him too but this guy had a different vibe to him. Serial killer, perhaps? She'd watched enough murder documentaries to be an expert.

Lana gave her best no-flirting-only-professional smile. "Gabriel? Is that right?"

"Yes, that's me."

"Just this way."

He followed her to her station. The salon was quiet. Wednesdays weren't a popular day. Mondays were for fixing weekend mistakes and Fridays were for getting ready for the weekend.

The in-between was mostly down time. Gabriel sat down and she wrapped the cape around his shoulders. He smelled like cedar and a pleasing spice she couldn't place. For a potential psychopath, he had good taste in cologne. He took off his glasses and set them on the counter.

She looked at him in the mirror. "What are you thinking?"

"Perhaps a bit more from the sides and top."

*Was that an accent?* It was unusual like his cologne. She was surprised she hadn't noticed it before, but it wasn't the only thing she hadn't noticed. Like his broad shoulders and muscular arms that made her want to fall into them, preferably without her shirt or bra on and maybe not her underwear either. Lana cleared her throat. "I'm going to be honest," she said. "I can't really go much shorter."

"Can you try, please?"

He definitely had an accent.

"Okay. You got it." Lana grabbed the clippers.

She turned it on and guided the clippers along his hair line. Flecks of brown hair floated to the ground. If he kept this up, he'd be sporting a buzz cut whether he wanted to or not. His skin was warm under her hand and she almost swore she felt electricity. She glanced up. The way he watched her in the mirror made her heart race.

"Are you from here?" Lana asked him. "I thought I caught an accent."

"I'm from Pumany. It's a small country in Europe."

"What made you come to Lake Covington?"

"A postcard."

Lana raised her eyebrows. "A postcard?"

"A friend of mine brought it home after visiting. It's a beautiful place."

Lana had lived in Lake Covington since elementary school. Her mom had always loved it, but it seemed too sleepy a town for Lana. Nothing exciting happened. At least nothing exciting to her. To an outsider, though, she could see the appeal. Lake Covington was the perfect postcard town with its lake, mountains, and overall vintage-themed downtown. It was like something out of a shabby chic magazine.

"And what do you do here?" Lana asked him.

"I teach history at the college. I just started this semester. It's my first time teaching."

That would explain why Collette didn't know anything about him. None of the cherubs in her gossip network had him on their radar. It was only a matter of time though. No one was immune from Collette.

"What about you?" he asked. "Have you been a hairstylist long?"

Lana brushed the hairs off the back of his neck. "A few years."

"You like it?"

Lana shrugged. "For now. I'm good at it and it's good money. It's something I can do anywhere."

"You don't like Lake Covington?"

"It's not that. I grew up here. You know how it is."

"Yes," he said. "I do."

Something in the way he said that made Lana wonder if he was trying to escape something himself—hopefully not a criminal past.

Lana changed out her clippers. She was almost finished. Even if it took a quarter of the usual time, she was still charging him the same rate as her other regular clients. She supposed she could consider Gabriel as one.

Lana ran some gel through his hair and then took off the cloak. "All finished," she said. "What do you think?"

He inspected himself in the mirror. "Well done, thank you."

"Great. Follow me." Lana walked to the counter. Collette started making smooching noises at her as she passed. "Stop it," Lana hissed at her. "It's not like that."

"Sure, it isn't, *ma chérie.*"

Lana ignored Collette and signed onto the computer. She gave Gabriel the total and he pulled out his wallet. Credit cards lined every slot and she saw a thick fold of cash. A college professor must be a lucrative career these days.

He handed her several bills. "I don't need any change."

It was more than a generous tip—much more than what he'd left the last few times.

"Is there anything you'd suggest in Lake Covington for a new fellow in town?" he asked.

A big tip always made her feel especially happy to help.

"There's The Impulse," Lana said. "That's a club downtown and really busy on the weekends. There are some great places to eat like Chez Charbon. I have a friend who works there. It's a nice place. You could also join the Sweatbox."

"The Sweatbox?"

"It's a gym. It has everything. Tons of workout equipment and a lot of the usual classes. Crossfit, Spin, Zumba, if you're into that. Yoga is my thing."

Gabriel nodded. "The Sweatbox, huh? Maybe I'll see you there sometime."

***

Lana circled the parking lot of the Sweatbox. It was busier than usual and cars crammed every space. A spot opened and she quickly parked and grabbed her yoga mat from the trunk. Lana ran inside, dodging sweaty guys coming out of the weight room and hordes of kids going to their swimming lessons. She headed up the steps to the second floor, taking them two at a time with her head down like she was on a mission, and stopped when she rammed someone with her rolled up mat.

Lana glanced up, ready with an apology on her lips, but disbelief silenced her. It was Gabriel from the salon. He was grabbing his groin.

"Oh my God," Lana said, hand over her mouth. "I didn't mean—"

"It's...okay." He grimaced. "I'm fine. I'm going to sit in a corner now."

"Shit. Here, let me help you." Lana grabbed his arm and walked with him up the stairs. "I can't believe I did that."

"At least it's obvious you work out. You had some oomph behind that swing."

Lana shook her head. "I'm so sorry. I should have been paying attention. It's just that I didn't get out of the salon until late and then the parking ... are you sure you're okay?"

"Don't worry about it," he said with his cute accent. "I take it since you're lugging a battering ram, you're going to yoga?"

"Yeah."

"Me too. The six o'clock class, right?

Lana raised an eyebrow. "You're going to Buti Yoga?"

"Sure. I was heading down to get my water before, you know, and then was going to the class. I might still." He lifted each leg in turn and twisted back and forth at the waist. "I think I'm good now."

"Have you taken it before? It's not your typical yoga class."

"All the time ..." The look on his face was classic clueless. "It might be a bit different here," he said, "but I think I should be able to keep up. Do you mind if I walk in with you?"

Lana wasn't buying Gabriel's enthusiasm for yoga. Didn't serial killers stalk their victims? She narrowed her eyes. It seemed too much out of the realm of chance that he happened to be here at the same time as she was, but the gym was a public place, not some dark back alley. Walking him to class was the least she could do after hitting him in the balls, she supposed. She hadn't done that to anyone since the second grade when Shane Miller tried to kiss her at recess. "Okay."

Melody, the instructor, was greeting people at the door. As soon as she saw Lana, she waved her over. "Good to see you, girl. How are you?"

"Good. Just crazy at the Curly Q. You know how Collette gets."

"You don't need to tell me. I saw her yesterday." Melody was smiling at Gabriel. "And who's this?"

"Gabriel," he said, stepping forward and shaking Melody's hand.

"Are you here for Buti?" Melody asked.

Gabriel's face reddened. "Um ... I'm not sure how to, ah ..."

"He is," Lana said for him. "Apparently, Gabriel here is a real fan."

Melody's eyes widened. "Is that so?"

"It is." Gabriel nodded. "I've been known to do a little Buti back home."

Melody looked him up and down. "I bet you have, honey."

Lana brought her hand to her mouth to stop from chuckling.

"We should get started," Melody said, grinning like a cat with a full belly. "Let me show you where you can get a mat, Gabriel."

Lana stepped aside to allow him to follow Melody. The room was almost full. Lana went toward the back, took off her flipflops, and pulled her hair back.

Gabriel came over next to her. "This spot taken?"

"I don't know," Lana said. "It's going to be hard keeping up with such a master. Don't you think you'd be better up front?"

He laid his mat out. "I mean, I wouldn't want to intimidate anyone."

Melody stood at the front of class. She whipped off her shirt, revealing her tie-dyed sports bra. "Okay ladies ... and *gentleman*. It's time to Buti."

Melody cranked up the music.

As the class progressed from warming up to the high-energy, fast paced movement of hip tics, plank jacks, and the tribal dancing that she was used to, she looked over at Gabriel. He was doing his best, but the confusion on his face, especially during the static shake was nearly enough to send her rolling on her mat. She watched him stumble through the balance poses, the ab track, and finally collapse when it was time for vinyasa.

"That was a good try," Lana told him as she rolled up her mat.

"Was it?" Gabriel asked, panting.

"I've seen worse."

Lana waited outside the meditation room for Gabriel. She should be running to her car and locking the doors, but something about him made her want to climb on top of him instead. Despite stumbling through the class, the sweat trickling down his chest was a major turn-on and several other women noticed as well, including Melody who descended upon him like a fly on a fresh piece of meat. That accent of his was just more glaze over the sweetness. Pangs of jealousy crept up Lana's throat and she forced herself to swallow them down.

Gabriel came out and stopped when he saw her.

"Want to get a drink?" Lana asked. "It's on me."

"Thought you'd never ask."

They went to the juice bar. In addition to every smoothie combination imaginable, it also carried a good selection of beer and wine. Lana ordered them both a chardonnay while Gabriel snagged them an empty table in the corner.

Lana carried the drinks over. "I have to say," she said, setting the glasses down. "I haven't been that entertained in a while."

"That bad, huh?" Gabriel asked. "Well, I have to admit, it was worth the embarrassment. It got a drink with you, didn't it?"

"You could have just asked me out."

He raised his eyebrows. "That's what I've been trying to do for weeks. Figured I was going to have to go bald before I could get the nerve. Good thing you beat me to it."

Lana smiled. She couldn't help but like him. He had gone to Buti yoga for her after all. That was more than most guys had done. The men she'd dated in the past would treat her as if she didn't have brains because she opted for hairdressing instead of college. Dinner never lasted longer than the appetizer before Lana was telling them where they could shove their egos. Having to deal with that time and time again, she hadn't realized how unapproachable she'd become.

One drink led to another and somewhere along the line—Lana couldn't remember if it was her or him—one of them suggested going to the hot tub. Luckily, they had it to themselves. Lana stripped down to her sports bra and underwear and Gabriel took off his shirt. She felt herself warm at the sight of his muscular chest. Everything about him had gotten hotter in the last hour. Maybe it was the booze or maybe it was her inhibitions bubbling away like the jets in the tub, but she wanted him.

Lana ran her fingers along the strap of her sports bra. "Have you done any dating since you've been here?"

Gabriel gave her a boyish smile. "Does this count?"

"Is this a date?" Lana smirked. "Does this mean you're going to kiss me at the end of the night?"

"Why wait?"

Lana's heart was hammering as Gabriel crossed the small space and pulled her toward him. His eyes watched her mouth as he brought his lips to hers. His kiss was sweet, soft. Opening her mouth, she coaxed his tongue with her own. Lana slid onto his lap. His erection was large and stiff underneath her. She pressed against him and he responded eagerly. She took his hand and guided his fingers under her underwear. A moan escaped her throat as she felt him enter her, going slowly at first and then faster. She looked toward the glass doors of the gym. At any moment, someone could walk through them, but right then she didn't care.

Lana's groans became rawer, louder, and within minutes Gabriel had her shuddering against his chest.

She ran her tongue along the lobe of his ear. "You want to get out of here?"

***

Lana woke up the next morning in a cloud of down pillows and comforters. The smell of bacon cooking wafted up the stairs. Gabriel was *that* guy and she liked it. There was a lot of things she liked about him. Like the way he ate her for so long that she was practically begging for him to bend her over the couch. Or when he fucked her in the shower while holding the shower nozzle to her clit. Or how he groaned when she took his entire length into her mouth as if no other woman had ever done that for him before.

Lana slipped on her underwear and chose a shirt from his dresser. She went into the living room where sunlight beamed in through the floor-to-ceiling windows that overlooked the lake. Everything in his condo was either mahogany, granite, or leather. All this on a professor's salary? A warning bell went off in the back of her mind, but it quickly dulled at the sight of Gabriel's handsome face.

"Good morning," he said in his adorable accent. "I hope you're hungry. I thought we could have breakfast on the deck. You like coffee?"

"Love coffee. You're in the U.S. now. That's a safe assumption."

She grabbed a blanket off the couch and went out onto the second-story deck. It was like something out of a magazine. There was a perfectly laid out table with orange juice and champagne, coffee, two white plates, linen napkins with gleaming silverware, a bowl of fruit, and even a centerpiece of mums and daisies. The lake glimmered in the distance, holding the promise of a beautiful summer day. It was so sweet she almost expected to be serenaded by tiny mice.

Gabriel came out with a skillet and dished eggs onto her plate. He put some on his own before setting the skillet aside. He poured them each a mimosa.

Lana picked up her fork. "This is amazing."

"*You're* amazing," he said with a wink.

She felt her chest warm and wondered if Gabriel would be able to see her blushing. "How do you get anything done with this view?"

"It's difficult, I'll admit. You get out on the lake much?"

"No," she said. "I'd love to, but I work all the time."

"Well there is this thing coming up. There's an open bar." He handed her an invitation. "I was hoping you'd go with me."

"You had me at open bar." She glanced down at the invitation.

"Ah, yes," she said. "More Mary McClellan and the Lady of the Lake myth. People here can't get enough of it."

Gabriel watched her with confusion.

Lana shook her head. "You've never heard of the infamous Lady of the Lake? She's like the Cupid of Lake Covington, only she's a mermaid who takes jewelry as payment. Mary McClellan and Percy Covington were supposedly her first match. For a History Professor you don't know much of the history of where you live."

"Ouch," Gabriel said, jerking back. "Now that one hurt more than getting rammed in the balloons yesterday."

Lana grinned as she took a piece of bacon but stopped short from taking a bite when she heard the slamming of multiple car doors. She looked at Gabriel.

His eyes widened as he jumped up and stood at the edge of the balcony. Lana came to his side to see what the fuss was. Below were several black sedans with men in suits rushing up the steps. Gabriel's hands gripped the wooden railing as he stared down at them with his jaw clenched. She felt herself pale. Whoever they were, they were there for him.

"Oh, God." Lana backed away. "Who is that? The State Police? The FBI?"

Gabriel turned toward her but didn't say a word.

Lana jumped at the sound of knocking reverberating through the condo.

Gabriel went to answer the door with Lana on his heels firing questions.

"I knew this place was too swanky for a history professor," she said. "What did you do? Rob a bank? Kill someone? Will you answer me? Is there a basement full of body parts?"

He stopped at the door with his hand on the knob. "I'm afraid it's much worse than that."

Lana felt the little bit of eggs she'd eaten turn in her stomach.

Gabriel took a breath and opened the door. "Hello, Julien. This is a surprise."

"Prince Gabriel." The man bowed his head. His hair was feathered over to hide a bald spot. "Didn't you get my email confirming today? The King and Queen—" The man looked up and balked. "Good lord, Sire. What have you done to your hair?"

Lana's mouth opened and shut. Prince. Sire. King and Queen. Her head was reeling. What was going on? This had to be some kind of a joke. Something Collette set up, because this was too crazy to believe. Gabriel was a psychopathic murderer or a con artist. That made more sense than a prince.

The man named Julien stepped forward. "You went to some place probably with the word *Puff* in it, didn't you? Americans love their nonsense names—" He glanced over at Lana. She suddenly felt very sleazy with just a blanket around her, wearing nothing more than her underwear and Gabriel's shirt. "Oh, hello," he said, awkwardly, before turning back to Gabriel. "I'm sorry, Sire. I didn't realize you were ... entertaining."

"This is Lana," Gabriel said. "She's my hairstylist."

Julien reddened as he glanced back at Gabriel's hair. "Oh, I see."

Lana felt her chest tighten. Hairstylist? That was all she was?

The room quickly began to flood with what Lana could only guess were Gabriel's personnel. They politely adverted their gazes, but she could still see their expressions and the looks of disgust on their faces. She was nothing more than a piece of secondhand furniture on a showcase floor. Probably one of many that Gabriel had brought home.

Julien cleared his throat. "Will she be needing a car?"

Gabriel turned toward Lana, waiting for her answer. What was this? A dismissal? He'd gotten what he wanted, and she was no longer needed. Gabriel was no better than any other man in this town, prince or not, and she'd been an idiot to think otherwise.

Lana gritted her teeth. "No, *she* won't."

She hurried back to the bedroom and threw on her workout clothes from yesterday and grabbed her purse. Despite it all, she had hoped that Gabriel would follow her, reassure her that she meant more to him, but he hadn't, and she didn't.

Without so much as a backward glance, she rushed out the front door. As she drove away, she could see the lake glistening in the rearview, but nothing about it was sweet anymore.

*** 

After her ritual stop at Cuppa Café, Lana pushed open the glass door to the Curly Q. The moment she entered, Collette ran toward her, shaking with so much pent up excitement that she reminded Lana of a fuzzy dog about to piddle on the carpet.

Collette's glittery mouth stretched from cheek to cheek. "I got the scoop on your mystery client. And you're not going to BE-lieve what I'm about to dish—"

"He's a prince," Lana interrupted.

Collette's face deflated like a bargain-basement air mattress. "How did you find out, *mon petite?*"

"Don't ask."

"Oh *non, non, non,* love. You *have* to tell me. That is like my air. Would you have me suffocate?"

"Today, I wouldn't mind," Lana mumbled.

Lana finished her coffee and went to her station. She wanted to forget all about the hot tub, Gabriel's condo, and the burn of her departure. It was just a fling. No, worse. A one-night stand. Gabriel wasn't serious about anything other than getting into her yoga pants. Cindrellas only existed in stories and Hollywood movies. Not real life.

As Lana got ready for her day, Collette whisked past her. "Your nine-thirty is here."

"I don't have a nine-thirty. My first appointment is at ten."

Collette smirked, "You do now."

Lana peeked around the corner. Gabriel sat in his usual seat, magazine in hand, waiting for a haircut. She felt her stomach drop to her heels.

"Send him away," Lana said.

"You know I cannot do that. A customer is a customer, *n'est pas?*"

"He's not a customer and you know it."

"I know nothing, *ma chaton.*"

"Give him to Krista. Shouldn't she be here by now?"

"Krista? I couldn't possibly. Did you know she allowed one of her clients to set her up on a blind date with her son? Talking about grandbabies and such tackiness." Collette reapplied her lipstick. "*Non.* This one, he is yours."

Lana groaned. "Fine."

She went out into the lobby. Gabriel looked up at her. His eyes were warm. Just like they were that morning at breakfast when Lana thought that maybe she could have a relationship with him. But that was before his entourage showed up.

"You know the drill," she said.

He followed her back to her chair. Lana went through the motions of putting the cape on him, trying to pretend he was only another customer. No one special. She refused to meet his gaze in the mirror.

"Lana ..." he said her name as if he were sorry, but she'd known men like him before. He wasn't.

"What will it be today, *Prince* Gabriel?"

He flinched. "I wanted to tell you."

"I get it," she said. "When could you have brought it up? Not all the times you sat here, or in the hot tub, or in your bed, or during breakfast. Why would you? I mean, I'm just your hairstylist ... You know what, I'm thinking a little off the top should do the trick." She grabbed her clippers and ran them down the middle of his head. "Done. Let Julien know this is a Lana Montgomery Special. It's very on trend."

"Okay, I might deserve that."

"You can pay on your way out."

She started to remove his cape and he stopped her, placing his hand over hers.

"Please Lana. I didn't know what to do."

"You could have started by not treating me like one of your subjects. Or, you know, your hairstylist."

"I panicked. I didn't expect you to find out..."

Lana crossed her arms and raised her eyebrows.

"I didn't expect you to find out *that* way. I was planning to tell you at the launch of *Mary's Jewel* when you couldn't run because we were on a boat."

"Good plan."

"Listen Lana ... my title, my parents, it's only one part of me. It's not all of me and you were the first person to like me as a history professor and not because I was a prince. You can't fault me for not rushing to burst that illusion, can you? And Julien's coming changed all that and I knew it would change you."

"It didn't," Lana said. "It changed you—into an ass."

Gabriel nodded. "You're right and I'm sorry. I was an ass. You have no idea how sorry I am. It's just that it's happened to me before. Many times in fact. And I'm not even the prince. I'm *a* prince. I have two older brothers."

Gabriel stood and turned to Lana before dropping on one knee. Her heart felt like it was about to beat out of her chest.

"Lana. If you allow me, I will always treat you like my lady, my princess, my queen. I want you by my side. I want the world to see you at my side. All I need is one more chance and I'll prove it to you. I swear it."

Gabriel looked up at her expectantly. It was hard to take him seriously with a single buzz down his head, but as much she wanted to send him on his way, skunk stripe and all, she couldn't.

"What are you waiting for, *ma chérie?*" She heard Collette say. "Snap that man up."

Lana rolled her eyes at her boss. "Eavesdropping again?"

"Oh, don't be so surprised. Eavesdropping is part of the gossip's repertoire. Now will you two get on with it already? The cherubs are waiting to share the news. Oh, I do not think even my great, great grandmother Joséphine had anything so juicy in all her time."

Gabriel's voice pulled her back into the moment. "Lana?"

She stared into his eyes. His words had been sincere. He meant what he'd said and, despite herself, she liked him. Really liked him. She knew that if she let Gabriel walk out that door, she'd lose her chance at something special—maybe her very own fairy tale.

Lana said, "I have one condition."

"Anything."

"Before we get into the world traveling and parades and all that jazz, how about you take me on a date first?"

Gabriel smiled as he got back to his feet. "That's a deal."

He took Lana into his arms and she leaned against him, breathing in the scent of his cologne. His lips brushed against her neck and moved up along her jaw until they pressed against her own. The kiss was tender, but then turned deeper, hungrier. She pulled away before Collette got more than eyeful. Not that Lana doubted she'd mind.

Lana looked up at Gabriel, feeling something she hadn't in years: happiness.

"Aren't you supposed to come with glass slippers and a basket of doves?" she asked him.

"If you give me a second, I can get Julien on it."

"Tell him I'll throw in a haircut."

# Lake Covington Herald

## This Day in Lake Covington
**CONNOR LANE**

On June 16, 1870, the courthouse gracing Main Street was dedicated in a quiet ceremony four years after it was completed. Most county employees were hard at work at their desks, unaware that Mayor Herbert Golligher and architect Jean Bemis were outside with a handful of people from the city council. They included a painter to mark the occasion, a reporter from the newly created *Lake Covington Herald*, and a giant pair of scissors.

The ribbon-cutting ceremony had been scheduled in 1866, but Bemis insisted the festivities be delayed until the addition of a clock tower atop the courthouse was completed. Due to a shortage of bricks, however, construction went on another 16 months. The bricks had to be brought in by wagon from Duquette, fifty miles away. In the end, construction of the clock tower cost more than the entire building.

"But look at it," Mayor Golligher was quoted in the *Herald*. "No town west of the Mississippi has anything as grand."

As for the local citizenry, they're glad construction went forward on the tower. "It looks like Big Ben," said not one, but all the visitors I spoke to. Indeed, its similarity in design is attributed to a fondness between Jean Bemis and Augustus Pugin, the man who designed the London marvel.

Lake Covington has one of the world's lowest crime rates per capita. Perhaps that's a credit to a courthouse far too big for such a small town. Coupled with the mayor's sprawling mansion ripped from a Jane Austen novel, it seems what Lake Covington lacks in originality, it makes up for in size.

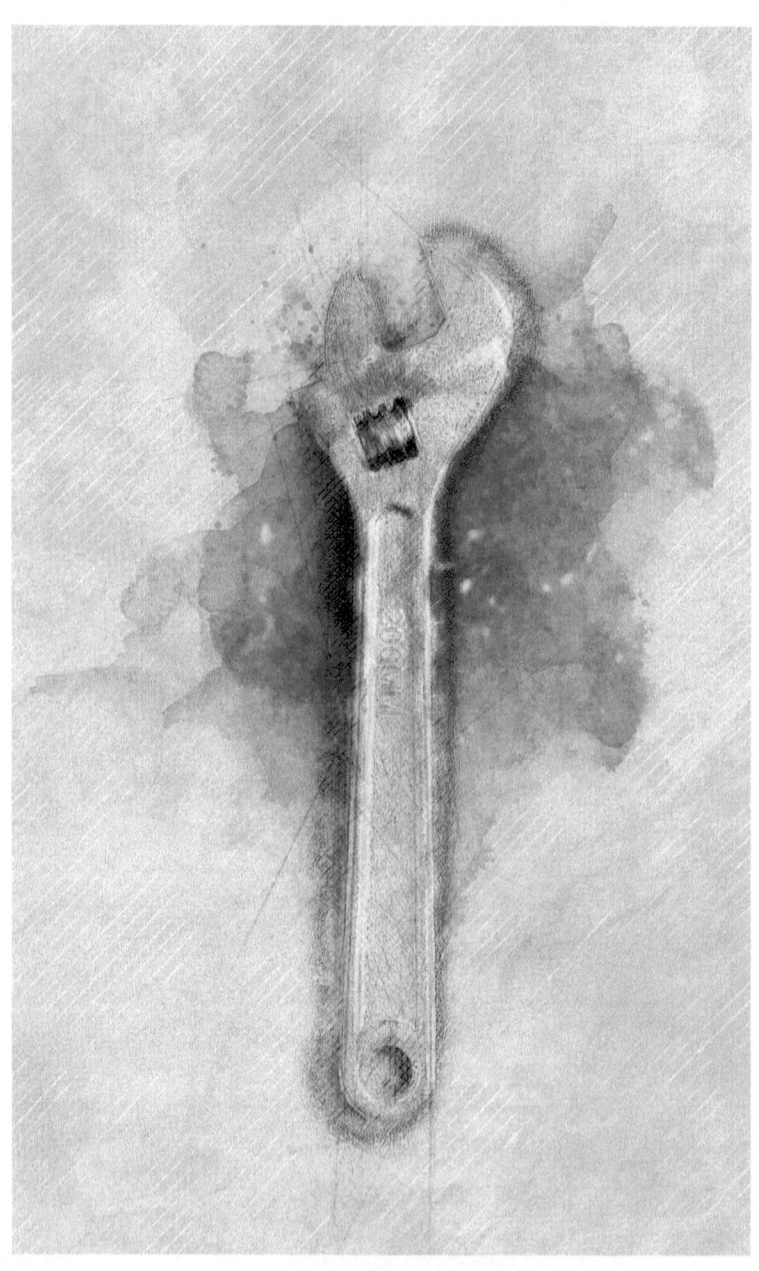

**LAKE COVINGTON**

# Heel and Toe

## LAURA POWERS

### Chapter 1
### Anderson

*A*s I pull into town, the great lake spans out to my right, with a picturesque sign that states, *Welcome to Lake Covington.* I can already feel myself decompress as I scan over the town with its quaint boardwalk lining the crystal-clear water, the shoreline dotted with couples, fishermen, and people out for a stroll.

"Yeah, you were right, Leticia, this town is gorgeous," I say on speakerphone. "This place might be exactly what I need."

Leticia is my good friend and literary agent. She's been with me through it all. In the eight years we've been together, she's stood by my side with all four novels, and as I attempt to write the fifth, she has shown support—albeit, in her own way.

She says, "I'll never lead you astray, my dear Anderson. I told you my hometown was perfect." There's a small pause in our conversation, a hesitation in her voice when she continues. "Don't beat yourself up about missing the deadline. You'll make it up."

"Perhaps." I chuckle. "Every author hits a lull, right?" It's what I tell myself, but I'm not confident.

Leticia's voice is perhaps a little too warm. "Just get some R&R and get back to me, love."

It kills me when she calls me *love*. I've done my best to keep out of any kind of personal relationship with her, but she seems determined. If she keeps pushing it, I'm not sure how much longer our partnership will last. Leticia has been great, she's done a lot for me, but I've never seen her as someone I could date.

My train of thought quickly shifts when I hear a loud clanking under the hood of my car. "Dammit!"

"What is it?" Leticia asks, concerned. "Are you okay?"

"There's something wrong with the Jeep. Is there a place where I can take it?"

"Nash's Fix & Fill, nice shiny red and chrome building, you can't miss it. Mr. Nash was always the best." She mumbles something else, but I only catch the word *daughter*. "Keep me posted. I'll be in town to visit my mother and we can grab some lunch."

"Sure thing." I hang up and search for the shop.

I spot the mechanic's joint and roll into the lot as the Jeep sputters to a stop. I get out and wait for someone to greet me. After nearly ten minutes, I realize no one is coming. *The best, huh?* Clearly, Leticia hasn't been back home in a while. I walk towards the open bay doors and take in the shop. There is one car up on a lift, another propped up with some jacks, and a door that leads to the front office. As I search for any sign of humanity, I spot a pair of work boots sticking out of the jacked-up car.

## Chapter 2
### Kelly

*Tap, tap, tap.*

Why do people think that is ok?

I look over at the brand new sneakers visible from my place under the car. Before I can even open my mouth to respond, there's another round of tapping above me.

"Excuse me, sir." I hear a voice say. "I'm in need of assistance."

*Calm down, Kelly.* Being a woman in a male-dominated field is a constant uphill battle, one I've been fighting all my life.

I nearly jump out of my skin at another round of tapping.

I finish loosening the filter and push my creeper out from under the car, the words falling out of my mouth before I can stop them. "You're in my shop, pal, cool your jets."

The man's eyes widen in surprise as he runs his hand through his dirty blond hair. I have that effect on people.

He starts to stammer out an apology, but I wave him off. It's not the first time it's happened. Besides, if I'm going to be stereotyped, at least it's by a good-looking stranger. His enticing green eyes send a shiver of desire down my spine.

"You're not from around here, are you?"

"What gave it away?"

"Because everyone in Lake Covington knows I inherited the shop when Pops passed away."

"Years of male mechanics make one assume." He offers his hand. "Anderson Culp."

*Why does that name sound familiar?*

I hold up my palm, displaying the grime caked into each crevice. "Kelly Nash." I tip my head towards the bay doors. "Is that your Jeep?"

"Yes," he says, dropping his hand and heading outside. "It started acting up."

I follow him, noticing how well his jeans fit. "Time limit?"

"I'll be staying in town, so no real rush." He reaches in the Jeep and pops the hood. "Do you know where I can rent a car?"

"Best bet would be the airport. They usually have a decent selection."

I ask him questions while inspecting the engine. I have a pretty good idea of what's wrong. Doing this all my life has given some insight on what makes engines tick.

"It sounds like it might be your alternator," I say. "I'd have to really get in there to make sure. It could get pricey though. Usually once the alternator goes, there's other issues, but—" I give him a playful nudge. "—don't worry, I don't gouge. I'm not that kind of lady."

"You seem like you know what you're doing."

Our gaze locks together, longer than it should. The way he watches me causes heat to course through my veins and pool in my gut. I've been hoping for some fresh meat in this town. The men here are a bore. Most of them won't look me in the eye anymore; something about being a strong-willed woman frightens them. This man doesn't seem to mind.

I give him my sexiest smile. I'm not sure how it appears on my grease-smeared face. "Would you like to get coffee tomorrow morning?"

"Yeah, that sounds great."

I can't remove the grin spreading on my lips. "Good," I say. "In the meantime, why don't you park in the side lot and go inside and see Patty. She'll call you an Uber."

"That's okay. I can call my own." He turns to get inside the Jeep and gives me a full view of his tight butt. He is delectable in every way. From his easygoing attitude, to his intense stare. I'm pulled toward him, as if we were always on course to meet. This one just might satisfy me.

"It's part of our policy," I say. "Besides, the Uber can take you to get the rental."

I dig through the top pocket of my coveralls and grab a card, trying my best not to cover it in oil. "Text me your number and I'll let you know a time for coffee tomorrow."

He takes it. His fingers graze mine and I swear I feel a jolt of electricity.

"Nice meeting you Kelly."

"And you."

I give a little wave and try to keep my cool as I walk back towards the garage to finish Mrs. Penbrook's oil change.

I'm practically skipping as I make it inside, lay back down on the creeper, and roll under her car. I pick up a wrench and hold it to my chest. Who is this guy who'd just rolled into my life? He had to have felt that chemistry. I'm still buzzing with it. If it's like that with just one brief interaction, a night with Anderson could be explosive.

A girl can only dream.

### Chapter 3
### Anderson

Kelly and I agreed to meet at Cuppa Café at five in the morning before she had to go to work. I'm not usually nervous. It's weird to feel a flutter in my chest over a woman, but Kelly brings that out in me. Normally I write fantasy, but after meeting her and the strong connection I instantly felt, I'm wondering if I should dabble in romance. She inspires me in that way.

As Kelly enters the café, my heart pounds against my chest. No longer is she hidden beneath greasy coveralls. Now her curvy body is on full display in skinny jeans and a tight tank top. Her brown locks that yesterday were pulled up in a tight ponytail, now have a slight curl as they cascade down over her shoulders. Hazel eyes peer out from thick eyelashes and plush lips hold a hint of a curve as she makes her way over to me.

"You all right there, Anderson?" Her voice is playful, no business straining it. She waves towards the counter. "Did you already order?"

"No," I say, standing up. "I was waiting for you."

I walk with her and as soon as we get there, the barista greets Kelly in a happy tone.

"The usual?"

"You know it, Aryn. Thanks." Kelly looks over at me and, for a moment, I cannot help but get lost in those hazel pools, the green and gold capturing me in their intensity.

"How about you?" Aryn asks, snapping me back to reality.

I blink and face the barista. "I'll have what she's having."

"Two black coffees coming up." Aryn gives me a wink before moving towards the coffee pot.

My brows shoot up towards my hairline. Kelly is nothing like any woman I've ever met. "Black? Really?"

"Helps wake me up in the morning. You get used to it." She turns her full attention towards me.

Being an author is not an aphrodisiac. Most women don't hit on you because you've written a *New York Times* bestseller. At least that hasn't been my experience. Lately, the women I've been with have had their hands in the publishing world. From boisterous writers to career-driven publishers and CEOs. Maybe that's why Leticia seems to think I'd be interested when I'm not. Kelly is different and I like that, but she also has me feeling like a nervous wreck.

She asks, "So what brings you to Lake Covington?".

"A friend from here suggested I stay at the bed and breakfast to recharge my batteries."

"What's your friend's name? Perhaps I can thank them for sending you my way."

"Leticia Rosemond."

"Oh." A shadow crosses her face. She looks away, her jaw clenching. It's clear there is bad blood there, but I cannot bring myself to ask.

Aryn hands over our coffees, breaking the awkwardness between us. "Here you two go."

We head back to the table.

As I sit, I say, "I'm staying at the B&B. Lake Cottage, I think it's called. It's nice. Can't beat the view."

I'm hoping to pull Kelly out of whatever mood the mention of Leticia has caused. Whatever went on between those two must have been bad.

Kelly twisted the coffee cup in her hands. "Why do you need to recharge your batteries?" she asks.

"I'm an author. I just finished a book-signing tour for my latest work. Problem is I can't seem to get inspiration to write the next one. Every time I try, there's nothing."

"What do you write?" Curiosity lights up her eyes, all thoughts of Leticia seem to be gone or nearly gone.

"Have you heard of *The War of Tides?*"

Her mouth drops open. "I knew your name sounded familiar. I read that in two days flat. I almost messed up an oil change trying to finish a chapter." She laughs, and the sound is like music to my ears.

"I'm glad you like it. Hopefully, the next book will meet your expectations, if I ever write it."

She leans forward. My gaze does its best to focus on her face, but having her chest propped up before me makes that difficult.

"Maybe what you need is a distraction," She says and places her hand on my thigh. "I'll be more than happy to be that distraction."

I cannot help but jump when she squeezes my leg.

"I can most definitely go for a distraction," I say, leaning forward, ready for whatever Kelly was interested in doing.

Someone clears her throat and it breaks the trance between us.

"Ms. Nash?"

I look up and see an older woman giving me a once-over before turning her disapproving eyes towards Kelly. "I'm glad I caught you here," she says. "I wanted to say thank you for the speedy oil change yesterday. Great work as usual. Your father would be proud." She makes a "tsk" noise at me and adds, "Of your work."

Kelly doesn't even bother looking towards the woman. "You're welcome, Mrs. Penbrook. Have a great day."

Mrs. Penbrook shakes her head as she heads to the counter. Once the older woman is out of earshot, Kelly sighs. "We have a deep-rooted gossip mill here and I don't want to be the bearing of bad news, but you're now in it."

"Am I?"

"Is that going to be a problem?"

I can feel her foot on the side of my leg. It sends an urge to claim her straight through me. It takes every ounce of willpower to hold onto my sanity and my coffee cup.

"N...no. Not for me. For you?"

"No. I'm used to it."

I hear a small clunk on the floor just before her now bare foot travels up the inside of my leg. I jolt slightly in my seat as her toes brush against my inner thigh and continue to slide over my groin.

"You do seem to know your way around an engine."

Her foot trails down my leg. The brush of her toes sends a pleasant shiver down my spine. "I'm quite the pro."

Kelly comes around the table and sits beside me. Her lips are on mine and, at first, my mind cannot keep up. She's a woman who clearly knows what she wants, and it takes me by surprise. But then, I pull her into me, wrapping my arms around her back as my tongue slips into her mouth. Our once soft kiss is now full of heat and passion. I wonder what poor old Mrs. Penbrook is thinking now.

### Chapter 4
### Kelly

A magnetic attraction to the new stud in town courses over my flesh as I stand beside Anderson's Jeep. I need his sign-off for some parts then I can get started, but it's hard to think about work when all I want to do is think about him.

After our coffee, I rushed home and quickly changed for the shop. As much as I enjoy putting on a cute outfit and makeup, it does little for me at work. No one will take a mechanic seriously in that getup. As it were, it took several years for the older locals to even trust me with their cars after Dad died. Even though I was eight when I rebuilt my first engine and know more about cars than anyone within a fifty-mile radius, I struggle to prove myself every day.

My mind is still on Anderson as I make my way through the garage. I cannot help but get stuck on one major detail. He's friends with Leticia—the woman who spread rumors around town that I'm a slut. Sure, I've had my romps in the sack, but slut? Come on. Not even close. It all started after I slept with Leticia's boyfriend in high school. It wasn't intentional. He'd told me they were broken up. I told Leticia and tried to apologize, but that didn't matter to her. Honestly, I don't know why she was so mad in the first place. I was doing her a favor. That guy was a terrible lay. But since then, I became Leticia's extra special pet project on her list of lives she wanted to destroy. The best thing that ever happened to me was when she finally left town. I thought my time with Leticia was over, but now there's Anderson and he's connected to her. Of course, it would have to be her, but I refuse to let Leticia ruin this for me.

Anderson's rental pulls into the lot and parks near the bay doors. As soon as he spots me, his features light up with a bright smile.

I've never felt this kind of attraction for a man before. Most men in my life were quick flings or drawn out, dreadful relationships where they think I'm just some damsel in distress who needs to be saved from my garage and be in a kitchen where I belong. It's not like that with Anderson. He listens to me when I talk. He engages with me and cares about my opinion. Anderson makes me believe that really good guys are out there.

He says, "Good morning, beautiful."

I know my oil-smeared cheeks are flushed, and right now, I couldn't care less.

I nod to the Jeep. "I have everything figured out. I just need you to sign off before I get started."

"What do you have in mind?"

I grab my tablet and begin going over everything.

"Looks perfect. Where do I sign?"

I hand him my tablet. When he's finished, he leans over and nuzzles my neck. "How about I take you out tonight?" His voice is smooth as he whispers in my ear before pulling away.

He's growing bolder by the minute and it excites me, but I wonder if his bravery would falter if I were to climb him right here, right now. "Sounds like fun to me. Maybe dinner? Dancing?"

"What time?"

"How about six? My place. I'll text you the address."

Anderson leaves, and I spend the rest of my working hours getting his Jeep fixed, doing what I can with the parts I have, and trying to stay focused on the task at hand and not the fun tasks I have planned tonight.

Once I get home, I waste no time getting dressed. After a quick shower, I get my makeup done, do my hair, and decide which dress will accent my curves. Even with it being summer, the nights are still mild in Lake Covington. I throw on a V-neck dress that goes down to mid-thigh and a pair of leather boots. I don't know where we're going, but this dress should fit every venue for dinner around Lake Covington.

Before I can second guess myself, the doorbell rings and my core clenches in anticipation. I pause and gather myself before opening the door. Anderson is standing on the other side in a pair of black slacks and white button-up shirt that fits nicely against his body, giving way to his well-toned form.

One look at him and I'm almost tempted to eat in and spend the night in bed, but I could use a night on the town. Letting it all loose is definitely on the agenda.

### Chapter 5
### Anderson

My breath catches when I see Kelly. I can't believe I was lucky enough to meet a woman like her. She's fun, quirky, her positive attitude lifts my spirits, and she's drop-dead gorgeous.

"Hello, beautiful."

I want to grab her and slam the door behind us as I search for her bedroom, but I mentally shake myself and take a deep breath. I don't want to come on too strong.

"Hey, handsome. Where are you taking me tonight?"

She grabs her purse and shuts the door, not bothering to lock it.

I grin. "I have a few ideas."

We eat at Chez Charbon, the nicest restaurant I could find. Once the meal is over, we head to The Impulse. The brick building is easy to spot with its orange neon sign. I groan when I see the line. It's long and wraps around the building. I glance over at Kelly, but she seems undeterred. We park and get out of the car and take our places at the end. In front of us is a sea of plunging necklines, unbuttoned shirts, six-inch heels, and too much cologne. There's a slight chill in the air and Kelly snuggles against me. I wrap my arm around her, suddenly not caring if we stand out here all night. The music thumps in our chests as we inch closer to the front.

Before I know it, we're heading inside. Not surprisingly, the club is packed. We push our way to the crowded bar. It takes up the entire right wall with staff running in and out from behind its oaken surface. As we stand there and wait for the bartender, I search for a place to sit. Tables and booths dot the perimeter, but most are taken. We get our drinks and drift towards the dance floor. It's lit up with several lights from the ceiling, basking the dancers in their multi-color hues. The DJ is at a raised table surrounded by massive speakers. While we watch, waitresses make their rounds, expertly maneuvering around all levels of inebriation.

Kelly points out an empty table and we snatch it. As soon as we set our drinks down, she grabs my arm and pulls me to the dance floor. I am not usually one to dance, but I'm happy to find any reason to wrap her in my arms. With the pulsing beat, her body grinds against me, with her thigh pressed against my crotch. Her breasts, which have been on display all night, are rubbing against my chest, and her lithe fingers graze over my skin as they slide underneath my shirt.

My hands move on their own accord as they make their way to her ass and give a squeeze. Within a matter of minutes, there is little of us not plastered to one another, including our lips.

It's nearly two in the morning when we finally find our way out of the club.

Kelly's voice is breathless. "Let's go to your room at the Lake Cottage and give those old Talleys something to talk about."

The Talleys are the nice elderly couple who own the Lake Cottage. While I'm not one to pass up a night of wild unrestraint, for the Talley's sake, I hope they're sleeping with ear plugs.

We try our best to be quiet as we enter the quaint little home that was converted into a B&B. Our bodies are interwoven as Kelly slams me into the stone fireplace in the small living area. Letting out a breath, I coax her towards the winding staircase that leads to my room. Once there, I push Kelly up against the solid oak door labeled 204. Our lips lock and her hands begin to unbutton my shirt while I do my best to find the key in my pocket.

Our momentum is disrupted by Leticia's shrill voice calling from down the hall.

"Kelly Nash, you have got to be kidding me."

I feel Kelly stiffen.

Kelly's features turn cold and a look of pure hate falls over her face. I've never seen that much distain aimed at anyone, and for the first time since meeting Kelly, I wonder if this was a mistake.

She grits her teeth. "Leticia fucking Rosemond, what the hell are you doing here?"

"I'd ask you the same question, but I'm sure you practically live in every B&B, hotel, and motel in town." Leticia turns to me, shaking her head. "You cannot be serious, Anderson. After everything we've been through, you're sleeping with this slut?"

Kelly responds in a hearty laugh. "Didn't realize he was taken, especially by such an uptight bitch like you." She steps closer to Leticia and narrows her eyes. "Perhaps there is something to be said that your men don't let on they're spoken for."

Leticia huffs. Any more of this and fists are going to start flying instead of words. I step between them.

Kelly stares up at me. Her eyes are no longer full of that fun I'd loved all night. "Your car will be ready in the morning."

With that, Kelly leaves.

I snarl at Leticia. "What was that about? Who I date is none of your business."

"I know," she says, her voice full of sympathy as runs her hands over my bare chest. "I'm just looking out for you. It is not my fault she assumed we were together. Listen, Kelly is just a whore. She's slept with every available man in this town. I'm saving you the heartache."

I run my hand through my hair. How can I have any kind of professional relationship with her if this is how she's going to act? "Just leave, Leticia."

"Leave?" Her eyes turn furious and she snarls, "You think you can just cast me off? Don't forget that if it wasn't for me, you'd still be in that studio apartment with that barely functioning laptop. My father didn't want to take you. He didn't think your novels would sell. But I did. I believed in you. Just remember that before you even think about pursuing something with that bitch Kelly."

Mr. Talley comes up the stairs in a beige robe with matching slippers. "What's all the commotion. Is everything all right up here?"

"Yes, Mr. Talley," Leticia says with a smile that could charm a yeti. "Everything's fine. I'm just having a discussion with my client." She looks at me and lowers her voice. "It's me or her, Anderson. If you value your career, I wouldn't make the wrong choice."

## Chapter 6
### Kelly

I should have figured Leticia had already sank her teeth into Anderson. What could I have expected? She exists to ruin my life. What had they talked about after I left? I'm sure Leticia painted me in the worst color she could. I could only imagine what Anderson thought of me now.

I study Anderson's car on the lift. Even though my head is pounding, I finish all the work. He's expected to pick up his car this morning. The sooner the better.

"Is it safe to come in?"

Anderson's voice sends a painful shiver down my spine. I plaster on a mask of professionalism before I turn.

"You're early," I say. "We're not technically open, but if you give me a few I can get your car down." I walk over to the lift and begin lowering it back to the ground.

"About, last night..."

I cringe. A part of me wants to hear him out, but I've allowed myself to give men the benefit of the doubt before and it's bit me in the ass.

"I get it," I say. "On vacation, want some excitement. I should have guessed you and Leticia were together when you said her name. No harm, no foul. I just hope you're not in the doghouse."

He shifts his weight. "Can I explain? Please?"

He sounds sincere and I can't help but want to hear what he has to say.

The car hits the floor and the hydraulics shut off. "You've got five minutes."

"Leticia and I have never been together. She's just my agent. That's all there is between us. I swear."

*Just your agent, huh?* I cross my arms over my chest. "Listen, it doesn't matter what you two have got going on. We were just going to have a little fun until you left town. It's fine. Really."

He steps forward until he's close enough that I can see the lines of his chest under his shirt. "Only a little fun? Really? That's all I was to you?"

I look up at him. "No. Not all." At that moment, I can feel it, feel the attraction radiating off him and I do something I promised I'd never do again. I kiss a man belonging to Leticia Rosemond.

Anderson pushes me up against the Jeep. His lips find mine and my mouth opens so he can claim it. The shy, sweet Anderson is now fierce and full of wanting.

I grab his shirt and pull him closer. "Tell me again that nothing is happening between you and Leticia."

"I have no desire to ever be with Leticia. I want you. Only you."

I gaze into his eyes. He's telling the truth.

My breath is shallow and short as I whisper, "I have an apartment upstairs."

Before he can respond, I grab his hand and run up the metal steps in the back leading to the small studio apartment. I slam the door behind us and throw him against it. I'm like a wild animal ready to stake its claim, and he seems eager to be owned.

Buttons fly in every direction as I rip open his shirt. I make quick work of his pants as his hands work the zipper of my coveralls. Before I know it, we're on the bed, naked, and ravaging each other in feral need.

His lips trail my body, leaving gooseflesh lingering in his wake as they inch closer to my core. Our desire burns bright and we both fall into a wanton passion until he pushes me over the edge into a toe-curling orgasm.

### Six Months Later
### Kelly

We make our way into town. Anderson seems nervous, but I tell him not to be. He has finished his next book and it's brilliant. All that's left is dropping the final manuscript at the post office.

Leticia is no longer his agent. Anderson told her that he wouldn't choose, and he wanted to be with me. They parted ways amicably—at least that's what the legal work said. He's free to move on to another agent and free to be with me as well.

Anderson says I'm his muse, but the truth is he's mine, and he inspires me to see a future full of love. No one knows if something is forever, but for once, I feel like such a thing exists.

**LAKE COVINGTON**

# Lipstick Stain

**NATALIE NIXON**

## Lake Covington, 1956

The atmosphere at the dinner table suddenly shifted, and Charlotte sensed that her parents' appetites had just changed.

"Goodbye, Charlotte."

Charlotte set her fork down. "But Mother, I was hoping to discuss St. Mary's College—"

"*Charlotte.*" Her mother's eyes burned into her father's. "Take some bills from my purse and go."

In the foyer, she found her mother's handbag and the money waiting for her—as always on the days her father was expected back from the city. Charlotte took three dollars and paused, listening. They had moved into the formal sitting room. She crept forward, peering into the room.

Her father's normally intimidating bulk was crouched on a low footstool, his gaze fixed upward on his wife's face. Her mother stood with her back to Charlotte. She raised her foot, and delicately planted one stiletto on her father's thigh. Charlotte watched his thigh dimple as the heel dug in deep, his breath a sudden hiss.

\*\*\*

Charlotte pedaled her bike furiously down their long driveway, her Schwinn lurching in the gravel.

Why had she spied on her parents? She knew what their reunion nights were like. When she was younger, she would retreat to her bedroom, turn on her record player, and The Four Aces drowned out the sounds. But since moving to Lake Covington three years ago, Charlotte was considered old enough to fend for herself, and expected to vacate the house.

When she arrived at the movie theater, she locked her bicycle to the rack and waited to purchase a ticket.

The poster for an upcoming movie caught her eye: The Man Who Knew Too Much. She liked Hitchcock features. The strange twists gave her something to think about during her forced evictions.

"What's today's movie?" she asked the cashier.

"*Baby Doll* by Tennessee Williams."

Charlotte shrugged. It didn't really matter. She had to kill time.

There were two people working the concession counter, a woman, and the handsome bow-tied fellow she had often noticed working the late shift. Acutely aware of her disheveled cleaning clothes, she ordered popcorn from the young woman. In the theater, an usher lit the aisle as she found a seat. She sank into the cushions with a tired sigh. Since four o'clock that morning, she'd been scrubbing the house beside her mother. When her father was gone for weeks at a time, Charlotte and her mother lived an independent, and admittedly untidy life. Her mother despised the images of perfect women in advertisements: Hoovering their carpets in ketchup-hued lipstick and matching heels. Only on days when her father made the long drive home did the house, and her mother, get polished.

The movie opened with scenes of a ruined plantation house, and a man named Archie peeping through a hole in a wall at a young woman sleeping and sucking her thumb. The young woman was Baby Doll, Archie's childlike, virgin wife. Charlotte shifted uncomfortably in her seat as the story unfolded. Baby

Doll had been forced to marry Archie but refused to consummate the marriage. Archie groped her despite her screams.

After the second showing, Charlotte pushed her way outside the theater. She fished a stolen cigarette and one of her father's lighters out of the bag on her bike. Slipping the cigarette between her lips, she tried to strike the flint, but her hands trembled.

Her sophomore year, when she was new to town, she had tried her best to fit in. But all the other girls at the women's college prep school had known each other from birth. Charlotte dressed the part, wore her hair like theirs, even tried going steady with a prep-school boy. When he jabbed his tongue in and out of her mouth, she wondered how anyone could enjoy such a thing. When he wanted more she refused, like any proper girl would. He shoved her against a wall one evening and forced his hands under her blouse.

She plucked the cigarette out of her mouth and ground it under her heel.

Back inside the theater, the only worker at the concession counter now was the young man, but Charlotte could care less about her grubby appearance as her thoughts churned around the film. She ordered a hotdog, but the bow-tied fellow frowned apologetically. "Sorry, we didn't think we would have any customers for the midnight show. The movie has been... unpopular. We shut off the grill an hour ago."

Charlotte's belly rumbled. She glanced at the neon clock in the lobby, but it was still too early to go home. "Well I *am* staying for the midnight showing. And I'm *hungry*. So, what do you propose..." she glanced at his name badge, "*William?*"

He ran a knuckle over the bridge of his nose, but then smiled. "I don't want my last customer angry, so how about this? Anything in the counter is on the house. What do you say?"

She looked through the glass counter and pointed to a bag of peanuts.

William handed them to her and asked, "So, what do you think of *Baby Doll?* I noticed you've been here since the eight o'clock show. You must have an educated opinion by now."

Charlotte thought about the men in the movie, all ruthlessly manipulating Baby Doll over her virginity. And the strange way Baby Doll glowed under the attention.

"It's abrasive. And titillating. And— outrageous!"

William's eyebrows shot up under his uniform cap. *"Disturbing,* right?" He said the word with relish. "Did you notice the way the director uses lighting, bright spots and shadows, to convey emotion?"

"You've seen it?"

"Six times so far."

*Baby Doll* was a dark story. What kind of person was William who'd watch it six times? Charlotte ordered a fountain drink to get William's disconcerting blue eyes focused on something besides her. She frowned as she went back to her seat.

During the final show, Charlotte paid attention to the lighting in the scenes. She noticed the way the dialogue moved from innocent to disquieting at the exact moment the characters passed into a shadow. *Disturbing.*

As Charlotte left the empty theater, heavy raindrops took her by surprise. The rain came down in sheets. With a shiver, she straddled her bike, flicked the headlight on, and pushed off tiredly in the direction of home.

A hot rod backfired as it sped by. Charlotte shrieked, nearly losing her grip on the wet handlebars. She wanted to be home. She wanted to crawl into bed and sleep till noon. But she had to be up at dawn again. Had to properly doll herself up and meet with her recently graduated senior class to beautify the Grange for the annual Sweetheart Dance.

Charlotte almost screamed again when a two-door Belvedere paralleled her and the driver yelled, "Hey!"

She braked hard, her Schwinn skidding.

"Lousy weather to be on a bike," the driver said.

"Who's that?" she demanded, blinking rain from her eyes.

"It's William, the jerk from the theater who had no hotdogs."

Charlotte walked her bicycle closer to the window. He looked older in his shirtsleeves.

"Do you want a ride?"

"I live way out, on Lake View Road."

"Shit, if you don't get in, you might drown upright before you get there."

She glanced toward the back of the car. "What about my bike?"

"Here—" He hopped out of his car and took her handlebars "—there's a bike rack across the street at the drugstore. What's the combination to your lock?"

The numbers were out of her mouth before she realized she was speaking. Numb, she opened the passenger door and slid into the seat. William jumped back in and they pulled away.

He raked a hand through his wet hair with a laugh. "Now we are a pair of drowned rats." He glanced at her before looking back to the road. "Sorry I don't have a coat to offer you."

Charlotte looked down; the white seams of her brassiere showed through her soaked shirt like a plus sign over each breast. She hugged her chest tight. "So how do you know so much about movies, anyway?"

"They're my greatest interest, you could say. Hopefully my future too. I've been working two jobs the last year, saving up money to move to Hollywood."

She stared at his profile, noticed the play of muscle in his arm as he shifted the car. "Do you plan to audition for roles?"

He laughed. "Nah, I want to work behind the cameras. I will start at the bottom, cutting film, but eventually, I want to direct. Tell stories visually, the way they do in the best movies."

"Is *Baby Doll* one of the best movies?"

"You said it was abrasive, titillating, and outrageous. It's definitely a twisted coming of age story. Twisted family dynamics. Like life. Real life, anyway."

Charlotte was quiet. *Twisted family dynamics...real life.* Her mother's stiletto sinking into her father's thigh flashed into her mind.

William turned the radio on. *Heartbreak Hotel* was playing. "I hope the DJs play some Elvis at the Grange next weekend." He chuckled. "Be nice if this sleepy town got shaken up a bit."

"Will you be at the dance?" Charlotte asked, coming back to the present.

William turned up the drive to Charlotte's house. "It's more of a couples thing, isn't it?" He parked his car.

"I guess so." She opened her door and made to heft herself out, but suddenly sank back into the seat. "Oh no. Oh, damn!"

"What is it?"

"I have to be at the Grange at nine o'clock tomorrow. My senior class volunteered to decorate. But my bike is at the drugstore. If I walk, it'll take me an hour."

"Shit, umm." He looked guilty. "Can your parents give you a lift?"

"They will be...otherwise occupied." She hung her head with exhaustion.

"Okay, look, I can give you a ride. This rain will put my construction job on hold till the site dries out, so I'll be free in the morning. I'll pick you up, okay?"

*\*\*\**

Charlotte crept upstairs to her bedroom, and let her wet clothes lay where they fell. Under her blankets, habit guided her hand between her legs, but she was dreaming before her fingers found their mark.

When William arrived in the morning, Charlotte apologized for being such a nosebleed the night before. He waved her apology off, "I was the jackass who talked you into leaving your bike." As they drove toward town he asked, "So, what are you doing at the Grange, exactly?"

"I've been tasked with hanging lighting—electric bulbs and lanterns."

He frowned. "The ceiling is mighty high in that old barn. Do you have ladders?"

"I'm not sure."

"The rain put my other job on hold for a day or two. If it's okay, I'd like to help out—to make up for locking your bike up last night."

"Oh ..." Charlotte hesitated, unsure of herself around this stranger, but exhaustion still hovered. "That would be great."

He smiled. "I can get a ladder from the toolshed at my job site. Just need to stop at home and grab the key."

\*\*\*

It was strange, and fascinating, to be alone in William's bedroom while he went to retrieve a ladder since a construction site was no place for a "lady." He'd explained that the house would be empty, his father gone, working.

"And your mother?"

He stroked the bridge of his nose. "My mother hasn't lived here for years."

"Divorce?" she asked quietly.

"No..." he paused. "Mutual agreement. After my little brother died, it was too hard for her to be here anymore."

Charlotte learned that William's little brother Clyde had been born with a hole in his heart. "Doctors told us he wouldn't make it to his fifth birthday. We celebrated his eighth." He smiled with sad pride.

Alone now, Charlotte looked at photographs of the brothers. William strong and healthy, Clyde frail and stunted. Both goofy and loving in the photos.

Charlotte took liberties. She peered into William's closet. Stretched out on top of his bed, rubbing her face into his pillow, inhaling his scent. Between the bed and the wall, something was wedged. She pulled out a magazine, jumping when she opened it and saw a naked woman posing in a sheer robe. She turned every page, reading articles with titles like "Will She, or Won't She?" There was an advertisement for prophylactics with the phrase "I take one everywhere I take my penis!" emblazoned across the top. Charlotte closed the magazine, frowning. Men wanted women who could be had, apparently at the drop of a hat. Fathers sent their daughters to schools run by nuns to ensure their daughters' virginity. Did real life happen somewhere between those two extremes?

When William arrived back home with a ladder tied to the roof of his Belvedere, Charlotte was examining his collection of movie posters. He smiled, pointing to a poster for *Treasure Island*. "One of Clyde's favorites," he said. "Anything adventurous. He was too weak to do much. He lived through the movies. I used to save every penny to take him. We'd stuff ourselves with popcorn and candy and watch a film at least three times in a row."

She motioned toward a group of posters featuring Jane Russell in sexy poses. "Are these William's favorites?" she asked, eyebrows raised.

William chuckled. "You probably won't believe me, but Clyde's favorites too. He had a thing for brunettes. I swear."

"At age seven?"

"He was an old soul. Dealing with everything he had to deal with...it matured him."

Charlotte curled her forefinger at William, beckoning him closer. She pointed at Jane Russell. Squinting his eyes, he looked from Charlotte's perspective. The light from his window revealed smudges over Jane Russell's mouth—smudges in the shape of lip marks.

"Oh, ha!" he barked. "Also Clyde. He used to come in here to bug me. He'd stand on his tiptoes, smooch Jane, and say 'Willy, kiss a real girl for me one day.'" His voice choked up.

Charlotte saw the glint of tears in his eyes as he cleared his throat. Without thinking, she closed the gap between them, mouth pressing against his, hands clenching his T-shirt. His body was stiff with surprise for a second, before his arms wrapped around her. His lips were warm, and firm. The kiss lengthened. Charlotte opened her mouth, felt his breath pause. She kissed him deeper, until their moist lips clung together.

"For Clyde?" she whispered.

"Hell no. For me." And this time he kissed *her*.

***

The Grange was a historic barn from Lake Covington's first dairy. It now belonged to the town, and every June it held the Sweetheart Dance. As Charlotte and William parked in the dirt lot beside the barn, the mermaid weathervane on the roof spun in a warm breeze. Charlotte was forgiven for being late when she announced to the other girls that she had brought help.

When it came time to hang the electric bulbs on the interior beams, William's ladder was not quite tall enough. Looking up, he spotted the floor of a hay loft directly above the dance floor.

"If we could get up to the hay loft, we could work from there," he said. "Let's look outside."

They circled the barn. "Here." William pointed. Just out of reach, a wooden ladder was nailed to the wall, and led to high doors, mounted on sliding rails.

"Boost me," Charlotte said. Her hands found a rung and she scrambled up. At the top, she was able to shove one of the doors open wide enough to squeeze in.

"How is it?" He asked when she reappeared.

She grinned down at him. "This will work."

He brought his ladder around outside and climbed up, the ropes of lights looped over his body. Inside the dark space, they felt their way to the edge of the loft, where the lip protruded over the dance floor. William could step from the lip onto the beams where the lights needed to be hung. Charlotte fed the strings of lights across to him, while the girls below admired his balancing act.

***

When their work was done, William dropped her off at the drugstore to get her bike.

"See you tomorrow?" he asked as she stepped out onto the curb.

"Okay." She shut the door on her awkward reply and his car pulled away. Her head was full. She wanted to sit by herself and think. She went inside, ordered a float from a young lady in a crisp white dress, and sat at the counter. People came and went: some to the cigarette counter, some to the pharmacy. A knot of girls perused the cosmetics.

"Peggy." The pharmacist beckoned the girl from the soda fountain. "Come watch my counter while I take my break."

"Be right there." Peggy turned to Charlotte. "Do you need anything else? He always takes at least thirty minutes this time of the evening."

"No, thank you."

The front door opened and a man walked to the pharmacy. Peggy chirped. "Are you here to pick up an order?"

"Umm ..." The man glanced around. "Is the doctor in?"

"No, he took his break. Name on your order?"

"Well, look, I need some..."

"Yes?"

He peered over his shoulder before saying, "I need a pack of Trojans."

"Oh, I'm not sure what that is. Hold on, let me ask. Dollie!" Peggy hailed the older woman at the cigarette counter. "This fellow needs a pack of Trojans, but I don't know—"

Dollie barreled out from behind the cigarette case. "Out! Get out!" she yelled at the man. She shooed Peggy into the back, then faced the man over the counter. "How dare you talk to a little girl like that? For shame!"

"Look, lady. I'm *married*, alright?" The man was obviously embarrassed. "Just sell me what I need so I can get back to the missus. Then I will scram."

Dollie huffed as she opened a drawer, pulling out a small tin. She took the man's bills, stalking him as he left the store. From the entrance, Dollie turned around to glare at the customers who had stopped to stare. Charlotte averted her gaze to the dregs of her float.

The next few nights saw more thunderstorms blossom over the town. William showed up each morning, rubbing the bridge of his nose when Charlotte made him nervous, and kissing her passionately in his car when she chose to let him in. When Wednesday dawned dry, Charlotte bicycled to the Grange alone. She wove garlands of silk flowers with the other young women and decorated the DJ's dais. Everyone chatted about their upcoming moves to various colleges.

"St. Mary's," Charlotte said when she was asked her destination.

"A good school, but you don't seem very excited," remarked Veronica, the former class president.

Charlotte shrugged. "It's my father's chosen school. Not mine. I would prefer to go elsewhere and not be under his thumb."

Veronica nodded. "If you don't mind my asking, what's your sudden interest in William Talley?"

"I don't think that is anyone's concern but mine," Charlotte said coolly.

Veronica's hands stilled from their work. "Are you college material, or not? A woman's reputation as an intelligent equal is hard enough to maintain when she associates with the right people. William's achievements are mediocre at best."

***

That afternoon, Charlotte's thoughts churned as she rode home. She pulled her Schwinn into the garage and kicked the stand down. Her hand rested on something bulky in her bag and she realized it was the lighter she had filched from her father's car on Friday night. Opening the passenger door of his Lincoln, she unlatched the glovebox to shove the lighter inside and a bright yellow lady's glove fell out. She picked it up. It was too large to be her mother's. Reaching into the compartment again she pulled out the matching glove, and one of her father's monogrammed handkerchiefs. She stared at the bright red lipstick blotted on it.

"Mother!" Charlotte charged into the house, sobbing. "Mother!"

Her mother rushed down the stairs. "What is it?"

Charlotte held out the gloves and handkerchief.

Her mother took them, confused. She stared at the handkerchief with the lipstick stain. Lipstick in a shade she did not wear.

"Oh, my dear." Her mother's eyes shone with sudden emotion.

"They were in his car. Who is she?"

Her mother paired the gloves together and folded the handkerchief. "I am so sorry, Charlotte, that you had to find out this way."

"Wait." She shook her head. "*You knew?*"

"Oh my love, life is complicated. You'll find out for yourself soon, how difficult things can be. Your father and I have an unspoken agreement. He works for weeks at a time, in the city. It doesn't change my feelings for him. But, you have to understand, it's not a one-way street. Charlotte, I couldn't stand for that. If I meet the right man ..."

Unable to believe what she was hearing, Charlotte sank down on the sofa.

Her mother crouched in front of her and took her hand.

"There are many things that we take for granted in polite society: perfect homes, perfect families. It's just a show. *Real life* is so much more complex. The most important thing is to be true to *yourself*. Know where *you* find happiness. It's so hard for us women, Charlotte. We put on a happy show, and struggle for our own power."

Charlotte realized that her mother had dealt with the same confusions that she wrestled with. Propriety? Femininity? Who was the all-important judge? In her own way, her mother fought the same double standard that *Baby Doll* had made so clear to Charlotte in black and white. She hoped that her mother had found happiness in her compromise, but Charlotte would not put on a show.

***

By Thursday afternoon Charlotte had come to several decisions. Her parents loved each other, but she'd assumed that meant fidelity. Her innocence was gone now. She had listened to her mother. Now, she wanted an explanation from her father.

Charlotte walked into the living room. She wore the gown she had chosen for tomorrow's dance. Behind her back she held a token of power: the gloves and lipstick stained handkerchief. Her mother might choose to let things go unspoken, but Charlotte had decided that the spotlight would shine on the truth in her own life.

Her father sat on the sofa, surrounded by trade magazines.

"Father, can I talk to you?"

He looked up from the newspaper he was reading. "Certainly. What is it..." Charlotte saw his eyes appraise her new look, "...young lady?"

Her back straightened. Normally he called her "my girl."

"Why do you love Mother?"

His newspaper lowered incrementally. He was silent, thinking. A man of precise words, he did not speak lightly.

"Do you recall, that when I was an adolescent, my Aunt Amelia taught ballroom dancing?"

She nodded; her father was an excellent dancer.

"I was her assistant, traveling town-to-town. Eventually, I hated it. The nickel she paid me each night was nothing, but my parents insisted. One of my duties was to dance with every wallflower. Every meek, voiceless teenage girl. I detested their shrinking bodies, their limp waltzes." His eyes did not waver from hers. "The night I met your mother, she asked me to dance." He paused, and Charlotte understood. Her mother had impressed this intelligent man by being unconventional. By making her own decision and acting on it.

"And the woman with the yellow gloves?" She held the gloves and handkerchief out toward him.

For a second, Charlotte claimed the heady victory of his surprise. The newspaper lowered to his lap. She felt as though she were looking down upon her father from the ceiling.

The newspaper rose again. "That woman is a puppet. A regular Howdy Doody."

\*\*\*

On Friday evening, Charlotte's mother dropped her off at the drugstore. Charlotte claimed she was meeting some of her former classmates for a fountain drink before the dance. Thirty minutes later, William pulled up outside the movie theater where Charlotte was waiting for him. He moved around his car, tripping on the curb as he stepped up, opening her door for her. "You look absolutely glamorous."

She smiled, settling into the bench seat. "Thank you for agreeing to escort me."

"I have to admit, I was trying to work up the courage to ask you, but you beat me to it."

William's sun-bleached hair was combed back. His jaw was pink from a fresh shave. He wore khaki slacks, a button up shirt and blazer. He kept glancing at her as they drove.

At the Grange, she left her coat in his car, but kept her little purse with her, dangling from her wrist on its strap.

They walked into the dance hall, and heads turned in their direction. While most of the young women sported dresses in the latest polka dotted and paisley designs, her solid green gown glowed like a jewel in the light of the lanterns overhead. Her hair was pinned into a French twist and, around her neck, she wore a choker of tiny opalescent pearls. People whispered as she pulled William into a slow dance. But she didn't care.

They danced the Boogie Woogie, the Lindy, and the Jitterbug. To cool off, they perched on the hood of William's car, sipping brandy from a flask, laughing and talking about their futures.

Back inside, the DJ played sultry hits from the R&B Race Charts. The lights dimmed and Charlotte swiveled her hips in slow circles, running her hands down her own body, feeling the pulse of the new hit "Fever," by Little Willie John, and clearly seeing the effect this had on William.

During the next slow dance, Charlotte's hands circled the back of his neck, fingers playing with his hair.

"What's in your purse, anyway?" he chuckled, "It's been whacking me all night."

She pulled his head down and whispered in his ear, "A tin of Trojans."

He froze.

"William, will you be with me? Tonight? I'm not asking more of you. I know we can't date. Our lives are moving in different directions. But I want to be in charge of my own life. I want to choose when, and *who*, I want to be with. I want to be with you."

William kept his head tucked down, breathing softly into her neck, as he moved them back into the rhythm of the music. The song ended and he looked into her eyes. "Yes."

Outside, William parked his car against the back wall of the Grange. He tucked her coat under his arm. When no one was in sight, they climbed to the roof of the Belvedere, and then scaled the ladder to the hay loft.

Inside, they moved to the side of the loft, well back from where anyone below could catch a glimpse of them. The rough wood of the roof slanted down to the floor of the loft, making the space to one side feel smaller, and cozy. They laid Charlotte's coat down on the thick planks of the floor. Gaps between some of the boards allowed beams of colored light to stab upward through the dust they stirred. Music and laughter rose from below. They sat cross legged, and she pulled the tin from her purse.

William shook his head, bemused. Charlotte detected a spark of respect in his eye.

"I stole them," she said. "I sent Peggy into the back for a non-existent prescription, then I leaned over the counter, and took them."

"What?"

"I knew the druggist wouldn't sell them to me, so I timed it for when he took his break."

William stared at her.

Charlotte was suddenly laughing and then crying, tears slipping down her cheeks. She rubbed them away, went to wipe her hands on her skirt, but William caught them. Looking into her eyes, he brought her hand to his lips and kissed it. He turned her hand over and kissed her open palm. Then he slid her fingers into his mouth. All the sensation in her body was instantly concentrated in her fingers; she felt the ridged edges of his teeth, gently pressing against the pads of her fingertips. Pleasure washed up her wrist, through the hollow of her elbow, fanning a warmth into her breasts. And this was only the beginning. Her breath caught in her throat.

*** 

A week before departing for St. Mary's, Charlotte moved beneath William in his bed. Her climax subsiding, she clung to him, her arms around his shoulders, legs twined over his thighs. He cried out, his body stiffening. The hammering of her heart slowed as his arms collapsed by degrees, his weight settling on top of her. She stroked the damp lines of his back, his buttocks, his face pressed into her hair.

William discarded the prophylactic and they settled themselves, him on his back, Charlotte tucked against his side.

"William?"

"Hmm?" His fingers stroked her hair behind her ear, rhythmically.

"I have some news."

His fingers stilled.

"My father and I have come to an agreement. After a semester at St. Mary's, if I decide I want to transfer to another school, he will support my choice." She rolled on top of him and looked into his eyes. "One of the other colleges we've looked into is in California. Los Angeles to be precise."

William's face went from startled to ecstatic, his cheeks flushing as he lifted her above him, laughing happily. He lowered her back to his chest, fingers tangling in her hair, and he pulled her head down into a hard, promise laden kiss.

Charlotte kissed him back knowing that this was what she wanted. *This* was what made her happy. This was where real life happened.

# Lake Covington Herald

July 4, 2019

## This Day in Lake Covington
**CONNOR LANE**

It was in 1946 that the first annual Independence Day Regatta was held on Lake Covington. The race consisted of eight races ran by ten teams. Each team was headed by a designated captain, a serviceman having recently returned from the Pacific or European theaters. Each ship's mainsail and prow were decorated with patriotic symbols, and the red, white, and blue streaked across Lake Covington in celebration and triumph.

The winner of that first regatta was MacArthur's Return, captained by Sergeant Nicholas Bixby of the 37th Infantry, who had been with General MacArthur for his recapture of Manila from the Japanese. When asked what the victory meant to him, he broke down in tears and was unable to respond.

Since the first regatta in '46, the event has grown to eighteen races ran by fifteen teams. The patriotic theme has continued, but the sail and hull designs have gotten more colorful. The red, white, and blue are still always on display, but so are all the other colors of the rainbow.

The Fourth of July Regatta has become a local staple, bringing sailing buffs and veterans from all over the country, and drawing everyone out to the docks and the lake shore to watch.

Charlotte Talley, owner of the Lake Cottage that boasts the best views of the lake, tells me, "That week we're always booked months in advance."

Last year, Reggie Sharpe kicked off the festivities when he parachuted into the lake trailing a fifty-foot American flag. This year, a flyover by four F-18 Hornets is scheduled. As always, the races will be capped by a trophy presentation for the winners, and fireworks over the lake at sundown. A brilliant way to honor our veterans and a great way to spend a day, it's no wonder the citizens of Lake Covington wait all year for the Fourth.

181       **LAKE COVINGTON**

# Jump Into Love

## NALA HENKEL-AISLINN

### Chapter 1
### Tessa

Tessa leaned forward in her antique chair, a creak echoing through the tall-ceilinged room of her majestic office in the courthouse. She made a final mark with her red pen and let the pages fall back into place. *Clean*, she thought. Looking at the clock, she sighed. Only two-thirty.

"Why don't you mark up the pdf like a normal person?" asked Carl, her assistant district attorney. He paused to analyze where he could set the drink tray down. She slid her Harper Lee paperweight aside to make room. "Or drink cold drinks on a hot August afternoon?" He arched an eyebrow at her as he handed over her Americano.

"Like a normal person?" She flipped the case folder closed and picked up the coffee. Cracking the lid, she inhaled the scent and let out a luxurious sigh. "I like ink and paper, and I love hot coffee. Call me old school. You've been my ADA for over a year. When are you going to figure out I'm not normal?"

"I think I already have." He laughed. "You work long hours at a job that you could probably do in half a day."

"I'm meticulous."

"You don't party or drink."

"What do you call this?" She waved her hand between them. "And you don't date."

"I'm choosy," she replied, but she couldn't meet his eyes on that one, not after what happened two nights ago. Right on the spot where he was sitting, actually.

"I accuse you of weirdness on all counts, prosecutor," Carl finished, taking a long drink of his Frappuccino. "Laura, drinks are in," he called through the adjoining door between their offices. Although he didn't need to raise his voice since every sound echoed off the oak paneling.

Tessa said, "I plead guilty to weirdness," as her assistant, Laura, strolled in.

"It's about time you did." Laura picked up her iced tea lemonade. "But I think I heard you say Tessa doesn't date, and I object to that statement. The weirdo in question," she hitched a thumb at Tessa, "had a nice long coffee conversation with Reggie Sharp."

Tessa channeled her courtroom-calm demeanor, hoping the blood draining out of her face didn't give anything away.

"What's this?" Carl gasped.

Tessa faked a regretful expression. "If only that were true. I was at the Cuppa Café and a man had a question—"

"Not just a *man*. Reggie Sharp, the skydiving hottie!" Laura fanned herself. "Think Jane Austin hero crossed with a sexy soccer player. He's got a wicked sense of humor and he *kills* at karaoke," she said, pointing her lemonade at Carl. "I've seen him at Mojo's. He rewrites funny lyrics off the top of his head."

Karaoke wasn't in Tessa's wheelhouse, but she had to fight to keep a naughty smile from forming at the mention of his name. Reggie Sharp. The shaggy-haired, mocha-eyed man in question. The man who'd been laying on this very desk two days ago, and sent her paperweight flying. She put a palm down on the wood surface, almost able to channel the energy through her skin.

"Oh, no. No, no, no," Carl said, shaking his head. "That's impossible. Tessa and Reggie Sharp?"

Tessa straightened in her chair. "Not that there was anything between us, but why couldn't there have been?" she asked.

"First," Carl started. "We're talking about you. You, Tessa Rose. Ms. Nose-in-a-Law-Book. You, date a skydiver? Someone who's adventurous? Someone who has a sense of humor?" He looked at Laura.

"Definitely funny," she agreed. "You know, in that dry, British way."

Carl snorted. "Yeah, no. Not you, Ms. Rose."

Tessa scrunched her nose at him. "You make me sound like somebody's old Aunt Mary. I have an adventurous side," she grumbled, but deep down she knew she didn't. She'd cultivated an untouchable, professional veneer, believing it served the role she'd stepped into. The few times she had dated, it was other lawyers. Humorless, boring, buttoned-down lawyers she thought were safe choices.

"*Right*, you're adventurous," he laughed. "Next, you'll tell me you're going camping next week."

"I might camp," she muttered down at her coffee. "Someday."

"Let's get back to the facts," Laura argued. "I have it on good authority that you two had a cozy coffee chat for almost an hour on Tuesday."

"Yes, I went to Cuppa Café." She paused. "For coffee. And Reggie Sharp was there. He had a legal question to ask about his marketing tagline over bucket lists, and—"

Laura let out a disappointed, "Ahhh."

"Now I get it," Carl said, rolling his eyes. "You were talking for an hour because you dredged up every precedent about poor Reggie's legal issue. I swear, lady, you need flirting lessons."

Tessa looked at them from under hooded eyebrows. Carl was close. It had started like that. But at some point, she'd gotten lost in Reggie's dark eyes and there'd been a whole lot of communication without any words being spoken.

She wasn't an innocent when it came to sex or relation-ships, but a few looks from Reggie had turned into some innu-endo-laced talk, and then a covert plan to avoid the security guard's rounds at her building and get to her office. Then two days later, chalking Reggie up as a fun romp, she was open to camping. *What's happening to me?*

"Anyway," Carl said, breaking into her reverie. "Another reason there can't be anything going between these two is be-cause he's already involved with someone."

"Who?" The two women demanded simultaneously.

"Jessie Harris."

"Ugh," Laura groaned. "She's the worst. Talk about someone getting their hooks into you. She invented the saying." Laura curled her other hand into a mock claw. "Maybe it's a rumor. This town is crazy for rumors."

The mention of the other woman's name made Tessa's brow crease, and she forced it to relax. She shouldn't care if Reggie was with someone. Their hookup had been all heat and spon-taneity, and something she'd thoroughly enjoyed. She had no plans to repeat it—just savor the memories. They were both adults and accountable to no one. And yet…something stirred an odd combination of giddiness and possessiveness. As if she might doodle his name with hearts around it, and then crumple it up and throw it in this Jessie's face. She squared her shoulders. She was the goddamned District Attorney, not some girl with a crush. She picked up the blue folder and tapped it on her desk.

"Okay, back to work, you two," she said. She held the folder out to Carl. "Changes are in red, but nothing major. As usual, your statement is impeccable. Good work. I'm just sorry that your talent is wasted on a graffiti charge."

She swore she detected a dusky blush in Carl's brown cheeks. He was never comfortable with compliments.

Once her staff had shrugged out to their desks, she shut the adjoining door.

*It wasn't a date,* she reassured herself. It wasn't anything. Just a fling. A one-time thing. *An awesome one-time thing,* she admitted.

Memories of him on her desk flickered through her mind but they were suddenly forgotten when the light in her office abruptly changed from its warm afternoon glow to tones of blue and green. *What the hell?*

Multi-colored fabric and several lines from of a parachute drifted over her tall office windows.

Carl yelled, "What is that?"

Laura teased. "Oh Tessa. I think your skydiving hottie is dropping in for a visit."

## Chapter 2
### Reggie

*Shit shit shit.* The words pulsed through Reggie's brain. He toggled to steer him and Jeff, the tandem client strapped to his chest, towards the broad gray roof. The next few seconds were a blur as he did his best to angle himself to take the impact of the landing first and then have Jeff land on top of him.

*Ooof,* he grunted as Jeff's weight thumped on his chest.

"I'm sorry," Jeff panted.

Reggie craned his neck to see his blue and green canopy glide over the courthouse's ornate clock tower. A miniature version of London's Big Ben. He wondered if he'd steered toward the only reminder of home he had here or if it was because his thoughts were always on the courthouse these days. And a certain woman who worked there.

The lines started to tug and drag them and the asphalt gravel bit into his back. When they came to an abrupt stop, his lungs unclenched enough for a few shallow breaths.

Jeff asked, "What happened?" He was an overweight fifty-something tax attorney from New Jersey, staying up at Lake Cottage for a reunion. He'd fallen hard—now, literally—for Reggie's brochure tagline: *Cross skydiving off your bucket list!*

"You panicked, mate, that's all. We're safe now," Reggie said, pouring on his UK accent a little thick. It usually calmed his nervous students, although it hadn't worked when Jeff lost it in the air and tried to undo his harness.

"Where are we?"

"We're on the roof of the courthouse," he said, unclipping the harness and letting Jeff roll off him. As soon as he did, he could finally breathe.

Jeff got to his feet. "Thank God we're alive," he said, patting his chest and legs as if he thought they might not be there.

"Yes, there is that." Mentally, Reggie groaned at the refund he felt obligated to process.

Reggie gripped the lines to the chute and started figuring out how to get it safely off the building without destroying it. As he worked, footsteps echoed from inside the clock tower.

He nodded toward the metal door. "I think we're about to be formally welcomed," he told Jeff. On cue, it flung open and hit the wall with a clang.

A security guard stumbled through the doorway, closely followed by Tessa. Sophisticated, haughty, gorgeous, out-of-his-league district attorney Tessa. The one woman in Lake Covington—hell, in the world—that he couldn't bring himself to talk to. Until Tuesday. His body tensed just thinking about that day.

"What the hell?" the security guard shouted. "You can't park that thing here!"

Reggie stared at Tessa, trapped into silence by her presence. Her mahogany hair was in its normal elegant twist, and her pale pink blouse with the little bow at her throat jumpstarted the pulse in his neck. If he wanted to get out of this with his sanity, he knew he shouldn't let his gaze slide down her calves to her black stilettos. *The land of no return.*

"This was all my fault," Jeff said, walking toward Tessa and the security guard. "I'll pay for any damages. But this man—" He turned to Reggie. "—this man saved my life. I freaked up there and if he hadn't acted quickly to get us down, we could have died. Probably *would* have died. He's a hero."

Reggie couldn't read Tessa's expression, but it didn't look impressed. In fact, her look of disdain was a turn on. *Was that even healthy?* he wondered, thinking back to how her haughty look had lit a slow burn in him in the Cuppa Café.

"A hero, huh?" she said. Her voice was all lawyer. She walked over to him with measured steps, her arms crossed.

Up close she was devastating. High cheekbones and full, pale lips. He remembered how her body was soft and strong at the same time. Her smirk made a dimple line pop on the right side of her mouth.

"Absolutely," Jeff answered, snapping Reggie out of his reverie.

"No," Reggie disagreed. "I'm trained to respond to any situation. I was just doing my job. Jeff's the brave one. He just made his first jump." He dragged his eyes away from Tessa to slap Jeff on the shoulder.

"My *last* jump, you mean," Jeff said.

Tessa smirked. "At least you can cross it off your bucket list, right?" She looked at him with a smug smile. He remembered her words the other night. *How smart is it to remind people of death before they jump out of a plane?* she'd asked, making him chuckle. He had to fight not to chuckle again.

The security guard turned to Reggie. "Sir, you've got to get that down before the Historical Society is up my ass."

Reggie nodded and refocused on gathering the chute lines. Jeff tried to help but he was getting more in the way than anything.

"Why don't you take a minute, mate?" he asked. "After a jump like that you're going to need to get your bearings."

"I think you're right," Jeff said, walking away.

With him gone, Tessa came over to Reggie. His pulse went into overtime at the scent of her perfume. He'd told himself she was out of his league, and—after Tuesday—out of his system. His heart rate said otherwise.

"Are you sure you don't need help to get your chute down?" she asked.

"No, but if you want it down quickly, I can call Jessie to come and help."

"Jessie," she murmured, her eyebrows lowering.

"Do you know her?"

She said, "no," but something about how she said it seemed uncertain. She looked over the town square and he followed her gaze. People shielded their eyes as they watched the action on the roof. He could see the sign for the Cuppa Café through the trees, another reminder of that night. He wondered if it reminded her too.

"You know, there's a trespassing ordinance you probably violated by landing on my roof," she said, pulling him out of his thoughts.

"*Your* roof?" he asked, arching his own brow back at her.

The corner of her mouth curled in a grin. "*The* roof," she corrected.

He held her gaze as he wound the lines around his arm.

"Are you going to press charges?" he teased, hoping she was picturing exactly what he'd like her to press against him.

He gloated when her lips parted to allow her tongue to flick over them. But it was short-lived when he saw her eyes had somehow deepened in color. *Cognac,* he mused. *They're like cognac.*

She turned toward the security guard. "Henry? Will you able to stay and help Mr. Sharp with his chute?"

"Yeah, I suppose."

Reggie gave Henry a grateful nod, which the older man rewarded with a scowl.

Tessa headed back to the access door. Reggie liked the way her hips moved when she walked.

"If you want to talk about those charges," Tessa called out, diverting his attention, "you can come back later. I'll be working late." Then she opened the door and disappeared.

## Chapter 3
### Tessa

A few hours later, Tessa stood in front of the bathroom mirror. The building was empty except for Henry.

The spontaneous invitation for Reggie to come back was a testament of what his sexy voice did to her. But now the excitement turned to reluctance. A one-night stand, by definition, was one night. One time. One amazing, fun, sexy encounter.

She thought about what Carl had said. He was right. She and Reggie had nothing in common. And as the District Attorney in small Lake Covington, she didn't want to impugn the integrity of her office with, well, a string of amazing, fun, sexy one-night stands.

*Oh, so now it's a string*, her mind teased her.

"Two isn't a string," she said out loud to the mirror and adjusted the bow on her collar. But she admitted there was something exhilarating about Reggie. He had a spark that she'd always felt was missing in herself. When they'd been together, she'd finally felt it, and she liked the feeling.

The generic ringtone of her cell phone jangled, the sound carrying down the now-quiet hallway. She hurried to her office and grabbed the phone from her desk. The screen announced *unknown caller*.

"Tessa Rose speaking."

"It's Reggie," came a husky voice.

"How did you get this number?"

"I stole one of your business cards when they fell off the desk the other night."

She ran a hand over her hair, feeling a blush rise out of her collar all over again at the sound of his voice.

"I have some things to finish up at the office. I thought maybe we could talk about bylaws and such over here?"

She blew out a breath of air. She was too old to melt because of an accent. Wasn't she? Thank God he couldn't see her expression. Heat raced up to her hairline. "I'll come over to your office."

"I should be done in an hour. Maybe we could...well, never mind. I guess I'll just see you then?" he finished on a questioning note.

"See you then," she said, disconnecting the call and pressing the phone against her chest. *He stole my business card*, she thought with a broad smile.

She circled her desk and plopped into the chair in front of her computer. Did this qualify as a date? Is that what had her acting like a teenager, overanalyzing everything?

As she contemplated how to get through the next hour, her thoughts wandered to Jessie. Clicking her mouse, Tessa opened her browser. The tab with the Sharp Skydiving website automatically opened.

"Smooth, counselor," she mocked herself. "Nothing like stalking your one-night stand."

Image after image of people jumping out of planes and floating in the sky slid across the homepage. She clicked on the *About* link and a photo of Reggie and a voluptuous blonde appeared.

Bright blue overalls strained across a rounded chest with the name Jessie stitched in elegant script. Her red lips smiled up at Reggie while her matching scarlet-tipped fingernails gripped his upper arm. Reggie and Jessie could have been models. Tessa glanced down at her own plain nails and her modest 36B chest.

Closing down her browser, she reached behind her for the *Lake Covington Ordinance* book. She turned the pages, trying to shove Jessie out of her thoughts without any luck. Jessie embodied the popular girls she'd seen at college. Everything was effortless when you had a killer body and that magical gift of confidence. Tessa had neither, which meant she deployed a strategy of impressing guys with the only weapon she had—her smarts. That was usually followed by the withering defeat of the guy in question backing away. Or in one case, running.

She propped her head on her hand and picked up the paperweight her dad had given her when she graduated from law school. She read the inscription:

*Watch carefully, the magic that occurs, when you give a person just enough comfort to be themselves.* —Atticus

Reggie stole *her* business card, invited *her* over. That was all that mattered.

## Chapter 4
### Reggie

Reggie set his cell phone down. Jessie's eyes pinned him from where she stood in the doorway.

"Jeff's all straightened away," she said as she strolled in. She fluttered a folder against her chest, pulling his eyes back to the zipper of her jumpsuit. It was just low enough to reveal a hint of shadowy cleavage.

"Great. Thanks, Jessie." He looked away to straighten some papers.

"He turned white when I gave him the free jump certificate, but he was stoked when I said he could gift it to his son. That..." She slid onto the corner of his desk. "...was a great idea."

"Yeah, well." He was sweaty and tired and had hoped to avoid Jessie. She was great at handling the clients and office work but was apt to drag out his workday with long conversations about nothing.

"So ... did I hear you say you're seeing someone in an hour?" she asked. "A hot date maybe?" She drawled the last words out in a teasing tone, but her eyes weren't smiling.

"No, just getting some advice after today's bail-out on the courthouse roof."

She looked surprised. "From our insurance rep?"

"No, from Tessa Rose."

"Tessa Rose. The DA, Tessa Rose?"

"Yes," he said, shutting down his computer.

"Why would she have advice about liability?"

"She has advice on the Lake Covington ordinances I may have broken when I landed on government property." He held back a smile as he remembered their rooftop banter.

Jessie stood and leaned over, offering a more direct view of her chest. He turned away to clean the whiteboard.

"Reggie, you should know that Tessa is, well, there are rumors about her around town."

"Oh?" He frowned. "What kind of rumors?"

"For one, she's never been romantically linked with anyone, and word is, now, I don't like to spread rumors..." She walked into his line of sight and leaned against the wall. Her face managed to look innocent and sneaky at the same time. "But I've heard she's a tease. Emotionally unavailable and not into the physical side of things, if you get my drift. And you're a physical, caring kind of guy. I'd hate to see you get your heart broken."

*Tessa, an emotionless tease?* An image of Tessa lying on her desk, her dark hair spread out underneath her, materialized in his mind.

"She's dated all the lawyers at the courthouse. Ask any of them about her."

"I've met her, and I didn't get that impression at all." He wagged a finger at Jessie. "You shouldn't spread gossip. I really mean that Jess."

Something flickered in her eyes and was gone. "I guess I just feel protective where you're concerned." She reached out to squeeze his arm. The movement pushed her breasts together.

Reggie sighed. Her tricks were getting old.

In the beginning, he would have dated Jessie if she wasn't an employee. But after working with her for a few months, he'd seen desperation in her when it came to relationships. It made him wary, but also sympathetic. He didn't have any siblings, but he'd started looking out for her like a troubled kid sister. Lately, though, her actions had gotten bold.

"Jessie..."

She released his arm.

"You're right," she said, her words dropping between them like ice cubes. "I'm sorry. Gossip is a hateful thing." She backed away.

He headed toward the bathroom. "I'm going to take a shower."

"I'd just hate to see you get your heart broken, Reggie. That's all."

"I appreciate the concern," he said over his shoulder. "I'll see you tomorrow."

He locked the bathroom door. Jessie was an excellent office manager, but their conversation felt dodgy. He didn't need complications in his business or personal life. He probably should have a formal talk with her, just to re-establish a more professional working relationship.

He started the shower and took off his jumpsuit. Upgrading the small bathroom had been brilliant, with the long hours he'd been putting into the business. The hot water was exactly what he needed, and he spent a good long time washing away the sweat and grime of the day.

Dressed in the spare clothes he kept in the bathroom, he walked out and heard the clicking of a keyboard. *Good grief, could she not take a hint?*

"Jessie, I said you could go," he said, walking into reception. He froze when he saw Tessa sitting in one of the waiting area's chairs, a thick book on her lap with her leather purse on top.

Jessie didn't look up from the computer monitor. "Tessa arrived, and I didn't want her to wait alone."

Tessa glanced up at him. "I told her it wasn't necessary—"

"Of course it's necessary," she said, cutting Tessa off and typing even faster, her voice as brittle as her keystrokes. "My job is to be at my desk when people come into the office."

Tessa stood, balancing the book and her purse. "Maybe this isn't a good time," she said, awkwardly.

"No." Reggie put his hand out to stop Tessa. "I'd like to go ahead with our discussion."

"It's late for a legal discussion," Jessie said, folding her hands together. "I'm sure you both had a long day."

Tessa pinched her lips together. "You're right, Jessie. It *has* been a long day." She turned toward Reggie before continuing.

"Maybe we should talk about the ordinances over a drink. At my place."

Tessa's eyes were blazing. Did he think they were the color of cognac? More like a slow-aged whiskey. She was a breathtaking contrast. Her blouse and tight black skirt exuded professionalism, but her loose hair that framed her jaw was pillow-top sensual. Man, she had a grip on him in a way no other woman ever had.

"What?" Jessie almost squeaked the word. He'd forgotten she was still there. He turned around, putting his hands on her desk and looking her in the eye.

Whatever swirling emotion that had controlled her face dropped away, and she jerked upright in her chair. "I mean..." Jessie started, her words full of icy disdain. "Don't you think that's inappropriate? Someone might misunderstand..."

"Jessie. Stop. Whatever you're doing, stop. I appreciate that you're looking out for me, but I don't need it. Okay?"

Jessie paled, and she looked as if she was teetering between tears and angry words.

"Let's talk more tomorrow," he said, covering Jessie's folded hands with one of his own. "You're a talented woman and this company wouldn't function half as well without you. But this possessiveness, however well-intentioned, has to stop. I don't need it."

Jessie took a deep breath and her expression softened.

"Okay," she said and gave him a wavering smile. Then she looked at Tessa. "Sorry. I guess it's been a long day for me, too."

Jessie hastily gathered her things and, a few seconds later, the door clicked shut and they were alone.

"I'm sorry about her," Reggie said.

"She's gone. It's fine."

Tessa walked around his small office. He watched her examine the clean lines of the white furniture, the pale gray walls and the lush potted palm in the corner. He'd aimed for a classy vibe and he found himself hoping she appreciated it. "I like your minimalist esthetic," she said.

"Come with me, Ms. Rose," he said in his sternest voice. He spun around and led her to his office, a smaller room in the back. It had the same look as the front office, except for the black and white photos of friends and families that circled the room.

He held the door open and enjoyed watching her saunter in and drop the heavy book on his desk with a bang. She leaned both her hands on the desktop, pushing as if to test its strength.

"Not as wide as mine, but it should do." She turned and positioned herself on the edge, the heat in her expression taking his breath away. He had to wrestle for a moment to steady his thoughts.

"I admit, I had ulterior motives behind inviting you here, but I've changed my mind." He'd only meant to tease her, but she blanched at his words. He took her hands in his, kissing them one at a time until the panic left her eyes.

"I mean," he continued, "if we end up back here, great. Even better would be ending up in one of our very comfortable beds. But what I really want is to take you out to dinner. And maybe a lunch. I'm tired of the casual dating scene. I'd like us to be a regular couple. That way the Jessies—"

"Or the Carls," she murmured.

"Or the Carls," he agreed. "All of Lake Covington will see that we are together. Because I want to be together with you, Tessa. I felt something when we first met, but I didn't really know that until I saw you sitting in my waiting room chair with that big old book on your lap."

Her shoulders relaxed with every word that left his lips. Looking into her eyes, his heart expanded and filled his whole chest, making it hard to breathe. Her response suddenly mattered more than any answered he'd ever waited for in his life.

"Do you know what you're getting into?" she asked, nodding toward the book. "I mean, this is just one of a hundred tomes that make up my life."

"I'm okay with that."

"And I will probably never skydive."

"I expected that."

"And don't push me to go camping. I mean, at least not right away."

His head jerked backward. "Who said anything about camping?"

Tessa slid off the desk and then wrapped her arms around his neck. His lips settled on hers, and everything around them disappeared. This woman who was sarcastic and smart and sexy and goofy when she let herself be...she mattered to him, more than he ever expected. She made him feel complete in a way he hadn't thought possible.

Their lips parted, and he looked into her wide eyes. There was no teasing, no veneer of a district attorney, just her perfect, authentic self gazing back at him.

"So, if I have permission to approach the bench," he murmured. "What do you think? Will you be my girl?"

"I will," she said, her voice echoing deep inside him.

"Good," he said with a grin. "Now who the heck is Carl?"

**LAKE COVINGTON**

# A Lot of Nerve

## T.L. SHERWOOD

Jaimie needed to make a decision fast. Vince Roberts was staring down at his phone, but he was headed right towards her. It was possible Jaimie could stroll past him without his noticing, but the better option was to duck into the Epicure. She might run into other clients there but none of their properties were so overpriced. Jaimie had shown Vince's colonial at least twice a week since it had gone on the market, but his house hadn't received an offer yet. Best to avoid him altogether.

The pneumatic doors of the trendy grocery store breathed open to allow a woman with a plastic tray of cupcakes to exit. Jaimie slipped in through the out door. Warm air rushed down from overhead vents. The blissful scent of ripe mangoes and fresh bread soothed her nerves.

Skirting the produce area, Jaimie set off for the deli section. She had Greek yogurt and a granola bar back at the office, but the soups here were amazing. She pulled a pale red ticket from the dispenser and waited for her number to be called.

The bearded guy a few places ahead of her tilted his head, obscuring the specials board with his man bun. Jaimie rolled up on her toes and spotted garlic curry on the list, her favorite, but maybe not the best choice since she had a showing in an hour.

A finger tapped Jaimie's shoulder. "Where do I know you from?"

Jaimie turned to find an attractive woman with mercurial blue eyes standing in front of her. What a lovely someone, she thought. Not that she was ready for love again.

"Did we go to camp Winnihaha together?" the woman asked, her smile hopeful, with a hint of flirtation.

Jaimie laughed nervously. This woman in a Lake Covington Prep tracksuit was gorgeous, her voice filled with the charming inflection of enthusiasm. If they'd met before, Jaimie definitely would have remembered. Fighting the impulse to blurt out something stupid, she squeaked out, "No, we didn't."

"Are you sure?" Twinkling lights from the distant pastry counter reflected in the woman's eyes, changing them from blue to green.

"My mother was never that frivolous with money."

The other woman's face clouded over; Jaimie grimaced. What was wrong with her? Spouting flip comments to a stranger–a potential client? Had she lost her mind?

"They offered scholarships when I attended." She glanced at the deli counter. The reprimand stung Jaimie like a scold from a headmistress. "I believe they still do."

"I'm sure they did. I mean *do.*" Jaimie wished she could start this conversation over. This woman stirred a tender longing deep within her and everything Jaimie said was coming out all wrong. She regrouped and put on her practiced expression. The one that said, *I am an assured woman capable of striking deals and following them through.* "I never went to camp. I had to babysit my sisters and brothers in the summer."

"Fifty-four!" a man bellowed.

The woman looked at the ticket in her hand and then stepped toward the counter to order.

Jaimie's shoulders drooped. Even if the woman was only reaching out to an old friend and not flirting, Jaimie had blown it. The sting of embarrassment filled her head while her heart raced with mortification. She knew better than to be confrontational about her upbringing. This town was willing to forgive the kids on the east side their poor starts in life, but only if they left their pasts in the past. Marianna had taught her that. Marianna had taught her a lot of things before she left last year. Jaimie turned her attention to the cases behind her filled with organic, free-range chicken breasts marinating in various spices while she worked up the courage to apologize. The man called out fifty-nine. Jaimie looked around. The woman with the curious blue eyes was gone.

***

The basketball thunk, thunk, thunked, then swished as Ariel went for the layup. "Nice job." Blake glanced at the clock. Excellent timing. She blew her whistle, halting the practice. "All right, you mangy cubs, enough for today. Hit the showers."

"Bears! Bears! Bears!" A chorus of young women shouted as they stormed towards the locker room.

"Remember, Saturday practice starts at seven sharp. Slackers are giving me fifty laps. Got it?"

There was muttering mixed with giggles. Blake gathered the two stray balls, put them on the rack, then pushed it against the far wall.

"Coach Wallace." Ariel had crept up soundlessly behind her, more cat than bear. "My Uncle Vince. He just got divorced." Every sentence Ariel spoke curled into a question. She held out a damp piece of paper towards Blake. Reluctantly, she accepted it. "He asked me to give you this number."

Blake stared at the girl, trying not to laugh or scream. Of all the bizarre pickup lines, this one was absolutely pathetic. Literally sending a girl to do a man's job. If this Uncle Vince approached her, Blake would tell him in no uncertain terms she didn't play for that team. No need to embarrass or upset Ariel though. The girl had enough self-esteem problems already. "Will do." Ariel gave a tiny smile then ran and joined her teammates in the locker room.

In her office, Blake texted Vince:

**T.L. SHERWOOD**     202

> You have a lot of nerve.

> Excuse me? Who is this?

> Blake. If you wanted to ask me out, why didn't you ask me yourself?

> I don't know any Blake and I haven't asked anyone out in months. You have the wrong number.

> This is the number Ariel Roberts gave me. She said her uncle just got a divorce and to call him.

A laughing emoji popped up.

She drew in a deep breath and stared at the half-empty Epicure takeout container on her desk before typing, each word a separate text.

> What

> Is

> So

> Damned

> Funny?

The bubble reappeared and showed activity for a long time, way past her endurance for a punchline. Blake tossed the takeout container into the trash then slid her phone into her back pocket. She locked the office door behind her, then checked the girls' locker room for stragglers. The boys' JV team was assembling near the locker room on the other side of the gym. Blake gave Coach Hammond a wave before leaving Lake Covington Prep and heading home.

***

Lakestar Lane, where Blake had grown up, exuded the uptight vibe it always had, full of old money, old families, and old-fashioned ideas about what was proper. It represented everything she had fought against from the time she was seven and realized she was different from most other girls. Turning onto the macadam, she pulled into the six-car garage. Her SUV was the only domestic in there. Brandon, her parents' driver, nodded to her as he made his way to the silver Rolls.

Blake's parents were in the foyer. Her mother was dabbing powder on her cheeks, while Blake Senior adjusted his French cuffs.

"You're not going to the Grange dressed like that," her mother said, snapping the compact closed.

"I wasn't planning on going to the Grange at all." Blake picked at a hangnail.

"Blakey, I told you, you must join us. It's the annual diabetes fundraiser. We have a table to fill."

She'd forgotten. Palming her car keys, Blake stared at the Klimt, the yellows and coppery orange tones of the painting brightened the entryway. "I'm not in the mood tonight, Mum."

"Blake Wallace, if you're going to be under this roof again, you will do what it takes to please your mother. I thought we were clear on this when we allowed you to move back after your... dalliances. "

*Ah, an upgrade from the last thing he'd called her relationships with women.* Not that there were many, but the last one threw her into a loop of pain. Blake had never felt so lost after Jean admitted to cheating on her with a man. Ok, fine, cheating on her and then accepting a marriage proposal. Jean neglected to tell Blake that she was bisexual when they met. Not sharing that vital piece information led to other lacks of candor. Oblivious to the many secrets Jean kept from her, Blake had believed they were committed to each other for five whole years. Blake swallowed back a retort and said, "I'll be ready in fifteen minutes."

***

There was a whisper from the dancing plastic when Jaimie pushed open the bifold door. To her left, three sad, empty dry cleaner bags swayed like ghosts on what had been Marianne's side of the closet. After selecting a pair of comfortable flats and her go-to black dress, Jaimie dropped her towel and prepared for the evening.

While brushing on lash elongating mascara in the tiny bathroom's mirror, she thought about the estimate she still had to do on the plumber's house with the leaking pipes. It made no sense to keep this apartment. It wasn't big enough and she could afford a nicer home, but the address was perfect. East Fenner Street in the land of Lake Covington was like Marvin Gardens in Monopoly. Not quite Boardwalk or Park Place—that was Lakestar Lane and McClellan Avenue—but there were no small houses on those streets. Maybe if she cut back on her work schedule and spent more time here, she'd be motivated to move somewhere else.

When Marianne had first left for Italy, Jaimie hated the constant reminders of their relationship. The Courthouse lawn where they attended a fiddler concert, Cuppa Cafe where they had their first kiss, the produce section at the Epicure where they selected mangos and papayas after the first time she'd spent the night. Now those places were comforts, if not roadblocks to a new relationship. Besides, she wasn't ready. It had only been ten months since she drove her love to the airport. It was possible that Marianne could change her mind, decide that Italy was a lousy place to live, and return.

*Right. And maybe gelato would be declared a diet food.*

Jaimie blotted her lipstick then checked her breath. Good to go. She settled a silvery shawl over her shoulders and took the elevator to the first floor.

***

Blake's father waited for the man to leave the table before narrowing his eyes at his daughter. "And what is wrong with David?"

"Nothing is wrong with David, but I'm not going to slow dance with him. Besides, my feet are aching." Blake cringed at the excuse. How many times had she used it as a child, teen, college student? "I run around on hardwood floors all day, you know."

"In gym shoes," her father growled, his exasperation obvious. "Now, I realize you're convinced you're —"

Blake cut him off. "Next song. I promise."

"Blake. Cynthia." Vince Roberts nodded as he approached the Wallace's table. His voice was nasally and high-pitched.

Cynthia leaned back in her chair. "Vince. Good to see you. Thought you'd be in France by now."

Blake caught her breath; this was Ariel's recently divorced uncle? The man had to be at least ten years older than her father.

Vince Roberts turned his attention to her mother. "Not this year." He took a sip of his drink. "Can't afford it."

"Come now."

"True, it's true. Unless something changes, of course." Vince Roberts winked at her. Blake flexed her back muscles as if she had wings and could fly away. "I'm hoping your daughter will make that happen." He giggled like one of Blake's students.

Unable to endure the next bit of banter, Blake excused herself before striding off to the restroom. If Jean hadn't left her, she never would have come back to her parents' home and their expectations, but until she saved up for her own place, she was stuck. Seated at the mirror, Blake touched up her eyeliner and reapplied her taupe lipstick, all with long, slow strokes.

Several women in flouncy skirts came and went while Blake waited for Vince to exhaust his small talk with her parents and slink away to wherever he belonged. She ran a comb through her short hair then pulled at the uncomfortable straps on her shoulders. Cautiously emerging from the powder room, Blake looked around but didn't see Vince. She meandered over to the bar.

Blake ran her tongue up against her teeth in an anticipatory arch as the bartender spritzed tonic over gin. She downed it in a gulp to settle her irritation then motioned for another.

"Tsk, tsk, running away like that."

Blake cringed at Vince's voice. Expecting an unwanted touch of his hand on her shoulder, she clenched her glass preparing to toss the contents in his face.

"Oh, Mr. Roberts, how good to see you," a female voice gushed.

Blake ventured a glance at the welcome interrupter and did a double take. It was the woman from the Epicure deli. The silver threads in her shawl accentuated the curve of her cheeks. Blake slid onto a barstool and angled her long body to eavesdrop more easily.

Vince said, "I thought you saw me wave to you earlier, dear."

"Did you? I must have missed it." The woman ordered a white wine. "They've done a lot of work in here." She paid for her drink then returned her attention to Vince. "This place is packed. I bet they beat last year's total. "

"Yes, yes. And if you actually manage to sell my house, darling, I could make a sizable donation."

Blake turned to stare at the woman. A real-estate agent. *Of course. That's where she knew her from.* Stein Realty signs dotted lawns all over town, the woman's face beaming from the center.

"I'm certain the foundation would appreciate that very much." Jaimie's eyes fell on Blake just as the band switched from a slow rock ballad to Benny Goodman's *Sing, Sing, Sing.* Jaimie turned back to Vince. "Oh, that's Geraldine Milner's favorite song." She placed her hand on his shoulder, directing him away from the bar. "You really should ask her to dance. She'd love that." Vince resisted long enough to pick up his drink before maneuvering through the tables. Once he was gone, Jaimie nodded. "Hello again."

Blake grinned. "Nice job. I was dodging him earlier." She held out her hand. "I'm Blake."

Jaimie squared her shoulders. "You're kidding."

"Excuse me?" Blake said, lowering her arm.

"Did you send me a text earlier today?"

"No, I didn't." Blake inhaled. "Wait. Maybe?"

"It was on the verge of threatening." Jaimie blinked, then shook her head.

"Look, it was the end of the day and I thought you were..." Blake checked the dance floor but didn't see Vince.

"Who? "

Blake gulped. "Vince Roberts. "

"What?" Jaimie sputtered.

"Yes. Well, see, I thought he sent his niece to ask me out."

"I take it you didn't see my last text."

Blake pulled the cell from her clutch and read the text. She raised her head with an awkward smile. "*You* thought *I* was a man?"

"All the Blakes I know are." Jaimie took a sip of her wine.

"Are there many?"

"No." With a wistful smile, Jaimie scanned the nearest table, raised her chin and took a step away from the bar.

"You're Jaimie, right?" Blake put as much lightness in her voice as possible. "I'd like to start again."

Jaimie turned back; her face looked pinched. She didn't speak.

Blake added, "Please?"

The real estate agent continued to regard the nearby table but remained where she stood. Blake held out her hand again.

"I'm Blake, and I'm pleased to meet you."

This time Jaimie took her hand and shook it. She said, "How do you do?"

"I *do* pretty badly at meeting new people it seems." Blake replied. "And I am sorry."

Jaimie's shoulders relaxed a bit.

Blake smiled broadly. "I'm going to make a lot of assumptions right now—and I know what they say about assuming things—but I take it Vince has a house he wants to sell me."

Jaimie grinned politely before taking another sip of her wine. "Well, at this point, he'd sell it to anybody."

"It's small, then?"

"It has a lot of charm."

"Tiny, huh?" Blake was pleased when Jaimie's chuckle joined hers. "Look, I could use some fresh air. Care to join me?"

Jaimie bowed her head then walked outside ahead of her. Blake followed leisurely. Given the cues, it was unlikely that Jaimie was interested in her. Their brief time together, the image of her curves, her exquisite silhouette at the deli counter, their shared laughter might be all they'd ever have. It would be unfortunate to have memories of such a lovely woman strewn about the places she frequented, but Blake knew that if someone wasn't attracted to her, there was no changing that, nor dwelling on what might have been.

The air outside the Grange was on the clammy side and the stars were muddled. Jaimie and Blake both nodded at a waitress smoking a cigarette in the shadows. Several drink-sneaking sons and daughters of the attendees were clumped near the white pines. Blake knew some of them from the prep school, repeating patterns of their parents. A few would force sex too early on partners too willing to forgive, fewer would explore the idea of liking members of their own sex and the fewest would discover true, forever love. Her parents were that type. Twenty-nine years of bliss.

Jaimie cleared her throat. "Have you lived in Lake Covington long?"

"Too long." Blake scratched her nose then glanced back inside at her parents' table. She didn't see either of them. "I was born here."

"Me, too." Jaimie ran a finger around the rim of her glass.

"Really? Small world, isn't it?"

Jaimie frowned. "It's a small town anyways."

"What year did you graduate?"

Before she could respond, a tall man walked up to them. "Blake, there you are." Blake Sr. said. "Where have you been? You promised your mother and me—"

"Dad, I was—"

Jaime turned toward Mr. Wallace. "My fault. I was telling her about Vince Roberts' house." Jumping into realtor mode, she stuck out her hand and introduced herself with confidence, turning the interrupted romantic encounter into a business negotiation.

Blake took a sip of her gin and tonic as Jaimie continued. "I was just saying to your daughter how she'd have to see the house to believe how charming it really is." Jaimie pivoted. "What do you say, Blake? Shall we run over there now? Get a feel for the place?"

Blake could tell that her father was as stunned as she was. She handed him her glass, kissed his cheek and said, "Tell Mum not to worry. I'll be right back."

*** 

Jaimie didn't know what had come over her. Blake was beyond beautiful. It was distracting, breathtaking even. When Blake Sr. came over—the only other Blake Jaimie had ever met—it felt like she was a kid again, deflecting a grownup's anger. But she was a grownup now, Blake was in her car, and Jaimie had lost her nerve. What next?

She put her foot on the brake and pressed the start button. "I'll have to stop in my office to get the keys."

"Oh, so we're really going to see the house, then?"

**T.L. SHERWOOD**

The flirtation in Blake's voice was undeniable, but now this was business.

"Well, yes. In case Vince or your father ask any questions."

Jaimie's curt answer stifled further conversation on the short drive. Their awkward conversation at the Epicure was still on her mind. Blake waited in the car while Jaimie retrieved her passkey. The conversation as they drove to McClellan Drive was sparse. Jaimie replied to the occasional questions Blake asked with one-word answers. Normally, Jaimie would be the one asking questions, probing in subtle ways and squirreling away tidbits. With Blake, she was afraid of the answers she might receive.

Jaimie parked on the street in front. Head-on was the best view of the Colonial and fortunately Vince had the outside lights on which focused on the Doric columns. "Shall we go in?" Jaimie asked after she was certain Blake had seen enough of the impressive façade. Walking up the steps beside her, she started her spiel. "It has three bedrooms and two full baths, it's on—"

"I'd like to see those bedrooms," Blake interjected. Jaimie's mouth dropped open, not knowing how to respond. Blake continued. "I mean, just because there are three doesn't mean any of them are big enough, you know?"

"Oh, of course." Jaimie put the key in upside down, tried again, then opened the front door and motioned Blake inside. "It has a generous entryway. You could put cubbies over there for your children's backpacks."

"No kids."

"Yes, well, and off to this side is the sunken living room." Jaimie briskly swept through it, which she knew better than to do. She stopped in the dining room and pointed out that the house came with a generous one point two acres, then entered the kitchen, flicking on all the lights. "All the appliances are less than five years old." Jaimie continued to walk and came out to the entry where they'd started the tour. "And then upstairs you'll find—"

"The good part?" Blake asked.

Jaimie felt her body flush from head to toe. She hurried up the carpeted steps and opened the master bedroom. Blake followed her in. Jaimie considered their reflection in the closet door mirrors. They made a cute couple. Inexplicably, Blake leaned toward Jaimie and smiled. Jaimie returned the smile before walking to the window.

Blake laughed and asked, "Why are you so fidgety?"

Under her breath, Jaimie muttered, "Because you're too beautiful." She cleared her throat and turned around. "To be honest, I wasn't expecting to show a house tonight."

Blake stood in front of her. "If you had, would you have walked through it a little slower?"

The attraction was undeniable. *Maybe I am ready to try again.* Startled by the thought, Jaimie said, "We should get back to the Grange."

"You haven't shown me the other bedrooms. I mean, what if Vince asks if I plan to turn the smallest one into a personal gym? I should at least know if there's room for a punching bag and a Nautilus, right?"

Relieved that Blake was now treating this as a showing, Jaimie slipped into her professional mode. She pointed out memorized details and began asking questions to help further this client's prospects of finding the perfect home.

Once they'd seen all the rooms, closets, and the basement, Jaimie said, "Let me run upstairs, make sure I turned out all the lights and then we can get back to Dancing Away Diabetes."

"Sure." Blake smiled.

When they returned to the fundraiser, there were no empty spaces near the entrance. Jaimie found a spot and parked. The distance and limited lighting gave Jaimie more confidence than she felt. "You're attractive, Blake, and maybe I misread the signals, but—"

"You misread nothing." Blake undid her seatbelt.

*Why did she have to interrupt?* "I just got out of a good relationship."

Blake turned in her seat. "Don't you mean a bad one?"

"If it had been bad..." She sighed. "Well no. The point is, I don't think I'm ready."

Jaimie glanced at her, attempted to leave the car, but the seatbelt was still secured. While she was undoing it, Blake grasped Jaimie's other hand. "When you are, make sure you let me know."

The touch, the look, the thought that maybe Blake would stick around made Jaimie's resistance crumble. This night— the whole day—had been exquisitely fraught. It was too much. It was so right. Jaimie swallowed, decided to be brassy and said, "Of course. I'll leave a voicemail saying, *You have a lot of nerve*, so you'll know it's me."

Blake laughed with her whole, lithe body. It was such a delightful response to her joke. When Blake regained her composure, she said, "I do, you know. I have a lot of nerve and that's why I'm going to insist on a kiss goodnight."

Jaimie held her breath. Was this really happening? "But it wasn't—"

"A date? No, not technically, but I still want to kiss you." Blake stared into Jaimie's eyes; she could spend hours in the depths of those oceans. Blake's next question was soft and vulnerable. "Unless you're opposed to..."

Jaimie leaned across the armrest, nestled Blake's cheek in her palm and kissed her. It was perfect. She fell back into her seat and pulled out her phone.

"You need to check your messages *now?*" Blake demanded.

Ignoring her, Jaimie typed and hit send. A second later, Blake's phone buzzed with the text Jaimie had just sent.

Blake stared at her. "Are you sure?"

"I think if we go slow I might be," Jaimie said.

"I can do slow." Blake took her hand again, kissed the underside of her wrist with a slight bite that sent thrills through Jaimie. "Real slow."

# Lake Covington Herald

July 14, 2019

## This Day in Lake Covington
**CONNOR LANE**

Before moving to Lake Covington, I've never known an American town to celebrate France's National Day. This is no means the first peculiarity I've noticed since relocating, but it is perhaps the most pleasurable. With almost as must as gusto as the Fourth of July, the citizens of Lake Covington cut absolutely no corners when it comes to the food on Bastille Day.

Main Street is lined with food carts and trucks, serving everything from coq au vin and cassoulet, to French fries smothered in duck fat gravy. Whether the French classics suit you, or you'd prefer a French spin on an American favorite, the Bastille Day block party has you covered.

The food is judged by a panel, which this year I have been invited to attend. Every restaurant in the county has a booth serving up their best in hopes of winning the top prize: bragging rights. Chef Henri Fontenot of Chez Charbon is the reigning champion, two years running.

When I asked about the origins of this strange tradition, I learned that the French have been well represented in Lake Covington for a hundred and fifty years.

"I guess you would have to blame old Mayor Golligher," Colette LaCoste, owner of the Curly Q Salon told me. "You know the one who built the big house on the hill? *Tres gauche.* He was fond of the French women, and he was personally responsible for employing at least ten in his household. My great, great grandmother, Joséphine, was one of them, so I guess without the old dog I might not be here today, *Cheri.*"

When I asked her what her Mademoiselle LaCoste did in Golligher's household, she laughed and said with a wink, "She was a maid, *mon chou.* They all were."

So, like so many things in Lake Covington, it seems Mayor Herbert Golligher's legacy is attached to Bastille Day in a somewhat curious manner. If the French population of Lake Covington started with ten French maids and grew to hundreds over the intervening generations, then the former mayor should be praised, and not blamed. If the food only halfway lives up to its reputation, this is one reporter who won't be complaining.

**LAKE COVINGTON**

# The Adult Section

## GREER ZEIGLER

*A*s Ann drove to the new airport, she took in its modern beauty. Lake Covington was a town stuck in its own history, but the airport expansion changed all that. Soon, she figured her quiet, content town would become something akin to a big, bustling city.

With her sister, Elsie, in the passenger seat, she found a place to park in the garage adjacent to the departing terminals. Elsie was catching a flight to London for a new job. It was the first time they'd be separated, and Ann's heart pulsated in her throat with each passing minute.

Elsie got out of the car and pulled her bag over her shoulder. "Don't have too much fun sorting through all of those returned library books while I'm gone."

Ann lifted Elsie's suitcase out of the trunk, blowing wisps of hair out of her eyes. "I quite enjoy putting books back where they belong. It gives me a sense of satisfaction to have everything back in its place, back to their little homes."

"You're such a nerd. How are we related again?"

"We share nearly fifty percent of our DNA."

"That's debatable." Elsie stuck her tongue out. "And that was a very nerd thing of you to say."

Although the two sisters were as close as buttons on a shirt, they were distinct opposites. Elsie was the tall raven-haired beauty that all the boys drooled after in school while Ann was short with curly, auburn hair that could never be contained, bouncing crazily around her heart shaped face. Her eyes were as blue as a Montana sky and freckles covered just about every inch of her body. As a child, she constantly faced bratty kids who picked on her for not being like them. She would cry to her mother about kids teasing her.

*Love yourself first, sweetie. That's all that truly matters.*

She'd remember those kind words, but the hurt from the past would occasionally reemerge. It haunted her. It made her believe she'd never be what anyone desired. Ann tried taking her mom's advice. She embraced her endless freckles, frizzy hair, and skin that easily burned when she went swimming at the lake. Despite all this, her self-consciousness got in the way of dating and the closest she ever got to experiencing a whirl-wind romance was when a new shipment of books came in.

At thirty, she wasn't a virgin, but still greatly inexperienced sexually. Ann longed for an adventurous romance she'd read about in novels. For a man who'd swoon over her, sweep her off her feet, and make the stars and moon appear from ecstasy.

Why couldn't she just let her hair down and do something daring like walk up to a guy and ask for his number? What was stopping her?

With Elsie's carry-on in tow, Ann followed her sister through the sliding doors inside the airport terminal. A little girl walked past them, carrying a book. Ann paused at the sight of her. The girl reminded Ann of herself at that age, her nose always in a story.

Elsie took a breath. "I can't believe I'm going loft hunting overseas. It's going to be like a different world." Ann started to frown and Elsie took her hand. "Don't look like that, sis. Everyone should spread their wings and fly from the nest sometimes. It's called *growth.*"

Growth. Not just in height and weight, but in experience. Ann understood the schematics behind it, but consistency and routine seemed better. Compared to most people she knew, Ann lived an uneventful life, filling her days and nights at the library. Yes, growth proved necessary, but change...Ann wasn't ready for that. She loved Lake Covington and its downhome, small town feel. Her parents were born here, and her grandparents too. Lake Covington wasn't just a tourist destination. It was home. She couldn't imagine leaving and going half a world away. That was Elsie. Not her.

She shook her head. "This is the only place I've ever known. And what about Mom? Ever since Dad had surgery, she's needed help with groceries and getting him his meds."

"Mom and Dad would be okay for a while." Elsie moved her hand, taking a step back. "And it wouldn't have to be forever. Take your nose out of those books for once and experience life."

Ann shrugged. "Maybe one day. Besides, I'm happy with my books."

"They won't keep you warm at night though."

"They would if I pile them on me," Ann said, smiling at her sister.

Elsie chuckled. "That's exactly what a crazy librarian would do."

Ann followed her sister's gaze as Elsie glanced toward the security area. The line was moving. It was time for her to go.

"Well," Elsie said with a sigh. "This is it. Wish me luck."

"Good luck," Ann said, hugging her, not wanting to let go. "Call me right when you land in London. I don't care how late it is. I mean it."

"Okay, I will. I promise."

Ann watched as her sister showed her ticket to the agent and then disappeared among a crowd of travelers. She wiped away a few tears and walked away.

\*\*\*

The Lake Covington Airport was flourishing since Dean Markham took the renovation job. He and his team updated the eateries, souvenir shops, and seating area. He'd touched about everything but the original murals. They were perfect just as they were.

Scenes of a peaceful town brushed on canvas, the murals were what newcomers to Lake Covington saw first, and eventually experienced, once they stepped out the front doors of the airport. Known for the beautiful views and serene setting, Lake Covington became the place you visited to escape the fast-paced world and the murals captured that way of life: children skipping on Main Street toward an ice cream truck, an older couple walking their dog, some reading the newspaper, and one that showcased the lake itself during the annual Fourth of July celebration—Dean's favorite.

Dean sat on a bench under that mural and satisfaction settled across him as he watched the heavy airport foot traffic. After winning the bid for the expansion he had moved *Dean Markham Construction Company* from New York City and immediately gotten to work. He relished in the fact that he helped turn the small airport into a modern transportation hub.

As the lead contractor, Dean oversaw all aspects of this endeavor, including planning and budgeting. By far, this was the largest job that his company procured. Who would believe that the little five-year-old who spent his time building towers with blocks would later land a multi-million-dollar expansion project? Certainly not Dean. With a lot of sleepless nights behind him, including neglecting to explore Lake Covington with all its beautiful streams and trees for as far as the horizon allowed, he finally had the chance to rest and relax.

*Community. Peace. Quiet.* That's what Lake Covington was to him, a stark difference from New York. He found a home here, but would he ever find love here, too? With all his success over the last year, Dean's love life had experienced the opposite. He struggled to find someone who matched his intellect, that understood the world the way he did. A few women tried to sway his attention, but none possessed that special something.

Did looks matter? Sure, but looks were second to conversation. He sought someone who could *stimulate* him in more ways than just the obvious sexual one. Dean had been with his share of women. They were looking for excitement, and he was happy to oblige. Yet, it got old. *He* was getting old. At thirty-five, he wanted more. A family, perhaps?

Lost in his own thoughts, he noticed a woman glancing around as if she wasn't sure which way to go. Dean watched as she found one of the map directories and pushed her curly red hair back with her hand to study it. The layout of the airport had changed, and it seemed people were still trying to get used to it. Dean got up. "Excuse me, miss," he said as he approached her. "Are you lost?"

She looked towards him, relief on her face. "Um...kind of. The airport is a maze now. It's changed so much. I'm glad to see my favorite mural is still here, though not in the same place that I remember it being." Her tone was delicate.

Dean said, "It's my favorite too."

A hint of happiness crossed her face. Dean found himself liking that.

"When was the last time you were here?" he asked her. "I'm assuming it was before the expansion."

She laughed shyly, "Maybe when I was five. We went to New York City to visit family."

"You don't say. That's where I'm from. Hey, listen, I know this place fairly well," he said. "Where do you need to go? I can help."

She glanced around. "I'm trying to find the parking garage."

"Okay. No problem." Dean turned to the map and started tracing a route with his finger. "First, you want to take Corridor A, which will lead you to the escalator, and then you'll see some automatic—"

Dean stopped and glanced over at her. She was wrinkling her freckled nose up in confusion. He thought it the cutest thing ever. "You know what," he said, "if you don't mind walking with a stranger, I'll get you to the garage."

She bit her lip. "Okay."

Dean pointed. "C'mon, this way."

As they walked, he stole sidelong glances at her. She wore plain, slightly oversized, light blue jeans and a simple white T-shirt. Her hair floated almost like a cloud— endless, bouncy lavender-scented curls that sculpted her freckled face. Soft and delicate like a flower blowing in the breeze.

"I'm Dean, by the way."

"Ann," she replied, slowly looking up at him.

His eyes went to her mouth. Her lips were peachy, moist, and pouty. He stifled a cough as he stepped off the escalator. "Did you drop someone off?" Dean asked. "A boyfriend, maybe?"

Ann blushed. "No. I don't have a boyfriend."

*That's good to know.*

Ann stepped up next to Dean, their arms grazed each other.

"It was my sister," she said. "She got a job overseas."

"You two close?" Dean asked.

"It's been a sad few days. Elsie, my sister, she's my best friend. Aside from my parents, she's all I've got." She shrugged. "But, she's in love with traveling."

"And you're not?"

"All of my traveling comes from the places I read about."

"You're a reader?" Dean asked.

"I should hope so," she said. "I'm the librarian at the Lake Covington Library."

Dean raised an eyebrow. "A librarian, huh? I think you're the first real librarian I've ever talked to."

Ann laughed, pushing some of her curly hair back. Her laugh was warm and silky, pleasuring his ears like a sweet melody.

She asked, "Not even in school?"

"School?" Dean scoffed. "You could say I was a bit of a bad boy. Nah...I was a bad boy. Not so good with the books. I work best with my hands. They got my company the bid to remodel the airport."

Ann raised her eyebrows. "You're the *Dean* of *Dean Markham Construction Company?*"

"The one and only."

They reached the parking lot sooner than he expected. Dean wasn't ready to part with Ann so quickly. She was the first person, outside of his employees, that he'd had a decent conversation with since moving here. She made it easy somehow, like slipping on a pair of worn gloves. He liked her. Liked being next to her.

Ann turned to him and held out her hand. "I love the expansion. I had my reservations, but it's beautiful. Thank you for the help. I'm parked just there around to the side."

"No problem, Ann," Dean said. He gripped her hand, and only reluctantly let it go when she pulled her soft fingers away.

The electric doors slid open and he watched as the most perfect round bottom he'd ever seen make its way down a row of hybrid SUVs and wagons.

"Do you need me to walk you to your car?"

When she looked back, tossing her hair in the movement, Dean nearly lost his train of thought. Her hair blew in wisps around her face. She was like an angel, brightening up the dimly lit parking deck.

"I think I can manage," Ann said.

"If it's cool with you," Dean started, "I might come check a book out. Got anything you'd recommend?"

Ann backpedaled as she spoke. "I'm sure I could find you something. You did help me get to my car, so I owe you. I work every day except Sundays."

Dean waited until Ann was out of sight, before turning on his heels and walking back the way he came. As he headed to his office, he thought about Ann—from her flaming hair and icy blue eyes to the freckles delicately peppering her cheeks and the bridge of her nose. It was as if she'd come out of nowhere and, he supposed, she had, and he couldn't ignore that he was undeniably attracted to her and that his attraction was growing.

*Well. I guess I'm heading to the library for the first time in years.*

***

The afternoon sun illuminated the library. While Ann took her time shelving the returned books, her mind kept returning to the guy from the airport. He was all she could think about.

*Tall.* That was the only adjective she could use about him. He had towered over her. He had to be six-three or six-four. His dark hair, much like Elsie's, fell in loose waves just at his temples, near bushy eyebrows. And his eyes. They were like two emerald stones plucked from a treasure chest and placed there just for her to admire. The New York accent of his sounded dangerous but alluring all at the same time. Her eyes kept wandering toward the entrance.

Every time the door opened, her heart leapt in her throat, wondering—hoping—it would be Dean, but he never showed his face. Even if he did, what would she say to this dreamy man? *Hi. I'm lame Ann. I wobble in heels as I walk, and my hair can swell to the size of an unshaven poodle in the rain. Oh, and I'm a thirty-year-old librarian that's only been with two men.*

He was tall, dark, and fucking hot. He was reminiscent of her favorite male lead from a romance story, as if he'd leapt off the page and into her path.

Yet, Dean seemed to like that she was a librarian. Not only that, she'd caught him staring at her form as if he was interested in more. Something about him made her feel pretty and wanted.

*Stop thinking about that guy*, she urged herself. It was days ago that he said he'd stop by and he hadn't. He wasn't interested. He was just being nice.

Ann placed the last of the books away and tidied up before leaving. "I'll see you guys tomorrow," she playfully whispered to the millions of stories waiting on shelves.

Ann's keys jangled as she locked the door.

"It's only five o'clock. You always close up this early?"

She gasped at the familiar deep voice behind her. *Dean.* Ann started to panic. Deep down, she hadn't really expected him to show up. Plain Ann. Quiet Ann. Boring Ann. No man like him had ever wanted to be with someone like her, but here he was. "Um, yes, the library closes at five on Wednesdays.

"Dang. I wanted to check a book out."

She took a breath as she turned to face him. He was in a simple black shirt with rugged brown boots and blue jeans. He did have a bad boy look, but something about him was softer. "I suppose since you're here, might as well see what we can find for you." His full lips had the pinkest shade, and his baritone voice oozed from between them, making her heart flutter.

As Ann led them back inside, she reminded herself that she was the librarian and he was simply another person in need of a good read. It helped her not focus on how close he was to her.

Dean shut the door behind him. "That's mighty nice of you, Librarian Ann. I'll remember closing time for future visits."

Ann fidgeted with her hair, twirling the curly strands around her finger while Dean looked around, taking the place in.

He said, "So, this is what one of these places look like? It's bigger than I expected."

Ann laughed. "Two stories and no modern technology. We still have an old rotary phone.

Dean watched her with a sly grin. "Can I get a tour?"

Ann nodded. "Of course, um, over there—" she pointed "—is the kids' reading area next to the young adult and children's books. Then crafts, cooking, and the arts. Upstairs is the adult fiction and nonfiction. That's where I think we'll find something for you."

"I see you enjoy your job," Dean said.

Ann felt her cheeks warm at the compliment. "Yes. I do." She placed her purse on the checkout desk. "What about you? Do you enjoy yours?"

"Like I said, I'm good with my hands. Been wanting to build things since I was little boy."

Dean took a few steps towards her. Ann was suddenly self-conscious about what she was wearing—a frugal grey blouse and a floral skirt. If she'd known that today would be the day he'd show, she would have worn something less librarian-ish.

"Right, so..." Ann started. "What kind of books do you like?"

"Honestly, I'm not really sure."

Ann smoothed a few loose locks away from her face. "We'll it's a good thing I'm a great librarian."

He lowered his eyes. "What else are you good at?"

"Reading," she answered as she awkwardly moved past him to go up the staircase.

Dean stepped up behind her. "I mean, what do you do *outside* of this place?"

Ann paused by the nonfiction section and looked at the row of books, grateful to have something to focus on instead of the way Dean's shirt stretched across his chest. "Nothing as of now. It's almost impossible to leave the library."

"If you could, what's something you'd like to do? Go to the movies? Head out on the lake? What?"

"I don't know." Ann shrugged. "My sister always thought I should get out more."

Dean said, "Maybe you should take her advice," Dean said. "You know, we could get out together. I am new in town. What do you say?"

"I wouldn't be opposed ..."

"Great. Why don't we start with that restaurant I keep hearing about. Chez Charbon? Wait—" Dean stopped and looked towards the right corner. "Does that say *Adult Reads?* Now that sounds interesting."

Ann shyly looked at him. "Adults need *stimulating* material as well."

"I'm all about stimulating." Dean walked over to the area and began skimming several of the titles aloud. "*From Dusk till Dawn: Tales of Multiple Orgasms. Clitoral Elevation: An Oral Guide to Pleasure. The Many Erogenous Zones of—*" He laughed. "I think this is my section."

Ann tilted her head to the side. "These books are checked out often. It's our more popular area."

"Oh, I bet." His finger grazed the shelf, stopping at one of the worn spines. "I might check out a few from here myself. Perhaps I can pick up a thing or two."

"You don't seem like the type that needs advice about how to please someone," she said amazed at her forwardness.

Dean moved toward her, stopping only when his body was mere inches away. "I've always believed old dogs can learn new tricks."

Ann cleared her throat. Heat drifted from his skin and it made her melt, down there. "I'm sure you know plenty."

Dean looked into her eyes. "So I've been told."

Ann bit her lip as Dean selected a few books to sample and sat at a nearby table. As she watched him ruffle through the pages, Ann couldn't help but wonder what he could teach her.

"*...The fastest way to bliss is asking her what she needs. What she wants. Mental sex is far superior to penetration when it comes to a woman...*"

Dean sat the book on the table. "And here all these years I thought if I ate her until she came that's what she wanted."

Ann's breath escaped her quicker than she wanted it too. "You...um...you just say whatever is on your mind, huh?"

"Yeah. Gave my parents the hardest time." He smirked. "They could never leave me around company long because I'd embarrass them."

Ann stared at Dean's lips as he resumed reading the book. She thought about what they could do to her; her imagination filled in all the delicious fiction. "Have you ever done something reckless. Like, without questioning it?" she asked.

"When I was a lot younger, I didn't know if I was finding trouble or if it was finding me." He laughed. "Though, I wouldn't suggest looking for trouble."

She was Bookworm Ann. Illicit affairs never happened. Life was ordinary and wrapped up in a perfect little bow, but she craved more.

"What if," she looked at him, her lips parted, "what if *I* wanted trouble?"

Dean raised his eyebrow. "What kind of trouble?"

Ann leaned closer to him, tentatively placing her fingertips on his arm. "Maybe a kiss?"

"That's what you consider trouble?"

She shrugged. "It's not every day I ask a guy I just met for one."

Dean watched her, not saying or doing anything.

Suddenly feeling foolish, Ann shook her head. "That was stupid, I'm sorry. I don't know what I was thinking." She started to get up. "I'll just—"

Dean's strong hands pulled her toward him. He brushed her lips with his, shocking her with the satin feel of them. He kissed her slowly, sucking both the top and bottom of her lips over and over again. She heard the tiniest moan. *Was that her?* Seconds later, they separated. She felt lightheaded and her mouth was tingling, as did other places.

Dean raised his eyebrows. "Was that enough trouble?"

Ann's chest rose and fell with the beat of her heart. *Not nearly enough.* She shook her head and stood, leaning her bottom against the table. "I could use a little more." She scooted until she was in front of Dean. She reached for his hand and placed it on her thigh.

He chuckled. "I could give you plenty of trouble, but is that what you want?" He squeezed her skin, searing trails of heat against it.

Ann looked down at him. "I want you to teach this librarian a few things."

She was wanting and ready and nervously waited for him to make a move. She loved the feel of his hands. Loved his warmth. Loved that this was so wrong, but it felt oh-so-deliciously good. Her sister had been right. She needed to experience life and Ann wanted this wicked adventure.

***

Dean waited for Ann to stop him as he slowly parted her blouse, pulling the cups of her black bra down, but she didn't. Ann's breasts spilled out, her nipples hard and waiting, her skin a beautiful contrast against the tone of the fabric. Dean had to taste her. *Had to.* He licked each nipple, ever so delicately.

Dean's lips skimmed the soft curvature of her breasts and Ann tilted her head back. He reached behind her and loosened her bun; curls cascaded down her back. She moaned and grabbed the nape of Dean's neck. He stood, his hands exploring as she pulled at his shirt, taking it off. Leaning back, Ann ran her fingers over his stomach, discovering his abs he'd chiseled to perfection.

***

Ann was growing restless of this long preamble. It had to happen now. She wanted to feel his hardness inside of her *now*.

Ann grabbed at his pants. His breathing became heavier as he helped her unbutton and then pull them down. Out of instinct, Ann reached in his boxers and circled her fingers around his length. Her thoughts ran rampant. She wanted to put him in her mouth, to let the softness of his skin and those big veins slide against her full lips. Somehow, time and desire reigned her back as she stroked his throbbing shaft.

Dean' eyes widened. "You know. I don't think you ever locked the front door."

Ann stroked him again and he hissed as if burned.

"I don't care who walks in right now," she said.

Dean's eyes filled with desire—*anticipation*—ready for anything she was willing to offer. Ann lifted her skirt and felt the fabric of her panties. She slid them over her flesh. He held Ann firmly while she lifted her hips. Ready.

Dean was slow about it, deliberately slow, and she wanted him to be. Ann stared into his eyes as Dean fell into her with all his hardness and girth, and she elicited a small gasp.

*** 

Her warmth surrounded him. *Covered him.* She was sweet and delicate. He grabbed a fistful of her hair, pulling a little rougher than he would like, but it allowed him to taste her neck. Ann shuddered against him, the vibrations from her moans thrummed against his lips.

He sucked and licked the same spot over and over, matching the stride of his pump. Each one taking her in more and more. He lifted Ann high, moving her up and down his length, feeling her dripping, melting around his cock and he wanted to keep this sensation forever. Ann's breasts bounced slightly and her hard nipples stuck out, begging for his tongue.

His words rushed out in a breath. "You feel so good to me."

*** 

Ann quivered. *Yes.* That deep power of his voice. It weakened her. Her tiny bud throbbed from desire and she ground her hips against his, wanting this so much. Sensations trickled down her spine and into her legs.

She sank down deeper, feeling lost in space. In another universe where it was just them. No books or shelves or tables. No time or specific place. They were drifting inside of bliss "Just... right there," she screamed, losing this reality.

*Faster. Deeper. Deeper. Faster.*

It was too much. It wasn't enough.

Dean placed her back onto the table, never leaving from inside of her. Stroke after stroke, he handled her in such a way that thrilled her very core. Her eyes closed, but she could see him still. Knew exactly where he was.

"Oh, god, I'm there. I'm...I'm...don't..." She started to tense up and shake, grasping him tighter as her legs went slack.

***

Dean heard her words, but kept his hands on her hips, enjoying the feel of Ann's spasming climax, throbbing and slick. He grunted, growling like a possessed animal when his own release came, pure lust washing over.

Dean stared into her blue eyes. He tried to leave her but couldn't. *Was it too soon to feel like this? To feel this rush of emotion?* He wanted to take her across town to his room, lay her in the bed and smooth her hair on the pillow and look into her beautiful eyes. To have long talks until the sun came up. But, at his heart, he was a bad boy.

"Was that enough trouble for you?" Dean asked.

*\*\*\**

Ann clung to him, still shaking from ecstasy. *Never.* She'd never felt like this. *Wanted. Desired.* Handled so roughly but tenderly at the same. Her breathing slowed and she felt her surroundings seeping in again. She looked up at Dean and felt herself blushing. She covered her face with her hand. Books might have taken her imagination to new worlds and experiences, but the real thing of his flesh pressed against hers, their breathing mixing in shallow harmony, was so much better. She hadn't a clue what was next or where the story would take them.

It was still unwritten.

233      **LAKE COVINGTON**

# Sailor's Delight

## MURIEL MCCANN

The surgery took eleven hours and left Lillian so tired her legs wobbled. It was like that for her sometimes, her focus so laser sharp in the operating room that when she finished, all the strength in her mind and body failed and left her shattered. It was worth it, though, for when she closed up Mrs. Lane, Lillian knew that the chest wall resection and reconstruction had been flawless, and her patient's broken body would heal. Even with the adrenaline gone and exhaustion threatening to take her, Lillian couldn't help but smile. She was good with broken things.

"Dr. Faris." A man ran up the hall toward her with a little girl. "Connor Lane. I just wanted to thank you for taking such good care of my mother."

Lillian took Connor in while she shook his hand. He was lean, with perfect teeth and fingers like a pianist. His smile was awkward, though, maybe forced. The little girl's made up for it, big and wide and perfect. She looked like Connor, Lillian thought, in the nose and cheeks.

"Thank you for fixing Grandma," she said.

Connor said, "This is Penny."

"Good to meet you, Penny." Lillian shook her hand as well. "And it was a pleasure fixing your grandmother. She was an excellent patient."

"You must be talking about a different woman," Connor said. "My mother is always difficult."

"Not under sedation."

They laughed and walked down the hall together. Lillian told them she was done for the day and Connor looked like he wanted to say something. Twice he opened his mouth and stopped. That strange smile came out a couple of times, but when they reached the hospital entrance, he looked serious again, thoughtful.

"Well," Lillian said, "It was nice to meet you."

The pause that followed stretched a beat too long, and it was Penny who jumped into it.

"I'm hungry," she said.

"That's fine, sweetie," Connor said. "We'll get something in just a minute."

"Can we go to the bakery?"

"We'll see, sweetie." Connor looked back at Lillian. "Thanks again—"

Penny cut him off. "Would you like to go with us?"

A blush rose in Connor's cheeks. "Penny, I'm sure she's busy."

Lillian didn't know what it was that made her speak up. God knew she didn't have time for a man, let alone one with a daughter. She'd tried dating, but her track record hadn't been too good of late. The long hours, the emergency calls, they were more than most men could handle. Something about Connor got to her, though. Maybe it was the way he looked at his daughter, or maybe it was that broken smile, but Lillian surprised herself by saying, "Actually, a cup of coffee sounds great."

Jansen's Dutch Bakery was on the old town square. A line stretched from the counter to the door. A baker dressed in all white brought out trays of steaming pastries to refill the display case while a uniformed police officer in an apron rang up customers.

When it was their turn, they got coffees for the adults and a hot chocolate for Penny along with a danish for each. The day was hot, but they sat outside at a wrought iron table and watched people go by.

"What do you do, Connor?" Lillian asked.

"I'm a journalist," he said. "Well, I was a journalist."

"You mean you're not anymore?"

"It's a different kind of journalism. I report on local issues, and I do a historical column, *This Day in Lake Covington*. The work is a lot slower here than in the city."

"Oh, I've read those," Lillian said. "You're new here, right? What brought you to Lake Covington?"

"My mommy died," Penny broke in, peering at them over the rim of her hot cocoa. The matter-of-fact tone she used stabbed at Lillian's heart.

"I'm so sorry," she said to both Connor and Penny.

"It happened a long time ago," Penny said. "When I was five. Daddy said we needed a fresh start."

Connor said nothing, just tried for a reassuring smile, which faltered and fell away.

***

They saw each other a few more times that week, each time at Connor's. His place was like Connor himself, Lillian noticed: well put together, sturdy, but in need of a woman's touch. They ate dinner and played board games with Penny until she could barely keep her eyes open, then Connor helped her into her pajamas and made sure she brushed her teeth before bed. The third night, Penny gave Lillian a hug and kissed her cheek before shuffling off to her room.

"She likes you," Connor said, watching after his daughter as she closed the bedroom door.

"I like her," Lillian said. "She's a wonderful girl."

Connor poured them each a glass of wine and they sat on the sofa, knees almost touching. "What should we toast to?" he said.

"How about to second chances?"

He clinked his glass to hers. "To new beginnings."

They drank and talked late into the night. The wine had Lillian buzzing not just from the alcohol but with new hopes and possibilities she hadn't known she wanted. Her focus had been on her career for so long that she had forgotten how nice a genuine connection could be.

"I should probably let you get to bed," she said. "I've been talking your ear off all night."

Connor's smile dropped as he looked at the clock on the wall. "I didn't realize. It's a good thing I have no deadlines looming. In fact, I don't have anything on my plate until the big party on the All-Aboard's new boat Friday night. They're expecting at least 200 people."

"Ooh, I heard about that. They say a prince is going to be there. Lake Covington is really moving up in the world. You're going to cover it?"

"I wouldn't miss it." He held up the bottle of wine. "How about you? You need to get home?"

Lilian held out her glass. "My rotation ended tonight. I'm off the next two days. Not even on call."

Connor split the last of the bottle between their glasses and they clinked and sipped. He leaned in and kissed Lillian. It took her by surprise, starting light and sweet, sending a thrilling flutter in Lillian's midsection. He kissed her harder, then abruptly pulled away. His eyes were alight with hunger and need but still something was stopping him.

Lillian took the initiative, kissed him back, and this time there was real heat to it, her mouth opening and his tongue exploring, tasting her. He put his hand on her neck and pulled her closer, kissing her deeply and stroking her cheek with his thumb. When he relaxed and pulled away, Lillian's face was flushed and her body tingled like an exposed wire.

She didn't know if it was the wine that got them carried away, or their mutual need. She grabbed Connor by the shirt and pulled him toward her. They melted together, their hands roaming over each other's bodies.

Connor was lean and muscled, his body taut under her fingertips. She undid his shirt and let those fingers wander over him, his tight belly and his smooth, almost hairless chest. All the while he was kissing her, stroking her, igniting the passion in her that had been dormant.

Connor's strong arms swept her up and he carried her into a dark bedroom. He switched on a corner lamp and she saw it wasn't a bedroom at all, but a converted office. He clicked the lock on the door and raised a finger to his lips, urging her to be silent.

It wasn't easy. He laid her down across his desk. With his lips, he explored her from her head to her belly, and at last between her legs. He was slow and methodical at first, kissing and licking and stroking until she whispered for him to go faster, then faster still as her heart raced and her body shuddered with a violent, yet silent, climax.

Then she had to have him. She tore at his belt and slid his pants down over his hips. He was rock hard and breathing in short, panting breaths as she grabbed the base of him and guided him inside her. He gasped, and it was her turn to put a finger to her lips. "Shhh..." she said, as he started to work his hips.

It had been so long, and it felt so good, she wanted to cry out. Something about having to be quiet intensified her pleasure, made every sensation even more profound, every part of her body more sensitive. She felt herself on the brink of another orgasm and she bit down on her lip and dug her nails into Connor's side as he arched his back and winced and—

"Daddy?" The doorknob rattled in its setting as Penny's voice came through the door. "Daddy?"

"One second, honey," Connor said, diving to the floor and scrambling for his pants.

"Why is the door locked?"

"I'm working, baby."

He threw on his shirt and did the first few buttons. When he looked back at Lillian, his eyes were wide as eggs sunny side up. Then, opening the door a crack, he squeezed through the gap and shut the door behind him.

Lillian plucked her bra off the floor but couldn't find her underwear. She could hear the muffled father-daughter conversation as she searched, but couldn't make out their words. Her cheeks blazed with shame. She had her jeans in hand, ready to go without her underwear, when she found them on the seat of the desk chair.

The voices had stopped, but Lillian didn't dare open the door in case Penny waited on the other side. She contemplated going out the window, but her purse and car keys were in the living room on the floor. By the time Connor came back, she'd almost done it anyway.

"She's back in bed," he said.

"That was close."

Connor was visibly shaken. He'd lost his usual color and when he took her hand, she noticed his was clammy. He pulled her from the office and into the living room. She didn't dare speak for fear of Penny hearing them.

If she was going to be with Connor, she didn't want Penny to find out like this. The girl had lost her mother, and that meant she needed to move carefully.

Connor found her purse and her phone and handed them over, and led her to the front door. When they were out on the porch, she broke the silence.

"Are you okay? Did Penny hear...anything?"

"No," he said. "I don't think so. She just had a bad dream. When I wasn't there when she came looking, she got frightened."

Lillian laughed, although she knew Connor didn't find any of this funny. She couldn't help it. It burst from her mouth faster than she could reach up a hand to stifle it.

"I guess we got a little carried away," she said, then traced a finger down his arm. "I would say it won't happen again, but I can't guarantee that."

She got on her toes and leaned in to kiss him, but he backed away.

"It can't happen again," he said. "That was irresponsible."

"It was," she agreed, "but you needed to let loose a little. God knows I did."

"Not while my daughter is in the house having a nightmare."

"Connor, people have been having sex at home when the kids go to sleep for centuries."

"But the difference is, you're not her mother."

His words stung, burning across her cheeks as though he'd slapped her. She could feel her mouth drop open, but she had no reply.

"Penny's my whole world," he went on. "I can't take my mind off that for a second. I'm all she's got. I don't think she's ready for me to have someone else in my life, in our life."

"You're right," Lillian said through gritted teeth. "You do have to think of Penny first, and I'm not her mother." She backed away, out of the reach of the porch light. "But I'm just not sure if it's Penny who isn't ready for someone new, or you."

She hurried toward her car. Connor called after her in a stage whisper, but she didn't turn. Tears poured from her eyes, and she used her sleeves to wipe them away. They kept coming until her vision blurred and her nose ran with snot. She sat behind the wheel and waited for it to pass. A few minutes later, Connor's porch light blinked out.

\*\*\*

For the next week, Lillian ignored Connor's calls. When he sent a text apologizing, she responded: *It's fine, just busy at work.* She wasn't lying. She was busy. Two valves and an emergency pacemaker surgery on Thursday alone. When Friday evening came, she was exhausted, and ready to be done with people and their problems and curl up at home in front of the TV.

When she got to her apartment, an envelope had been shoved under her door. There was no writing on it, and inside there was only one thing: a ticket for the inaugural voyage of *Mary's Jewel.*

Her first thought was of Connor. The fact that there was only one ticket and the sender chose to remain anonymous pointed at him.

Her next thought was to throw it away, to tear it up into little pieces and flush it down the toilet. She didn't need anything from him. She didn't want anything. Then she remembered the way he'd kissed her, the way he looked at her, and that curious, broken smile that had intrigued her. It wasn't like she hadn't been guilty in the past of saying something harsh. She supposed she owed Connor the chance to explain himself.

*Now*, she thought, *what to wear?*

\*\*\*

The ship was larger than the other dinner cruise liners that typically navigated Lake Covington. The deck towered above the dock and the flag waving on the mast was so high it almost scraped the clouds. It was scheduled to shove off from the docks at six, and the line of people waiting to board suggested more than the expected two hundred had bought tickets. It might be twice that, she thought.

She spotted Connor before she made it on the ship. He was on the upper deck at the railing, talking to a bald man in a tuxedo and a white bow tie. The man put a hand over his eyes to block the evening sun and scanned the crowd.

Someone bumped Lillian from behind.

"I'm sorry," he said.

It was Taylor Beckett, who owned the dog grooming shop and took care of her mother's beagle, Maxie. He was with a large, swarthy man with a thick head of dark hair and a rugged smile.

"No harm done," she said, but when she looked back to the rail, Connor and the man in the tuxedo were gone.

A checker took their tickets and they stepped onto the boat two-by-two like animals climbing aboard the ark. It was a little sad handing over her individual ticket and boarding alone, but she was determined not to let that ruin it for her. She took in the sights and sounds and looked for familiar faces as a man in a captain's hat and white shirt ushered them onto a grand platform at the stern, with padded benches and a covered area to sit out of the sun while taking in the lake.

"I'm your captain, Wes Stanton," the man said, addressing the crowd, "We'll start the tour around the lake shortly, but feel free to go through the glass doors to the ballroom, where we're serving drinks and hors d'oeuvres. If you have any questions, please ask one of the crew, or come see me in the engine room."

Lillian was amazed at the size of the ballroom. It was two stories of glass, running the width of the boat, providing a panoramic view of the lake on three sides. Toward the front of the ship was a parquet dance floor and a raised stage.

The bartender was Carla Ward, an old school friend of Lillian's. They chatted for a minute, then Lillian got a glass of Pinot Grigio.

"I don't want to forget to give you this," Carla said, flipping an envelope in the air and catching it with a flourish. She handed it to Lillian. It was beige stationery, with an *L* in flowing cursive on the back.

"What's this?" she asked.

Carla smiled. "Looks to me like someone has a secret admirer."

Lillian scanned the room for Connor, then took her drink and the envelope out on the deck. The ship's engines started and the captain's voice warned them they were about to head off. She braced herself, but the boat slid off the dock so smoothly she wouldn't have noticed they were moving if she'd had her eyes closed.

The seats on the observation deck filled as people came out with their drinks in hand. It was a beautiful evening, but the summer heat had everyone in the shade. Lillian chose to go to the rail, stand out in the sun and let it warm her skin as she watched the boat's wake foam up as white as snow on the wine-dark waves.

Twice more she saw Connor. First, he was at the enormous glass doors that led inside, then he was moving among the crowd, weaving in and out of the rows of benches. He snapped pictures, a huge camera tethered to his neck. He never came over to Lillian.

She always thought of journalists writing their stories and photographers taking the pictures, but she imagined in such a small town he had to do double duty. A pang of remorse for Connor shot through her, for all that he'd sacrificed, on top of all he'd lost, but she tamped that down.

Lillian was there, alone, watching couples laugh and kiss and enjoy themselves while he ignored her. Yes, he'd sacrificed. Yes, he'd suffered. When he'd had a chance to move on, though, he'd chickened out.

The part of Lillian that wanted to be sore at Connor warred with the part of her that wanted to fix everything. She'd seen it in him in the hallway, in that shy, unsure smile that showed hints of cracks beneath the veneer, that told her to go slow. It was like in surgery, the strength of the veins, the calcification of the arteries that indicated just how much a heart could handle. The signs had all been there with Connor, too, but she'd been swept away by need and loneliness and the comfort of his touch.

She opened the envelope. Inside was a folded slip of paper. She opened the note and saw two words: *Foredeck telescope.* She put the note back in the envelope and shook her head, the corner of her lip curling up in an involuntary smile.

A melodic laugh drifted to her ears, and she wheeled, expecting a woman behind her, but there was no one within fifteen feet. Then the speaker above her squawked and Captain Stanton addressed them.

"Ladies and gentlemen, if you look off to our starboard, you'll see the belfry of the Old Town Church. The church was one of the oldest buildings standing in Lake Covington when Moyer Dam broke in 1919. All of the town square was flooded. In fact, we're sailing over the cobblestones of the original Main Street now. Divers are still finding coins, vases, and other objects, and on a clear day, you can see the sun glinting off the church bells under the water."

Lillian headed around the boat's gunwale to the bow. A few couples had moved to that end, no doubt for a little more privacy. One couple was locked in an embrace right beside the telescope mounted to the rail. Lillian felt like an intruder as she slid up beside them but hanging from a piece of twine was another note.

"Excuse me," she said, embarrassed.

The couple moved apart, and Lillian recognized Joy Kinsey, who sometimes tended bar at Mojo's. The man with her was large, with a T-shirt that read *Police Academy* on the back. He looked flustered, and Lillian noticed he was holding something in his hand, a small jewelry box he clutched with white knuckles.

Lillian snatched the note and apologized for the interruption. She moved away from the couple before she opened it. Taped to the inside she found a golden skeleton key. The note read *Galley*.

The galley was the size of a restaurant kitchen and bustling with men and women in white chef's jackets. Their voices called out to each other as they worked their stations. Lillian caught a glimpse of Connor at the opposite end snapping pictures.

She was enjoying the cat and mouse, but she was ready to talk to Connor, ready to see why he wanted her there, but he ducked out and disappeared. A man tapped her on the shoulder and spoke to her in a French accent.

"Madame Lillian?"

"Yes."

He handed her a plate with a something fancy made of puff pastry and what looked like smoked salmon. On the edge of the plate was another piece of stationery. This one didn't have an L, but two earrings poked through the paper to dangle beneath. They were beautiful, with diamonds shaped like huge teardrops. The card read *Museum.*

Lillian climbed the stairs to the top level, where she found a sign in front of a door with a mermaid and the words *Lady of the Lake Museum.* She tried the handle, but the door was locked. Again, she thought she heard a woman's chuckle, but after a look around she was confident she was alone. The key in her palm looked too old to open such a modern door. She tried it in the lock anyway, and it gave with a soft click.

Inside was a collection of local art and artifacts under glass cases. There were sculptures and paintings and native American tools found in the area. On one velvet pad, there was something missing, and by the impression left in the material, Lillian guessed there had been a necklace and a pair of earrings.

The centerpiece of the display was a large portrait of a woman in a flowing gown, her hair spilling down her shoulders in tight curls, a beautiful ruby at her throat. Lillian didn't have to read the painting's caption to recognize Christian Jones' work.

"You look like her."

She turned, hoping to see Connor, but it was Wes Stanton in full captain's garb. He smiled while handing her a stunning gold necklace with a ruby pendant surrounded by glittering diamonds, along with another note. She held the necklace up. It was the same as the one Kate Sheffield wore in the painting. Lillian's heart leapt, and she felt her cheeks get hot. Her emotions were a mix of happiness and confusion that tumbled inside her belly and left her lightheaded.

Wes Stanton looked back to the painting.

"He was in love with her, I think. You'd have to be, wouldn't you?" He looked at his watch. "Uh-oh, better get going."

Then he was gone, and she stood with the necklace and the card in hand.

She wanted to call out to Connor, to tell him to show himself so she could hug him or shake him, whichever felt right at the moment. She opened the card. *Second deck, observation room two.*

It was as ornate as the ballroom, but with a carpeted floor and about a quarter the size. A chandelier hung from the ceiling and the lowering sun's light hit the crystals, sending glittering kaleidoscopic rainbows across the wall and floor. Televisions along one wall cycled through pictures of the ship, the decks full of people, the ballroom, and then wait—

Pictures of Lillian.

They were pictures Connor had taken. There she was with Carla at the bar, then at the entry to the kitchen, and at the railing with her eyes facing out to the lake. She'd only seen him a few times, but he'd been there all along, from the time she boarded the ship, to the moment she'd opened the door to the room in which she stood. The last picture on the reel wasn't of Lillian, but of Penny, holding another card out so she could read it: *Turn around.*

She followed the card's direction and there Penny was, in a white dress, her hair in spiral curls. She smiled wide and ran to Lillian. Penny wrapped her arms around Lillian's neck and held her tight.

"I miss you," Penny said. "Daddy misses you."

"Oh, Penny," Lillian said. "I've missed you, too."

"I asked Daddy where you've been, and he says he did something stupid."

Lillian couldn't help but smile. "Grownups do stupid things sometimes."

"I told him he'd better apologize."

"Yeah? What did he say?"

"He said he would have to do better than that."

Penny motioned for Lillian to come closer. She turned and plucked something off the table behind her and told Lillian to bend down. She smiled a toothy grin, and held a sparkling tiara. "You need to put on the earrings and necklace, too."

When Lillian was bedazzled to Penny's satisfaction, the little girl kissed her on the cheek and darted for the observation room door. Lillian was about to call her name, to ask where she was going, but seeing the figure filling the doorway made the words stick in her throat.

It was Connor, but gone was the camera around his neck, and the jeans and polo shirt he'd been wearing. He was in a suit, navy blue with an old-fashioned cut, his hair coiffed like a 50s movie star. He had a single white rose in hand.

He said, "You look amazing."

"Connor..." she started, but faltered. She didn't know what to say. Part of her wanted to let him know how much he'd hurt her. The look in his eyes, though, was vulnerable and tender. It melted her.

"I've been such an idiot." He held the rose out to her. "You were right about everything. I thought I was protecting Penny, but what I was really doing was preventing my own happiness. Our happiness. I'm so sorry, Lil. I was blind not to see how good you are with Penny. You didn't disrupt our family. You fixed it. We're broken without you."

Lillian stepped in closer and he kissed her. It was like their first kiss, only better, sweet and passionate, but without the hesitation he'd first shown. When their lips parted, she took a deep breath, opened her eyes, and saw the smile there.

"You're not broken," she said. "You're perfect."

A song filled the room and Connor took her in his arms and they started to dance. Lillian recognized it as *Swan Lake*, the Tchaikovsky waltz. He was light on his feet, if not graceful, and they stepped and turned and reveled in each other as the sky to the west turned a deep red with the setting of the sun.

When the song ended, the door opened and the man Lillian had seen with Connor on the observation deck came in. He rushed to Connor and Lillian and spoke in a near whisper.

"It is almost time, Mr. Lane."

He had a European accent that Lillian couldn't place, and he wasn't bald like she'd first thought, but his hair was shaved closer than a military buzz cut.

"Lillian, allow me to introduce Prince Gabriel of Pumany," Connor said. "He helped me set this all up. The jewelry you're wearing, he let us borrow it."

Lillian felt the jewel at her throat.

"They do not belong to me," Prince Gabriel assured her. "The jewels of Lady Kate Sheffield are on loan from the museum. They belong to Lake Covington. But I must confess," the prince said with a bow, "you were made to wear them."

The door closed behind the prince, leaving Lillian and Connor alone. He took her hand, then kissed her cheek. His lips felt warm and right.

"Where's Pumany?" Lillian asked.

Connor shrugged. "Who knows? Somewhere in Europe. Who can keep track?"

They went outside to the observation deck to await the arrival of the prince and his paramour. Penny sat with Connor's mother, who was snapping pictures with the big camera. Penny had saved them a seat.

Again, Lillian heard the woman's laugh. She whipped her head to follow the sound. All she saw were gentle waves lapping at the starboard side of the boat, and the glorious splash of purple and orange the sunset had painted across the sky.

"Did you hear that?" she asked Connor.

"Hear what?"

She looked out across the lake, sure the sound had come from that direction. Something rose out of the water in a spray of purple not far from the boat. It disappeared before she could be sure what she'd seen, but that laughter echoed with the ripples that danced across the water.

"Never mind." Lillian took Connor's hand and squeezed. "Don't you have to cover the event?"

"No." He kissed her on the cheek and whispered in her ear. "I've already got my story."

# About the Authors

Stacey Bryant lives in Minnesota with her husband (her real-life hero) and is happily owned by her two very talkative and rambunctious Siamese fur babies. She can completely lose track of time reading a good book and enjoys spending her summers outside after being holed-up over the long winter months. Hobbies include gardening, testing new recipes, visiting new wineries, and walking off the calories created by sampling new recipes and new wines. When she's not writing, she's teaching college freshman how to improve their reading and writing skills. www.stacey-bryant.com/

Nancy Canu was born and raised in New York City, and she and her husband dream of living someplace with better weather. The middle of nowhere would be nice, with land for their horses plus a big enough house to keep their Rottweiler and four cats happy. For the past twenty-six years, she's run her own dog-walking business in Manhattan by day, been a freelance editor by night, and written whenever she has the time. As J.J. Cassidy, she's published three M/M romance novellas, and two other novellas have been in anthologies with Dreamspinner Press. Writing under her own name, last year her short story, *Fathom*, was featured in a paranormal anthology.

Volanna Dal'Ziel spends most of her time tapping away at the keyboard, bringing to life the characters that refuse to remain quiet in her mind. They deserve love too, after all. She enjoys reading, painting, and all things crafty. When she's not engrossed in her latest romance novel, you can find her spending time with her friends in her local writing group, going on hikes and camping outdoors, or cuddled up next to her own true love, binge watching Netflix.

Nala Henkel-Aislinn was born in British Columbia, Canada. She's a part-time romance writer who also consults as a digital marketing specialist. Nala's also been a creative storyteller since first grade. She's written six contemporary romance novels in the Cranberry Hill Inn series, and has plans for two more series by the end of 2020. She loves bringing funny, strong female characters to life, and creating their complex, romantic Beta-male partners. Nala currently lives in Washington State, U.S. with her husband, Eric. Together they have a blended family of three daughters, one son, and one snuggly cat.

Chris Kanther may be a pharmacist by day, but by night he writes, draws, watches cartoons, drinks obscene amounts of caffeine, and collects way too many things. Chris cut his writing teeth on fan fiction and serves as one-half of the duo behind The Jewel Riders Archive, a fan site dedicated to the animated series Princess Gwenevere and the Jewel Riders. You can find him at www.chriskanther.com, @polychrome_pen on Instagram, and at www.jewelridersarchive.com.

Muriel McCann is a 68-year-old housewife, the mother of three young men, and proud grandmother of five. She lives in Grand Island, Nebraska with her husband and two golden retrievers. Muriel began writing as a youngster, and with no formal training was published in the *Church-Wellesley Review*, *First Statement*, and *HEAT*. Unable to find representation for her novels, she turned to ghostwriting romance, which she's done for almost twenty years.

Hannah Morse is an author of contemporary and paranormal romance novels. She lives in New Mexico with her high school sweetheart and too many Chihuahuas. She can be found binging Netflix shows or reading steamy novels when she isn't hard at work writing a happily ever after.

Natalie Nixon's work has appeared in literary magazines including *Reunion: The Dallas Review*, *Driftwood Press*, and *Cliterature*, among others. Raised on an island in Alaska, she spent her weekends in the woods, and gained a fascination for biology while dissecting creatures in her father's taxidermy studio. Literature and the sciences feed her endless curiosity, and she uses her experiences of both to color and enliven her work. She is currently finishing a fictional novel which incorporates earthquakes, lightning science, human evolutionary theory, psychic powers, and snake venom- she would like to thank the cast of characters that blossomed in her book, and took her on such a joy ride. She lives in Flagstaff, Arizona with her beloved children Hailey and Camron, and her partner-in-curiosity, David Gilley.

Laura Powers uses her small breaks from being a stay-at-home mother, wife, and full-time school volunteer to spark her imagination. Between the stories she weaves, the art itching at her fingertips, or hours spent crafting, Laura's love is creating things that make people feel joy. Literature has been bringing a reprieve to those in need for centuries, and she's hoping to leave even the smallest mark in the world in that regard.

HJ Reinhart has always been a sucker for a great romance. She discovered a love of the romance genre when she read *The India Fan* by Victoria Holt in high school and subsequently devoured all the books in Holt's collection before branching off. When she's not reading or writing, she likes to go thrift-store hunting for items she can repurpose and upcycle. She has an unapologetic addiction to coffee, M&M's, and scarves and lives full-time in her craft room.

T. L. Sherwood is the Managing Editor at *Literary Orphans*. Her work has appeared in *New World Writing, Jellyfish Review, Elm Leaves Journal, Page & Spine, Spelk, Vestal Review*, and *The Dead Mule School of Southern Literature* as well as other journals. She won the Gover Prize in 2016 and was the first ever London Independent Story Prize winner in 2018. Her work has also been a finalist for Best Small Fictions and nominated for Best of the Net and the Pushcart Prize. She lives in Springville, New York where she is editing a novel written this year during National Novel Writing Month.

Noel Stark, a life-long reader of romance, was excited to finally get the chance to use her Honours History degree on her first short-story *Flood Gates*. Hailing from small town Ontario, she now makes her home in West Hollywood, California with her young son, husband and, at random times, her three step-kids. Presently she is working on her debut contemporary romance novel, *Taking Direction*, the first of a four-part series.

Kat Vinson grew up in Oklahoma and lived in Scotland, England, Czech Republic, and several states before landing in Seattle, where she spends her days as a data scientist. Her evenings and weekends are dedicated to writing and she is currently working toward an MFA. One of her three cats is her muse, although she's not sure which one. You can find her at katvinson.com and @kvbooks on Twitter and Instagram.

Greer Zeigler, author of the self-published book, *Those Blue Skies*, has actively been writing for an audience since 2016. Currently living in Norfolk, VA, she works as a bookkeeper, and is a full-time single mother to Jaiden and Nyla.

# About the Anthology

This anthology is the result of a unique romance writing contest that opened for entries on Thanksgiving Day 2018. The SMOLDR Creative Group created a town, gave it a history, peppered it with characters, and connected it together with classic romance tropes. We invited writers from all over the world to take those individual pieces and create a story that would capture both the heart and soul of this magical lake town. We believe we achieved that goal. Here are the original character profiles that were given to each author:

### Forever Masterpiece

Christian Jones: Artist

Christian has had a paintbrush in his hands for as long as he could remember. Nothing is off limits, and that goes for his work and his love life. He throws himself wholeheartedly into both pleasurable pursuits. His muse is purely living, from the crowded markets on the docks, to the bustling streets of upper Main Street. He paints with every fiber of his being and if the colors don't always land on the canvas, who was he to complain?

Kate Sheffield: Housekeeper

Kate relishes the memories of her Grandmother's English gardens. It's one of the things she misses most about home. Being forced to move to America puts one's life into perspective, yet, she's found a sense of joy in her position as head housekeeper at the Mayor's House. Although taking care of another's home wasn't exactly her dream come true, it's a comfort that she's not on the streets. A small part of her hopes, however, that one day, her prince charming will find her.

Trope: Forbidden Love

A setup between two lovers under conditions that prevent their love from being fulfilled. Think Leonardo DiCaprio and Claire Danes in *Romeo and Juliet* or Ryan Gosling and Rachel McAdams in *The Notebook*.

Location: Mayor's House

The Mayor's House is a newly constructed, two-story brick home, with palatial columns and a wraparound porch. Located within the heart of Lake Covington, directly off Main Street, it's one of the largest homes within the township. No expense was spared, with manicured lawns and hedged-wall gardens, and generously placed rose bushes dispersed throughout. To enter the estate your carriage drives under a bricked archway, covered in ivy, up a cobbled drive that winds its way in front of the expansive porch. A three-tiered fountain made of marble trickles in welcome and stone pathways lined with wrought iron lanterns beckons you to tour the grounds.

Year: 1880

### *All I Want Is You*

Evan Jacobs: Start-Up Entrepreneur

Evan sits in the garage of the cottage he's renting in Lake Covington and dreams of riches. He has file, upon file of notes and diagrams all pointing to the next world changing invention. His friends worry he needs to fill his life with more than technical specs, but the ideas come faster than he can ever develop, leaving little time for him to take his eyes off the keyboard and appreciate the beauty around him.

## Aryn Keyes: Barista

Artistically gifted, Aryn flutters from thought-to-thought as easily as she does from cappuccino to Americano. She loves her current job at Cuppa Cafe and prides herself on her ability to create designs in foam to match each customer's aura. But her interactions with customers is fleeting and she longs for someone to add some passion to her personal design.

## Trope: Bookworm/Lovable Nerd

This trope involves a brilliant guy who's clueless when it comes to women. Social cues go over his head and he avoids embarrassing himself with members of the opposite sex by keeping himself immersed in his projects. But sometimes the right woman comes along and coaxes out his inner puppy dog. Think Leonard Hofstadter in *The Big Bang Theory*, Spencer Reid in *Criminal Minds,* or Temperance Brennan in *Bones*.

## Location: Chez Charbon

Chez Charbon is the chic place to dine in Lake Covington. Chef Henri creates a little piece of heaven in everything he touches. Situated on the edge of the lake, surrounded by flower and herb gardens, makes it a delightful place to wait, even when you have reservations.

## Year: Present Day

### *Wagging the Dog\**

## Taylor Beckett: Dog Groomer

Taylor loves dogs. And by love, one can safely assume obsessed. There was a time Taylor considered veterinary school, however, one summer grooming dogs to pay for college quickly changed Taylor's mind. Opening the first dog grooming business in Lake Covington turned out to be the smartest thing Taylor has ever done. Constantly busy and surrounded by furry companions is a dream come true.

Frankie Kaye: Dock Worker

Frankie isn't one to shy away from hard work, and there's nothing better than working out on the waters of Lake Covington. It'd been a family trade, one Frankie was happy to take over, maintaining the docks and boats. Long days often turn into long nights, and Frankie looks for any way to wind down, most notably with a fishing pole in his/her hand off the back of his/her father's old fishing boat. Frankie wouldn't mind sharing the solitude and beautiful view with someone else, if the moment was right.

Trope: Beautiful All Along

The tale of our ugly duckling, losing their glasses, taking down their hair and transforming into a beautiful swan. This trope is a lovely representation that looks aren't everything, it's all in the heart, and beauty is everywhere. Think Freddie Prinze Jr. and Rachael Leigh Cook in *She's All That* or Michael Vartan and Drew Barrymore in *Never Been Kissed*.

Location: The Pet Project

The Pet Project was once the old pharmacy within Lake Covington. Converted into a pet and kid friendly institution, it houses several rooms and areas for all sorts of four (or two) legged friends. A huge, wall-to-wall window graces the front entrance, where several puppies and kittens nap in the afternoon sun. Located on the east upper side of town, it gets plenty of foot traffic, much to pet store inhabitants' enjoyment.

Year: Present Day

### *Hooked*

Jude Hunt: Biologist

Jude has studied Biology, both molecular and cellular, for

what felt a lifetime. He's landed a pretty cool gig studying water conservations and Lake Covington seems to have all that he needs. There was nothing better than living life outdoors. Having spent a majority of his time in labs, studying the most minute facets of living organisms, it was freeing to finally be out within the forests surrounding his little town, picking up organic samples to study at a later time. And if a little romanced blossomed somewhere between the work and lands he was growing to love, he wouldn't mind, not one bit.

Amber Smith: Nurse

Amber has wanted to be a nurse since, well, forever. Spending so much time caring for others has put her love life on hold. She's never been afraid of hard work and running the emergency ward at Lake Covington Hospital is indeed difficult. Yet she enjoys it, most of the time. Night shifts are always the hardest and, after the adrenalin of saving another life begins to fade, loneliness sinks in. It makes a girl wish she were the one strapped to a bed, and a handsome fellow was taking care of her needs for a change.

Trope: Meet Cute

A meet cute trope is a staple of romantic comedies, involving two people who will form a future romance. A meet-cute is almost always rife with awkwardness, embarrassment, and sometimes outright hostility. Frequently, the meet-cute leads to a humorous clash of personality or beliefs, embarrassing situations, or comical misunderstandings that further drive the plot. Think Patrick Swayze and Jennifer Grey in *Dirty Dancing* or Richard Gere and Julia Roberts in *Pretty Woman*.

Location: Nash's Fix & Fill

Nash's Fix & Fill is a family owned and operated establishment. Seamlessly stuck in the 50's, its chrome encased, and shiny red building brings back memories of milkshakes and greased overalls. Located in the heart of downtown Lake Covington, it offers the best mechanic work and only petrol for the bustling little town.

Year: Present Day

### *Flood Gates*

Isaiah Wilson: Infantry Man

Isaiah was raised on a rural family farm at the South end of Lake Covington. Farming taught him the value of hard work, grit, and loyalty. He always dreamed of carrying on the farming life, raising children, and living off the land like his parents and grandparents. All that changed at the start of WW1 when, as soon as he was able, Isaiah enlisted to fight for his country.

Olivia McCray: College Student

Olivia seeks out adventure and loves a challenge. Always considered somewhat of a tomboy by her folks, Olivia has never been comfortable with societal expectations. Olivia spends her days outdoors, either hiking in the woods that surround Lake Covington or riding her horse along its shores. Olivia might be a tough one to catch, but not for someone with the mettle to accept the challenge.

Trope: Trapped in the same place

There's no faster way to get to know someone than to be trapped together. Add in the worst storm Lake Covington's ever seen, and you've got a recipe for excitement. Think Jennifer Lawrence and Chris Pratt in *Passengers*, Lora and Max in Karen Robards' *Wild Orchids*, or Dickie and Emmeline in the *Blue Lagoon*.

Location: McPherson's Cabin

Nestled in the woods north of the lake, the small post and beam cabin is just the perfect size for two. Its stone hearth and bearskin rug invite those on chilly nights to settle before its fire and enjoy the moment. Its small store of canned food is always stocked and there's several cords of firewood for the fireplace. Empty most of year, the McPherson Cabin is a welcomed oasis for those who find themselves lost in the forest. It is said to have been a miracle that it even survived the epic storm of 1919.

Year: Great Storm of 1919

### *The Lie that Binds*

Russ Kannier: Bouncer at The Impulse

There's more to Russ than eighteen-inch biceps and the build of an NFL linebacker, but that's the first thing people see. His muscled exterior makes him perfect for his job as a bouncer at Mojo's, but underneath is a man with ambitions of finishing school, going into business for himself, and raising a family. As much as he enjoys playing the tough guy, he'd love to meet someone who sees through that act to the man within.

Joy Kinsey: Kindergarten Teacher

The one thing Joy is missing from her life is the thing her mother named her for: Joy. It's not that she's unhappy. In fact, she draws great pleasure from her job and her students, but they take so much of her time and patience that Joy doesn't laugh like she used to. She's a no-nonsense type, who's looking for someone who can be honest and fun and help her find that laughter she craves.

Trope: Enemies to Lovers

These people don't like each other, or do they? Maybe they're just too similar, too bullheaded, or just at cross purposes, but when the circumstances are right, sometimes bitter enemies find that the white-hot fire that fuels their rivalry can turn into an all-consuming blaze. Think Mr. Darcy and Elizabeth in *Pride and Prejudice*, Wesley and Bianca in the *DUFF*, or Bridget and Mark in *Bridget Jones' Diary*.

Location: Mojos Bar

Lake Covington is known for its beauty, its charm, its classic style. Mojos might be the only exception to the rule. It's a tiny hole in the wall with a whole different kind of charm, where the locals go to escape their day-to-day and tourists flock to for its rock and roll music and devil may care attitude.

Year: Present Day

### *Much More in Store**

Casey Jansen: Baker

As a child, Casey learned the love of baking from watching his/her grandmother move around the kitchen like she was orchestrating a symphony. With a little love and a dash of flour, anything can be cured. But for something a little spicier, Casey knows just how to kick up the heat.

Morgan Cass: Police Officer

Morgan grew up wanting to catch bad guys like the super-heroes did on TV. The police academy was the most logical step—opting for a badge instead of a cape. Unfortunately, a cop in Lake Covington isn't as exciting as Morgan thought it was going to be, but occasionally, s/he does get to see a little action.

Trope: Childhood Friends

Two people who spend their childhood years together now find themselves developing romantic feelings for each other. Think Heathcliff and Catherine from *Wuthering Heights*, Will Turner and Elizabeth Swan from *Pirates of the Caribbean*, and Forrest Gump and Jenny from *Forrest Gump*.

Location: The Main Street General Store

The Main Street General Store is one of Lake Covington's original buildings from when it was founded and has operated in much the same way since its inception. You can find just about anything at the General Store, from cake mix to post-cards and everything in between. Preserved by the Historic Society of Lake Covington, it's columned front porch still in-vites passersby to sit for a spell on one of its two benches that frame its main door.

Year: Present Day

### *A Lana Montgomery Special*

Gabriel Hoffman: History Professor

Without studying the past, we are doomed to repeat ourselves—or so believes Gabriel, who has recently been teaching at the local college. For a history professor, Gabriel is far from stuffy, even if the topics of his lectures sometimes are. Lately, attendance has been booming, especially among females, in what was once an unpopular class.

Lana Montgomery: Hair Stylist

Lana has been steadily building her clientele since starting at the Curly Q Hair Salon. Clients of Lana are loyal, coming back to see her as often as once a week, especially the men. They say it's because she's so easy to talk to and that she makes them look good. But maybe it's something else about her—something they can't quite put their finger on—that brings them fluttering back like little moths to a burning flame.

Trope: Royalty

One of our lovers is descended from royalty (or nobility); this trope includes sheikhs, princes, etc. Think Danielle and Prince Henry in the movie *Ever After*, Paige and Eddie in *The Prince and Me*, and Ann and Jo in *Roman Holiday*.

Location: The Sweatbox

The Sweatbox is the go-to gym for Lake Covington residents and visitors to workout. Its state-of-the-art facility boasts three levels of workout equipment, two pools (one indoor and one out), tennis courts, basketball courts, four rooms for group exercise, and a sauna in each of the locker rooms. Personal trainers are on hand to offer one-on-one instruction. Once the workout is over, there's a café on site to grab a smoothie or a protein shake and an adult-only jacuzzi—a popular spot to unwind those sore muscles.

Year: Present Day

### *Heel and Toe*

Anderson Culp: Author

After four novels and eight years of hard work, it's all starting to pay off for Anderson. He's on the last leg of his first book tour and his agent tells him his sales numbers are better than expected. Driving through Lake Covington, the town's beauty and atmosphere catch his interest, and he decides it's time to stop and take a breather.

Kelly Nash: Mechanic

Kelly watched her father work on cars when she was young, and one day she asked if she could help. He'd laugh and put a wrench in her hand. Soon, he wasn't laughing, and he taught her all he knew. Now, she's the best mechanic in town. Her customers keep her busy, but she knows when it's time to put down the tools and have a good time.

Trope: Out of Towner

Everyone knows everyone in a small town. That can be a good thing, but it has its drawbacks. When a mysterious stranger blows into town, it can turn the run-of-the-mill into something exciting, making even the familiar fresh and new. Think James Spader and Andie MacDowell in *Sex, Lies, and Videotape*, Mickey Rourke and Kim Basinger in *9 ½ Weeks*, or Gene Kelly and Leslie Caron in *An American in Paris*.

Location: Cuppa Café

Cuppa Café is at the busiest corner in Lake Covington, across from the courthouse on historical Main Street. Despite the big-box coffee stores coming to town, it's still the spot the locals flock to for their caffeine fix. The staff is friendly, the views to die for, and the booths in the back corners are a great place to get some privacy and talk one-on-one.

Year: Present Day

## *Lipstick Stain*

**William Talley: Movie Theatre Concession Stand Worker**

From behind the concession stand, William sees a lot of couples walking arm-in-arm through the foyer of the theatre. Maybe that would have made other men jealous, but not William. He'd never had a steady girlfriend, not that girls weren't interested, he just wasn't that interested in them. They acted too silly and giggled more than talked. To William, the perfect girl was about as attainable as those on the silver screen ... or so he thought.

**Charlotte Knightly: Recent graduate of Lake Covington Prep**

Full of life, Charlotte holds the world on a string and knows it. As a recent graduate from Lake Covington Prep, the hazy summer nights ahead feel full of possibility and magic. Her well-to-do parents have other plans for her though, which include sending her away to an all-girls college. But Charlotte refuses to go without living a little first.

**Trope: Fish Out of Water**

One of our lovers doesn't fit in a social or professional environment, but that doesn't keep him/her from proving him/herself and winning the heart of the one s/he loves. Think Claire and Jaime in *Outlander*, Jane and Mr. Rochester in *Jane Eyre*, and Jack and Rose in *Titanic*.

**Location: The Grange**

Converted from a barn, the Grange is the official venue for many of Lake Covington's community events. From town meetings to pie contests, it's been a staple of Lake Covington life for as long as its residents can remember. Recently, the local rotary club has been hard at work transforming the Grange into a world of love and enchantment for the annual

Sweetheart Dance coming up this Saturday. It's the one time of the year where everyone has a chance of finding that special someone.

Year: 1956

### Jump Into Love

Reggie Sharp: Skydiving Instructor

To Reggie, nothing beats the adrenaline-rush he gets from skydiving. A little of a thrill-junkie, he takes every opportunity to get in the air, even going as far as starting a skydiving business at the new airport. The feeling he gets when he jumps is like nothing he's ever experienced before. That is, until he finds himself free falling for someone special.

Tessa Rose: Lawyer

Number one in debate team and class president all through high school, it was only natural that Tessa took the reigns as Lake Covington's sole district attorney. Only with the crime rate next to nil, the challenge from a new case is too far and few in between. Perhaps the thrill Tessa is seeking isn't in the courtroom.

Trope: Secret Romance

Our couple doesn't expect things to last beyond a night or maybe a few dates, but they can't stop thinking of each other and things start heating up. Think Sandy and Danny in *Grease*, Baby and Johnny in *Dirty Dancing*, Lloyd and Dianne in *Say Anything*.

Location: The Courthouse

The Lake Covington Courthouse was built by Jean Bemis in 1864 and designed in the Greek Revival style with red brick and marbled columns. Sitting on the corner of Main and 3rd Streets, it's one of the tallest buildings in downtown Lake Covington. It's rumored that the clock in its tower was designed by none other than August Pugin, the designer of Big Ben, as a favor to his long-time friend Jean.

Year: Present Day

## *A Lot of Nerve**

Blake Wallace: Basketball Coach

After surviving a heart wrenching breakup, Blake was resigned to return to the arms of family, delving into coaching basketball at the 113-year-old private school across the water, Lake Covington Prep. Blake hopes that focusing on the school's need for a championship will help keep all thoughts of romance at bay. Blake finds Lake Covington a bit sleepy, but maybe, just maybe, someone will come along to wake things up.

Jaimie Stein: Real Estate Agent

Helping couples find their dream home is not as fulfilling as it used to be. Listening to anxious couples bicker over the trivial use of closet space makes Jaimie want to scream, "Stop worrying about who has more shoes, at least you have each other!" Every night when Jaimie returns home, the void in the bedroom closest is a painful reminder of what was. A reminder of the void in Jaimie's heart, longing to be filled.

Trope: Second Chance at Love

Sometimes love lets you down hard, so hard that you don't think you want to risk putting yourself out there. But love has a way of finding you when you least expect it. Think *Under the Tuscan Sun*, *Home Again*, or *Enough Said.*

Location: The Epicure

The Epicure is Lake Covington's upscale organic-fair trade market. The market touts its local farm to table produce and humanly sourced meats. Tourists come for the import section with shelves brimming with foods with exotic labels and unusual ingredients.

Year: Present Day

## *The Adult Section*

Dean Markham: Construction Work Contractor/Handyman

Since Dean was five years old, he always had a hammer in his hand so starting Dean's Construction wasn't a surprise to any of his friends or family. He loves the freedom of working on his own, being his own boss, and accountable to no one. Despite being a little rough around the edges, Dean has no problems turning heads, but has yet to have someone turn his.

Ann Rogers: Librarian

Ann has always had a love of books. As the librarian for the Lake Covington Library, she prides herself on helping its patrons find just the right one. While she spends her days cataloging new releases, stocking the shelves, and helping both young and old, she spends her nights buried within the pages of her favorite romance novels. One of these days, Ann's love life is about to get as steamy as some of the characters she reads about.

Trope: Loveable Rogue

The male lead character is simultaneously desirable, and off-putting or threatening. Think Indiana Jones from the *Indiana Jones* series, Aragon from *Lord of Rings*, Captain Jack Sparrow from *Pirates of the Caribbean*.

Location: Lake Covington Airport

The recent addition of the airport has finally put Lake Covington on the map and made it possible for tourism to boost the local economy. Although not as large as airports in bigger cities, it's spacious eateries, gift shops, and murals of Lake Covington life give it a charm all its own.

Year: Present Day

Connor Lane: Journalist

Connor has loved and lost more than he could have ever imagined. Losing his wife in a tragic accident, the love from his little girl is the only thing keeping him going day-after-day. But being both mother and father, packing lunches and helping with homework, doesn't quite fill the void. He knows there's something more missing, but will his broken heart ever heal again to dream?

Lillian Faris: Surgeon

Lillian is a shark in the operating room. Being a cardiothoracic surgeon and a wiz in her field, she's often found working double shifts and sleeping in the on-call room. Needless to say, her love life is lacking. Spending hours every day holding someone else's heart in her hands can't keep her from hoping that one day, she'll be able to give her own heart away.

Trope: Broken/Healing Love

When the love interest is an Anti-Hero with a scar from the past that needs healing. Think Harry Connick Jr. and Sandra Bullock in *Hope Floats* or Richard Gere and Diane Lane in *Nights in Rodanthe*.

Location: Healing Waters Hospital

Healing Waters Hospital is a cutting-edge hospital with an advanced Level-1 Trauma Center. One of the most modernized buildings within Lake Covington, it houses several operating rooms, intensive care units, over 100 patient rooms, a morgue, and a chapel. Its recent renovation created a research center, focused solely on new medical and technologic advances, reigning it the number one medical facility in the county. Located right outside of downtown, it stands tall and proud, overlooking the west banks of the lake.

Year: Present Day

*Denotes gender-neutral character profile

To learn more about SMOLDR and to stay up-to-date with upcoming writing contests, please go to our website at www.smoldr.org

**SMOLDR**

www.ingramcontent.com/pod-product-compliance
Lightning Source LLC
Chambersburg PA
CBHW020726210626
46807CB00016B/258